THE SEARCH

by Megan White

Society of Young Inklings

SOCIETY OF YOUNG INKLINGS

The Search
Copyright © 2015 Megan White

Requests for information should be addressed to:
Society of Young Inklings. PO Box 3134, Los Altos, CA 94024

Editor: Jennifer Mazi
Cover Design: Debbie Bakker
Interior Design and Composition: Jennifer Mazi

Printed in the USA
First Printing: April 2015
ISBN 978-0-9910031-3-6

TABLE OF CONTENTS

CHAPTER ONE

 Rae

"Sweetie, we have to take you to a hospital. You're hurt," the woman in the front seat said. I shook my head.

"I'm fine. Just get me to California. My friend can … she's a doctor."

"Really, hon, it would be horribly irresponsible of us not to help you. We just want what's best," her husband said. I hadn't asked their names, and though they had asked mine, I hadn't told them. I just needed a ride as far as California. I couldn't risk the help of this elderly couple, as much as I may have wanted to.

"I understand that completely, but I'm very serious," I said. The man hit the blinker and peeled off onto a freeway exit, shaking his head.

Chapter One

"We are taking you to a hospital, and we are going to find your parents or someone to take care of you until you're better. I'm sorry," he growled. The ancient car squealed to a halt at a red light.

"No, I am. Thank you," I said, throwing open the car door. The woman screamed, and I dove out of the car and ran across the street. Hiding behind a wall beneath the freeway, I pressed my hand against the bullet wound in my stomach and suppressed the urge to cry. Black spots swirled across my vision, and I leaned against the wall until they faded, careful to stay out of sight.

I was exhausted, starving, sleep deprived, and injured. I'd been hitchhiking for nearly 200 miles, and was still three states from home. I'd have to find another stranger willing to feed me and take me as far as I could get before they tried to stick me in a hospital and find my parents, whom I hadn't seen in nearly five years.

Glancing out to check for the elderly couple and any cops that might be in the area, I pulled my hood up over the gash on the back of my head and zipped my sweatshirt over the red, oozing stain on my shirt.

I stepped out onto the street and stuck my fist out, thumb raised, hoping against all odds that I would make it home before I pushed my luck too far.

Maddie

I stared at Cole's blank, unreadable face. His pale brown hair was getting long, and a lock of it stuck to the sheen of sweat on his forehead. I had sat here, next to his hospital bed, for four days straight. Ever since I got home.

Home? Was that what this place was? After I left my own home for Camp Magic, California, I had called this home. Then my friends and I had started on the fatal mission that ended up bringing me here, beside this bed, wondering if my best-friend-maybe-more was actually going to make it.

After my week in the wilderness (long story, involving being a coyote for a while) I had come straight back here to help Cole. A new girl at camp, Jezzie, had explained what she knew. What she had done. She said that Cole had come to her when he got back, begging her to wipe his memory. That was Jezzie's power—causing amnesia. Unfortunately, she had absolutely no idea how to reverse it.

That was the "magic" part of Camp Magic. Every person here had a magical superpower, including me. I was a shape-shifter, and the only thing keeping me from being on top of the world was the fact that I still had an unsteady control over my powers, plus my … um … charming past sometimes tended to come back for a visit. Cole had super-speed. There were kids who could fly, kids who could heal people by touching them,

who could lift elephants as easily as I could lift a cat.

Cole stirred a little. I didn't get too excited, though. This happened a lot. His green eyes would open. His face would light up when he saw mine. And then he would moan and spiral back down into oblivion. Rebecca, the camp healer, spent almost as much time here as me. She tried curing him, but it was impossible. Something was off in his brain that she couldn't reach. She couldn't cure people who were in comas. I had learned that the hard way myself.

"Any change?" Jezzie touched my arm and leaned in close. Her long blonde hair fell over her shoulder

"Nothing. He has been sitting here smiling at me like that for four stupid days. Why can't he … why can't he wake up?" My voice cracked, and I had to pause to take a few deep breaths.

When I finally stopped and wiped my eyes, Cole moved again. His eyes flashed open. He stared at my face, and that faint and faraway smile that seemed permanently etched onto his pale face faltered. Then he was gone. His eyes closed. That stupid, idiot smile returned. He was a statue of still, calm, silent marble.

"I hope you know that this has never, ever happened. Most people forget. He passed out as soon as I touched his mind, and I don't know why. I never would have done it to him if I knew this would happen. I promise you," Jezzie assured me for the millionth time. I nodded.

"I know. I trust you, Jezzie." In the past few days, the

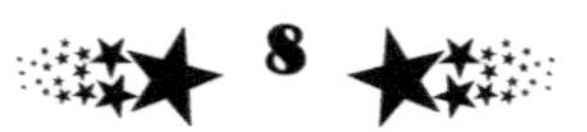

little girl and I had become good friends. She cared about people, was a really good listener, and gave good advice. Jezzie was on her way to becoming as good a friend as Cole, or Rae and Amanda. Well, just Cole. Tears threatened to take over again, and I had to look away from Cole's blank face. Jezzie pulled up a chair next to me and sat down.

"I have an idea. I'm going to try something new, something that might bring him back. I don't know if it'll work, but it can't hurt, right? I mean, even if it makes things worse, it can't actually get worse, right?"

She squirmed in her seat, twisting her fingers together as she waited for my approval. I nodded, trying to smile, but only managing a grimace. Of course it could get worse! At least right now he was alive. And he wasn't in pain. That was so much better than him being dead or screaming or hurt. So much better. But I nodded anyway, because that's what she wanted. She wanted to help. She wanted to repair the damage she had caused. And truthfully? Any change that happened now would at least be a change, something new to worry about.

"I'm going to start. If anything goes wrong, I'll stop. Promise." She placed her tiny hands on his head and took a deep, shaky breath.

Both of them started screaming.

Cole arched his back into a C on the narrow hospital bed, and Jezzie's fingers dug into his scalp, knuckles white, as she curled around her hands. Their screams rose in volume

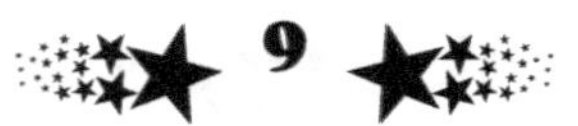

and pitch until I couldn't be near them anymore. I cringed from the noise and ran, faltering only when I reached the doors. I hadn't been outside in days, or at camp for weeks before that. There was no telling what it would be like out there. Maybe they bought pet dragons. Maybe everyone got matching tattoos. Maybe the sky turned yellow.

Jamie, the camp director, blasted through the doors, knocking me backwards into a table. A glass vase shattered on the floor, delicate flowers hand grown by a camper spilled across the tiles.

"What is happening?" she demanded. I couldn't put words together with the horrible screaming claiming my thoughts, so I pointed.

Campers started to flood through the doors, curiosity drawing them like mice to peanut butter. Jamie snapped at them, telling them to get outside and stay there.

I ignored her order and followed her back into Cole's room. I stuck my fingers in my ears to block out their horrible wails and stayed close to Jamie's side. Jamie was trying to tear Jezzie free from Cole, but her grip on his head was too strong. I was surprised that his skull didn't fracture. I came over and looked at the three of them. Then I ran back outside for Rebecca, the only person I trusted at this point.

I hurriedly explained my plan, and though she winced, she followed me in. Right outside the door to the hospital room, I blocked out the screams and focused on the change. It took longer than I wanted it to, because my thoughts were

so scattered, but eventually my skin rippled and grew hot
as I shrank down into a cold, metal crowbar. Rebecca picked
me up with a bit of difficulty and carried me in. Without eyes
or ears, my senses were numbed and frozen. I only had the
vague impression of my surroundings. Grimacing at the noise,
Rebecca hefted me up over her head and swung me back down.
I landed squarely on Jezzie's right arm. I only felt a dull thump,
but I heard a horrible crack as Jezzie's bone shattered, and
blood dripped to the floor. She released Cole. I used the intense
focus in my head to pop straight up into my own body. My ears
rang in the sudden silence. Rebecca grabbed Jezzie's wrist, and
what looked like golden dust motes began to swirl around her
hands, catching the light. The glitter converged around Jezzie's
wrist, and burrowed into her skin with the sound of the bone
crunching back into place. Jezzie sniffed back tears, cradling her
arm. Cole slipped into a shuddering, grimacing sleep. I pushed
away from Jamie, leaning over the bed.

"Cole! Cole, please talk to me!" I shrieked, watching him
thrash and shudder. I couldn't reach him. He might as well have
been locked into a glass coffin, for all the good my words did.
Jamie put a quivering hand on my shoulder.

"Good job, Maddie. You probably saved both of
them." Her voice was weak and shaky. As I swallowed hard
and touched Cole's sweaty forehead, Jezzie tried to explain
what happened. Jamie shushed her until Rebecca had left the
hospital.

"Okay, Jezzie. What was that?" she said.

Chapter One

"I don't know. I was going to try to dig into his mind. Part of the amnesia thing is invading the person's mind, and finding a place to hide the memories and hiding them there. I was going to go in and dig around to find that little pocket of memories. Instead, what I found was painful and sharp, and at the same time, it was like I was numb. I couldn't sense anything, and I couldn't escape from it. It was in my head, and it wasn't letting go. I couldn't feel my body. I guess that's why I was screaming and wouldn't let go of him." She looked sad, beaten, and … conflicted? Was she hiding something? I saw her glance at me from the corner of her eye.

"It's okay, Jezzie. You did your best." Jamie sent Jezzie back to her cabin and turned her attention to Cole. He was shivering, shaking, and mumbling. I never should have let her try this. He was in pain, and it was all my fault.

Memories flooded my brain. Since I had split up with Cole at the Others' lair, I had been able to forget everything that had happened in my past. But blaming myself for this sent it all rushing back, and it took everything in me to push them away.

"Maddie? I need you to leave. You have been in here for days. Go outside. Hang out, swim, do something. I'll see what I can do for Cole." Jamie shooed me outside and closed the door.

I had no idea what to do.

I had changed so much since I had last been out here. There was also the fact that my best friend and major crush was sick, possibly dying, and majorly out of it. My other two best friends and roommates were dead. Killed by the Others.

I closed my eyes. Flashes of my childhood flew across my eyelids. Hiding in my room as my parents screamed, my sister sitting next to me and stroking my hair and telling me that it would be okay. I shook off the images, before they could turn dark. Darker, anyway. I decided to go do something, anything other than standing here, an outsider in my own home. Most of the campers had disappeared into the dining hall for lunch. Jezzie was standing outside, absently rubbing her wrist, still slightly glowing as Rebecca's power continued to strengthen it.

When she saw me, she pounced, question ready. "Hey, Maddie. Any change? Good or bad?"

I knew that she already knew the answer, but I shook my head anyway. She sighed and pulled absently at her hair.

"I am so sorry. I was only trying to help him." Her voice was small and sad. She seemed so much older than her mere ten years.

"I know, Jezzie. I don't blame you for this." I touched the messy blonde braid on the back of my own head. I yanked the rubber band out and raked through the mass of knots and dirt with my fingers. Then I looked down at myself. I hadn't showered since I had been here last. People weren't breathing through their noses around me. I told Jezzie that I was going to go shower, and she nodded and entered the noisy, boisterous gathering in the dining hall. I went back to my cold, empty, cabin and took a long, hot, shower. The water ran black down the drain. When I was done soaking my sorrows in steam, I got dressed and ran a comb through my clean hair, wrestling

its wavy, wet length into a braid. I pushed my feet into a pair of flip-flops and walked back across the campus and into the dining hall. Food sounded amazing. Real, cooked food. I walked inside, and immediately the room went silent. I closed the giant wooden doors behind me, feeling conspicuous and self-conscious. All the eyes on me made me think of the day a mere few weeks ago when I walked into the dining hall completely unaware of the fact that I had accidentally given myself a tail. However, that day I'd had my friends to defend me, and Amanda to turn the bullies to stone. Now, I was completely alone.

Without warning, everyone started clapping. Even the people I hated, even the people who hated me. The room was filled with the deafening sound of rapturous applause. Stunned, I couldn't make myself move. I was frozen, my eyes slowly scanning the room. Jezzie got up and smiled at me, waving me over to her table.

"No one ever got to really thank you for saving the world. So we're doing it now," she said in that weirdly wise way. I ducked my head and the clapping started to trickle away. Soon it was replaced completely by the normal sounds of the camp dining hall.

"I didn't actually save anything at all. Cole did. I fell down and hit my head! I did nothing!" I protested.

"You helped him to get there. Anyway, we wanted to make you feel appreciated. Everyone knows you need it." Jezzie's comforting voice wasn't comforting at all. Everyone

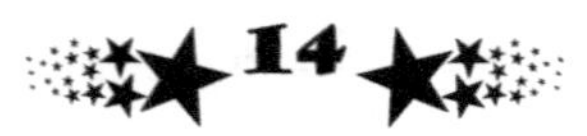

knows I need it? Did that mean that suddenly the entire camp knew about my insecurities? Jezzie seemed to notice her mistake, and amended her statement with a quick "because of Rae and Amanda. We're all going to miss them."

"Yeah. Of course." My knees were wobbling. That brief reminder of what had happened to them turned my entire body to jelly. I sat down and Jezzie shoved a tray of food across our little table towards me. The tray was loaded with steaming deliciousness. Pasta covered in a rich, creamy sauce and topped with a sprinkle of Parmesan cheese. A watermelon-flavored Italian soda with a Maraschino cherry bobbing on the surface, skewered with a tiny, pink plastic sword. A small dish of curly fries, seasoned just right. Best of all, a thick slice of cake. Red velvet with cream cheese frosting, and coated with pink sprinkles. The food was gone before I even really thought about it. I had lost a lot of weight in the past few weeks. Time to gain it back, I thought as I went for seconds and thirds. Jezzie laughed as I returned with my fourth heaping plate of food.

"You're going to explode!" she giggled. I laughed too, even though the action felt strangely wrong with all the tragedy surrounding me.

"Not before I try the chocolate cake." I stuffed a forkful of noodles into my mouth. Truthfully, I was already stuffed, but I couldn't stop. It was so good. Finally, I really couldn't eat any more. Jezzie kept me from going back for fifths, and we went outside into the fresh air instead. I was stuffed, and real movement seemed impossible, so we went into the garden

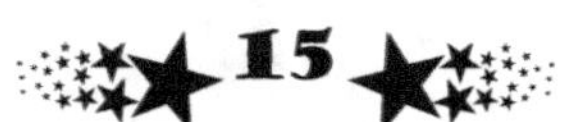

spiral. The camp was built around the main buildings, like the dining hall and the auditorium. Then there was a spiral of hedges circling out from it, decorated with statues and flowers. Outside the spiral were a few concentric circles of cabins. Outside that was the lake and a strip of forest, and then the fence.

Jezzie sat down at the feet of a particularly pretty statue of a girl. I sat next to her, though I couldn't make myself look at the statue. The girl's name had been Clarissa, before Amanda accidentally turned her to stone for laughing at me. Now Amanda was gone, and all that was left of her were a few statues, forever frozen in their cemented state. A few tears escaped me before I could stop them.

"What's wrong?" Jezzie reached for my hand. I couldn't push words past the lump in my throat, so I ignored her. Ten deep breaths later, I told her much of what I hadn't before, all about Amanda and Rachelle and the Others and me.

"Amanda was my roommate. She was my best friend, too. She defended me when no one else would. I mean, it was usually by turning people into statues, but at least she cared, right? Rachelle—Rae—was an amazing person, too. Her power was…I never know exactly how to describe it. She could talk anyone into anything. When she talked, it was like … like she was handing you a present, the most beautiful, perfect, expensive present ever, and asking a small favor in return, and you wanted to do whatever she said. The Others kidnapped her, then they got Amanda. Cole and I tried to save them, and

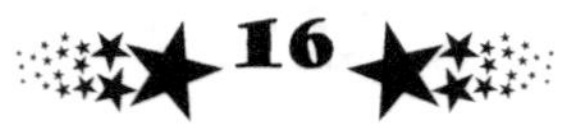

they got out, but we didn't, and then they came back for us. And then they got killed." That was all I could get out before I started crying. Jezzie wrapped her arms around me, and laid her little blonde head down on my shoulder. It was weird, Jezzie being almost five years younger than my only real friend and me. Of course, it was also weird that all my other friends were dead or almost dead.

"Who are the Others, again? I sorta forgot. Sorry," Jezzie said. Oh, the Others.

The stories I could tell about the Others.

"The Others are a terrorist sect of an alien race called the Oppos, or Opposites, made up of the Oppos of the heroes of our own race." This was the definition Jamie fed everyone at camp, but Jezzie looked even more confused after I said it than she had before. So I tried again.

"They are these freaky aliens, but they are exactly opposite of us. For every person on Earth, there is a perfectly opposite Oppo. Opposite in personality, likes, dislikes, everything. They look exactly like us, though. It's really disorienting. They know everything about us, because they are so perfectly different. Anyways, the Others are the Oppos of all the people with powers, like the ones here." Jezzie nodded, but she still had perplexed wrinkles between her eyebrows.

"Why are the Others here?"

"They want to destroy us. And themselves. They want to reset the universe. It's really stupid, actually. Our mission, the one Cole and Rae and Amanda and I went on, was to stop

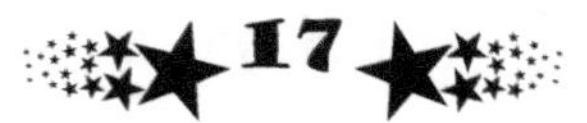

them from recreating the Big Bang and destroying the entire universe."

Memories assaulted me, their stings like a slap across my face. Rae's twisted expression right before she turned herself in, Amanda's tear streaked face as she told me what Rachelle had done. The beaten emotion on Cole's face as he watched me leave him in that jail cell, deep in the ground under miles of Others. Jamie's angry grimace when she heard what happened.

I couldn't sit there anymore.

"I'm going to go check on Cole and Jamie."

I got up and left without looking back at my little friend.

CHAPTER TWO

Cole

The blackness was peaceful, calm, quiet.

Blissful.

Sometimes, the darkness would recede, and a blinding light would burn my retinas. I saw a face whenever this happened. A beautiful face, marred slightly by worry lines and a frown. It was a girl, with freckles and icy blue eyes that were still somehow warm and blonde hair that tumbled over her shoulders and into my face. As soon as I began to see this girl, a searing pain burned through my head, and I sank back into the dark. At some point in the immeasurable time of this blackness, there was something. Hot fingers dug into me, burning their way through my skull. It hurt. So much I wanted to scream, but I didn't know how. I couldn't control my own body.

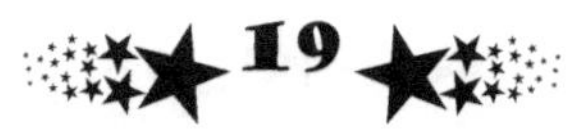

Chapter Two

Those flaming fingers felt like they were digging deep into my brain, probing, searching, and scalding. Finally they reached the deepest, darkest corner of my mind. In an instant, the pain went from excruciating to unbearable. That was when I found my voice, and the screams tore through my throat like knives. The dark was no longer comforting, no longer dark. Blinding white and yellow flashes tore across my vision, blurry pictures among them. As the scorching fingers dug deeper, the pain intensified. I wanted to tear at my head, rip my burning eyes out of their sockets. I wanted to die so that it would end. Just when I was about to start tearing at my eyes, at my hair, at anything that could make this pain go away, it disappeared. The fingers were sucked out of my head, like a needle after a shot. Instead of relief, though the fire burned on. Less, now, but a dull, stinging throb that seemed to be melting my brain.

"Cole! Cole, please talk to me!" A helpless and high-pitched voice. Fuzzy noises hit my ears like hammers, words unintelligible. The burn was spreading, down into my limbs and chest. I wanted to scream again, but that panic-tainted voice stopped me.

Cole. Please. Talk to me.

The voice reminded me of someone important. As the burn started to make my fingers itch, I groaned. The pain was worse than anything I'd ever experienced before.

"Cole? Are you waking up? It's Jamie. If you can hear me, lift your right hand. Please, Cole. Try." This was another voice, this one lower and rougher. Jamie. The name jumped into my smoldering brain, surprising me. Maddie. Jezzie. Amanda. Rachelle. Victoria. Names, with faces starting to accompany them. Ignoring the blazing torture in my arm, I lifted it. It took an incredible amount of energy, and it fell listlessly back at my side. A blistering wave of heat blew through me, and I gritted my teeth to hold back another scream. Something cool touched my hand.

"Cole! You can hear me! Can you wake up? Open your eyes? Can you speak?" Jamie's questions flew through my mind. Wake up? No, I couldn't do that. I didn't know how. Open my eyes? Maybe. I had done it when the darkness was enveloping me, anyway. I tried to open my eyes. I could feel the flame-streaked darkness receding, and a new brightness hit my eyes with a fierce burn. A bright light above me. No gorgeous face, though. Maddie. That had been Maddie.

"Oh, Cole. Can you talk? Or blink?" So demanding, Jamie. Okay, blinking. I could do that.

Dark-light.

Dark-light.

Dark-light.

Blinking.

Talking was next. I had a better understanding of where my body actually was, so I tried to open my mouth. A slow whine escaped me, and I snapped my jaw shut. I heard a door open, and then slam.

"Oh, god! Jamie, why didn't you call me? He's worse!"

Maddie. It was Maddie! I had to tell her that I was okay.

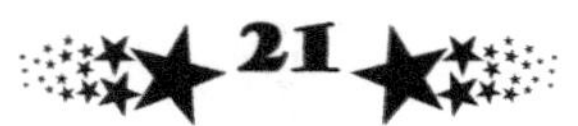

I had to make sure that she knew that as long as she was here, near me, the fiery burn was tolerable.

"Maddie, relax! I'm making progress, okay? He can hear me. He responded. He can move. I have this under control," Jamie assured her. This wouldn't be enough for the Maddie that I knew. I had to speak. My eyes flashed open, and I saw her. She had showered. Her hair was shining wet, in a loose braid over her shoulder. Those blue eyes flashed to mine, and I opened my mouth and spoke.

"Maddie," I croaked. "I missed you." The words made the fire recede, gave me the strength to stand. I walked over and hugged her, and then my mind went blank. I couldn't remember. Couldn't remember...Couldn't remember. My mind was blank. Not the cold, empty black of my time in the dark, but an empty, blank expanse that offered no words for my feelings. I couldn't find a single memory in my entire mind. Not one. I couldn't even identify the girl who had her arms wrapped tightly around me.

I was no one.

# Maddie

"Maddie, I missed you."

Those four words reminded me of all that I was missing. I had screwed up big time by rejecting him, throwing away the love he said he had for me. Now that I wanted it, needed it, even loved him back, it was too late. He was gone, off deep in his own head. As soon as he hugged me, he made a tiny noise, and seemed to forget everything. As Jamie and I tried to investigate further, we discovered that he really couldn't remember a thing. He could walk, talk, move, but his memories were gone. I tried to talk to him, but he would look at me like I was a crazy person on the street and walk away. He wandered uselessly around camp, unaware of anything. He couldn't even run.

My own life seemed to have no purpose. All my friends were gone, and the boredom was killing me. Anything would have been better than this bland, tasteless torture.

"Maddie! Catch!" I was sitting on the pier, dangling my toes in the warm, clear water of the lake. I reached up instinctively, and caught a small tangerine. I stared at it, at all the little pockmarks on its neon surface. Jezzie plopped down next to me.

"Cole isn't getting any better. Now quit staring at that orange, it isn't going to eat you." She reached over me and grabbed the fruit, tearing the peel off and throwing it out into the lake. She ate it fast, grinning at my expression. I sighed and looked back at the water, at the curved pieces of the orange peel floating on it.

"He should be better by now. He's gone, Jezzie. There's no hope now," I whispered. I knew it was true. If he were coming back, it would have happened by now. Jezzie and Jamie had been trying to wake him up for hours. He was gone.

23

Chapter Two

"Madison! Come here! There's something you need to see! Come on!" Victoria had appeared out of thin air right behind me, her hair puffed with static electricity the way it did when she teleported. Startled, I almost toppled over backwards off the pier. She grabbed my arm and pulled me back towards her, and then started dragging me through the camp.

"What is going on?" I pulled my arm free and glared at her.

"Rae is here."

I stopped dead. Victoria started pulling me along again, and I didn't resist. Rae? Alive? Tori seemed to think so, and it seemed like the entire camp was converging around the main road. As we rounded the little cluster of trees that separated the camp from the road, my heart dropped into my feet. There was a girl, lying on the ground, covered in blood and dirt. I started running, falling to my knees and skidding to a stop as I turned to look at her face. Buried under the filthy, matted, crusty, dark hair was a familiar face. Rachelle. I pushed the hair out of her face, and started crying. She was alive. Barely, but she was here. All the way from the Midwest, where the Others creepy lair was. Rebecca sank to her knees next to me, already searching for an injury. I watched, gripping my friend's hand.

"There's a huge gash on the back of her head. Looks like one of her ankles might be sprained, and there's a bullet wound here. This is going to take a while," Rebecca said, pointing to a blood-soaked stain on Rae's stomach. I nodded, unable to speak through my tears. Rae was alive. As Rebecca placed her healing

hands on the wounds, flecks of gold catching the light as they floated away from Rebecca, a thought punched me in the gut: If Rae was here, where was Amanda? Possibilities swam through my blurry mind for the entire six hours it took Rebecca to heal my friend. We had moved from the asphalt to the hospital as soon as Jamie found us. When Rebecca was done, she told me to help Rae get cleaned up and fed.

My skinned knees were stinging and my legs were cramping from being still, and as I helped an incoherent and wobbly Rachelle back to my cabin, I could barely hold her weight. She was healed, but weak from exhaustion and hunger. I took her straight into the bathroom, and helped her into the tub. I waited for the water from the handheld showerhead to heat up and began to rinse the dirt and blood off of her. I shampooed her hair and rinsed it, and then helped her back out. She changed by herself, and I led her to the dining hall. We sat down and I ordered a huge platter of snacks. A robotic waiter slowly set down a big tray. Rae immediately started eating.

Neither of us said anything. I slowly shredded a paper napkin, spreading the little white pieces across the table. Finally I had to ask. I had to know.

"What happened? Cole and I … we thought you were dead. The Others said you were dead. We left without you because you were dead. How are you not?" I asked, my voice rising in pitch with each question. Rae paused, pushing a cracker around on the plate.

"Amanda … yeah. She … I guess it's obvious, but she

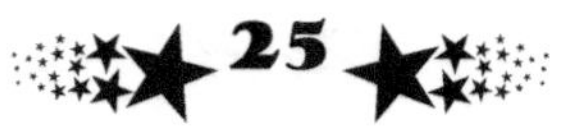

didn't … she…she didn't make it. We had both switched back, I don't know how, but we guessed that you got caught. We were running down the hallway when we heard shouts. Some guard shot at us, and he got Amanda in the side of the head. She went down, and I tried to convince the guard to stop, but they knew we were there, and he had earplugs in. He shot me in the stomach, and then called three other guys to come take us away. Amanda was still alive at that point, but she was bad, really bad. Her blood was absolutely everywhere. I was so scared, I never even thought of myself."

She absently rubbed her stomach, where the bullet wound must have been. "I was bleeding a lot, too. I was so scared. They took us and dumped us outside, because they probably thought we were already dead. Amanda sure looked it, and I guess I was half paralyzed at that point.

"They left us there. I thought that I could help Amanda, keep her alive until I found a way to contact you. We—I saw you guys leave, and I tried to yell, but I could barely move, and my voice wouldn't work. I saw Cole take off, and you disappeared, and I couldn't say anything. After a few hours, Amanda died."

Rae paused to wipe her eyes, though it didn't look like she was crying.

"I had done everything I could, but I couldn't save her. I wasn't even sure I could save myself. I couldn't take her anywhere, or even bury her, either. I had to leave her sitting on the side of that building, rotting in the sun."

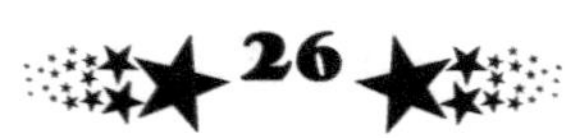

My eyes burned with impending tears, picturing my best friend lying broken on the side of a warehouse thousands of miles away.

"I had to crawl, and drag myself along. I knew I had to get back here. I hitchhiked for a few hundred miles too, and I managed to stay out of hospitals. We campers have to stay under the radar, you know? So I got some people to feed me and get me to Reno. I crawled from there."

"That's like, hundreds of miles," I squeaked.

"Yeah. It was really hard, especially when I figured out that my cuts were getting infected. The one on my head, and the one on my stomach a lot worse. I thought I was going to die out there, alone and with absolutely no one to know where I was. Just like Amanda."

She sobbed once, trying to disguise it as a cough. I was still trying to wrap my head around Amanda's death. People can't just disappear, can they? I knew that Brittney was still alive somewhere, and Mom was okay. No one I really cared about had ever died. I couldn't imagine Amanda never laughing again, never taking another step, diving into the crystal clear lake, getting angry enough to turn someone into stone. She couldn't be gone. It was impossible. Life couldn't jerk to a stop that way. Even when I believed that she and Rae were gone, I still hadn't really accepted it. But now I had no choice.

"Maddie? Are you okay?" Rae asked, tapping my arm. I had zoned out, and she looked worried.

"Yeah. Yeah, I'm fine. Sorry." Her face softened, and I

could see that she knew exactly what I had been thinking about.

"I know," she said.

"Is it possible that she made it anyway? You could've been wrong. Someone might have rescued her. Maybe she's on her way home right now!" I knew I was wrong, but I couldn't not hope. There had to be a chance, right?

"No. She was gone. I wouldn't have left her if she wasn't." Rachelle's voice was so firm, so determined and so sad, that I lost all hope. Amanda was dead. Permanently.

"Maddie, are you alright? I think I'm going to go get some rest. Do you want me to stay here with you?"

I shook my head, too lost in memories and guilt to speak. After an indeterminable amount of time, Jamie sat down next to me.

"I heard Rae's side of the story." She gently placed her hand over mine on the table.

"I am so sorry, Maddie. I know you two were practically sisters. Her loss will hit the camp hard." She was silent for a bit, watching me cry.

"I have some ideas for Cole, honey. You might want to pay attention, because Jezzie thinks that these might work too," she added.

I snapped to attention. "Tell me. I have to help him."

Jamie smiled a little.

"I know you do. We're going to try reminding him of things from his past. Amnesia patients often get their memories back when you find a certain key memory, something that

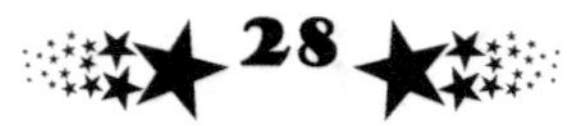

unlocks everything else. If we find that memory, and trigger it, then he should come back. I need your help to brainstorm some ideas, and to help trigger the memories."

Jamie looked excited, like we had a chance of helping him. That got me excited, and soon we had a good list of ideas. She led me to the hospital, and into a waiting room. Cole was sitting in a big, comfy chair in the corner, staring blankly into the distance. I looked at him, remembering all those moments where he had looked at me and I had looked at him and my heart felt like it was melting, and I couldn't think of anything but him. My lips warmed as I remembered the moment that he had kissed me, right before jumping straight into the Other's clutches. I hadn't told Jamie about that part. I still couldn't wrap my own head around it, and I didn't want her to know. It was too personal.

"Cole, this is Maddie. Say hello," Jamie instructed him.

"Hello, Maddie." He stood shakily, trying to get control of his legs. He looked like a little kid being introduced to their mother's friend in the supermarket. He didn't recognize me.

"Cole. We are going to experiment a little bit with your brain. Please be patient, and tell us if anything feels wrong," Jamie said. He nodded, and stepped back to sit down again. Jamie looked at me, and we began.

Cole

The girl named Maddie and the woman named Jamie started telling me things, showing me things, and acting out things. Every time I looked at something I should have known, a strange tickle nagged at the back of my mind. It was especially bad when I looked at that Maddie girl's face. When they showed me a smiling girl in a wheelchair, a splitting pain shot through my head.

I should remember. I should remember. I should remember.

Finally, after almost three hours of that kind of stuff, Maddie threw down the black cloaks she was holding and flopped into a chair, covering her face with her hands.

"None of this is helping! We might as well give up!" she screamed. Jamie scowled.

"We will find the trigger. It's a matter of finding the right memory!" she shot back.

My head was spinning. When I looked at Maddie's lips, an awful shudder went through me. There was something important about her, but I could not remember it at all. I blinked, and her eyes met mine. The clear, silvery blue sent another pang of emptiness through me. I should know this girl.

"I'm out of here. I'm not helping and this hurts too much," she muttered, stomping out of the room. She slammed the door behind her.

"Alright, Cole. You are free to wander again. I'm sorry I made you do that. Come straight to me or Maddie if you remember anything at all, okay?" Jamie said.

I nodded, forgetting how to use my voice, and she escorted me out of the hospital and out into the campground. I still got lost a lot, and I sort of walked around with no particular focus in mind. Jamie told me that everyone at camp had a superpower, and mine was super speed, but I couldn't get my feet to move properly. My body didn't always cooperate, and sometimes it was really hard to do things that should be easy, like writing or reading or walking or running or simply standing up.

As I walked past a stone statue in a rose garden, my head spun. Nothing made any sense anymore, with disconnected feelings and half-memories, all loosely fitted together and nonsensical. I rubbed my forehead, blinking away spots and trying to make my feet move. I walked and walked, around in circles, looking at everything, trying to find the elusive trigger Jamie kept talking about. I wanted my memories back. I wanted to know who the intangible Cole was. I wanted to be able to remember whom I liked and who my family was, and what had actually happened in my life.

I wanted to be me.

"Cole, wait up!" The little blonde girl, Jezzie, raced up and grabbed my wrist.

"Maddie has a another idea! This one really might work!"

She started pulling me towards the hospital again, but I

tripped and fell. I picked gravel out of my stinging knees. Why couldn't I move? I was supposed to be good at running! Jezzie helped me up and dragged me forwards at a slightly slower pace. We burst through the automatic doors, and skidded into the room I had spent the afternoon in. Jamie, Maddie, and another vaguely familiar girl were already there.

"Cole, say hello to Rachelle. She went on a journey with you and Maddie once. We need you to listen to her for a few minutes, alright?" Jamie asked.

"Hello," I said to the latest stranger who knew my name. Jamie asked me to sit down in the same chair as earlier. I stared at Rachelle. Warm brown eyes, long black hair, a guarded frown twisting the corners of her mouth down. I knew this girl, too. Her face made my head hurt almost as much as Maddie's.

"Cole, you need to remember. All those moments, memories from your past, they want to come out. I need you to open your mind and release them, let them go, remember them."

I did as she said. I had no choice. The problem was, as soon as I tried to open my mind, a searing, burning pain split through me. I cried out and curled in on myself, trying to close off my head again. Rachelle paused, uncertain of what to do next.

"Come on, Rae. This is what almost gave him his memories back before," Jamie encouraged. I blinked and lifted my head to look at Rachelle. She shrugged, wrinkles deepening between her eyebrows. Her voice slid over me like a cool breeze,

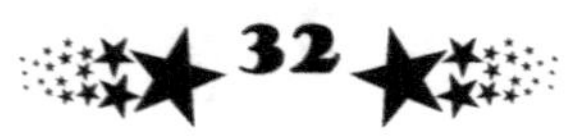

slow and soothing and comforting.

"Try to let go. Ignore the pain, and release your memories. You can do it. You want to. Don't hold yourself back." Her voice was as smooth as silk, as comforting as a warm blanket.

All I wanted to do was help her, do what she said. I tried to open my mind again, but the splitting, burning, fiery pain was too much, so I shut down again.

"Cole! Stop blocking me!" Rae insisted, but I couldn't let go. I couldn't.

"Let it go, Rae. Jamie, this is hurting him. He won't give in if we do it like this. Move on," Maddie pleaded. The insistent tone in her voice made Rachelle turn away from me and towards Jamie.

"She's right. I'm on full power and he's still resisting. Jamie, we have to find a different way." She walked towards the door, her expression remorseful.

"Rachelle, get back in here. Now. This is the only way," Jamie ordered. Maddie's mouth fell open. She glared at Jamie.

"Jamie, stop! You are going to hurt him!" she shot back. Jamie's eyes glowed.

"No! We have to get this done so you all can go back and save the world! We need him! Come on, Maddie, I know you want him back too!" Jamie screeched.

"Not if it hurts him!" Maddie's voice was a shriek. Jamie's face contorted, and then she gave up. She sat down on the chair and massaged her temples with her fingers.

"Oh, Maddie. Cole. Rachelle. I am so, so, so sorry. It's so much pressure to keep this camp going. It's so hard. I needed to do something right. I needed to get Cole back. It happened right under my nose. I wanted to get him back, to say I did something right. . And I need someone to help me with the Others. Things are only getting worse, and I need you. I need you all." Her head fell into her hands, and she wouldn't respond to any of our pleas.

"Jamie? We're going to go now. I'll see you later, okay?"

Without lifting her head, Jamie waved us on. I stumbled on the way out.

"Cole! Stop being so clumsy! It is driving me insane!" Maddie yelled. Rae took off, mumbling something about cleaning her room. That left Maddie and me, standing in the middle of camp, wondering what to do next. She said that she was my best friend, but I didn't know her. Not at all.

"Maybe we should start over. Create new memories to replace the ones I lost," I suggested. Maddie looked me over, skeptical.

"Uh, sure. Do you want to meet me at the pier? Tonight? Watch the sunset?"

"Okay. I guess I'll see you there." Maddie smiled slightly and turned around. I saw her shoulders shudder as she took a deep, deep breath, and then she walked away. I was left there, unsure of how to proceed, unsure of anything. Yes, I knew I knew her, but I didn't know how. I couldn't remember her at all. Meanwhile, she and Jamie and Rae and Jezzie and the entire

stupid camp were freaking out and trying to help. Truthfully, I didn't have a whole lot of hope left.

It's not like I had anything to remember anyway.

CHAPTER THREE

Maddie

When I left Cole, I ended up right where I knew I would—the little patch of sand by the lake, too small to get crowded. I watched the gentle waves lap up against the sand, wakes from the small motorboat that raced back and forth across the little lake, towing skiers. Far out in the water, a fish leaped into the air and splashed back down.

Campers were experimenting with their powers all over the place. A short boy with spiked black hair ran across the surface of the lake, racing a girl and her six clones in a canoe. A kid with laser vision shot the rocks another one threw right out of the air. A girl with control over the water sat on the pier shooting streams of lake at any one who came too close.

I spread my arms out and fell back onto the beach. The warmth from the sand spread through my skin, wiping away the cold, empty feeling that filled me when I was near Cole. The soft sound of the water washing up on the beach was soothing; in sharp contrast to the turmoil that was the rest of my life.

"Hey! Maddie!" Jezzie called. I sat up, sand pouring off

of me like a waterfall. I shook out my hair, causing more sand to cascade down. She plopped down next to me, and immediately started digging her toes into the beach.

"Hi! I haven't been able to talk to you in a while. How is it going? Jamie said there was still no change."

I shrugged. "Nothing. Still. I'm starting to think that nothing ever is going to change. I really need some time, Jezzie. If you don't mind, I'm going to go take a walk."
Jezzie's face fell a little, and she lowered her gaze. I paused, feeling bad for leaving her, but decided that it didn't matter. Jezzie would understand. She knew me well enough by now to realize that this mess was tearing me apart.

"Bye then. Hope you feel better," she called.

I waved over my shoulder at her, and went back to my cabin. The door squeaked a little as I opened it. I hit the light switch and flopped down on a bed. Amanda's. I jumped up again, smoothed down the blanket, and fell on my own bed. Touching Amanda's stuff felt wrong. It was my fault she was dead, after all.

It was you.

I let out a small scream, flipping around to face the wall behind me.

"Brittney? Is that you?" I whispered. Brittney, the sister who abandoned me. The sister who made sure I knew that my father's mistakes were my fault. She was my father's first daughter, with his first wife, Lindsay. But my dad cheated on Brittney's mom, with a woman named Rosalie. My mother.

Dad left Lindsay and married Rosalie. Brittney couldn't stand it. When she was seventeen, she ran away with her boyfriend. But before she left she told me that it was my fault that Dad left Lindsay. My fault that her life was ruined. The last thing she ever said to me was, "I want you to know that it was you. You ruined my life." Ever since I failed my mission, with Cole and Amanda and Rae, I had heard Brittney in my head. Every mistake I made caused me to hear those words again. It had been a while, though. I had hoped that she was gone. I guessed that was too much to ask for.

"Maddie? You in there?" someone called. A few seconds later, the door opened. It was Rae.

"Hey, girl. Are you okay? Jezzie said you weren't feeling great," she said. I shrugged.

"Good enough. A little depressed, I guess."

"I don't blame you. I talked to Cole a little. He doesn't remember me at all, either. You know, if that helps at all. He was my best friend before he was yours." Rae tried to squeeze out a laugh, but ended up coughing. I patted the bed next to me, and slid over a little to make room.

"I know he was. I remember. But he really doesn't remember you at all? Does he remember his family? Did you ask?"

"No, no, and yes."

Rae pulled one of my pillows close to her chest. "I've tried asking him about everything I know he should know. Not a trace. That Jezzie is pretty powerful, really."

"What are we going to do, Rae? I don't think his memories are in there at all. You know how people in movies recreate situations that should unearth old memories? Or they like, say a word that is so important to them that it brings all their memories back?"

"Yeah. Didn't you try that, though?"

"Mhm. That's why I think his memories are gone. We spent three hours trying to find a trigger, and there isn't one!" I shouted. There was no reason for me to yell, but I couldn't hold in my frustration.

"Hey, calm down. They have to be there. Remember when I was trying to talk him out of the amnesia? He almost had it. It was painful, not impossible. Remember? This isn't hopeless, Maddie. I promise you," she said. A warm, tingly feeling floated through me, and was utterly convinced of her words. Deep inside, I knew she was using her power, but somehow I still believed what she said.

"I have to go to my training session with Jamie. Talk to you later?" Rae said. I nodded. She left, closing the door gently behind her. I sat there for a minute, stewing over Rae's words. The longer she was gone, the more my doubt increased. The more I wanted to cry.

"Maybe tonight will work. With the sunset. Maybe," I told myself. My voice cracked on the word "maybe."

I needed to shower. Something about hot water helped me think, and I really needed to think right now. I grabbed a towel off the rack and turned on the water. I spent a long time

standing under the gentle rain, wondering. Wondering and wondering and wondering. By the time I shut off the water, steam wafted thickly through the bathroom.

I wrapped a towel around myself and smeared the fog from the mirror. I looked at my face for a minute, wondering what Cole saw there, now that I was a stranger to him.

I left the bathroom and pulled on a pair of shorts and a tank top. I brushed out my hair and put on my gray flip-flops. The small digital clock on the wall said 6:30. Time to go to dinner. As I touched the doorknob, someone knocked. Rae stood on the grass outside.

"It's time for dinner. Ready to go?" she asked.

I smiled a little and nodded. We walked to the dining hall and towards our old table in the corner.

Worn, dark wood shimmered under the bright lights, and the clinking of glasses and silverware and plates filled the cavernous room. We sat down at our four-person table, the two empty seats opposite us a painful reminder that we weren't the same, and that we never would be again.

"Maddie, Rachelle," Jamie said.

We both jumped.

"Cole's here. Be nice." She walked away without another word. Cole appeared, looking awkward and uncomfortable. Rae and I both cringed as he sat down in the chair that had always been Amanda's, across from Rae.

"What's up?"

Before, way back before our lives turned upside down, he

would never say that. He would sit down and say some random fact, something crazy and random and interesting. Something like, "Did you know that sometimes a sloth will mistake it's own arm for a branch and fall to its death?" Never, ever would he say something so normal and stereotypical as "What's up?"

"Hi, Cole," Rae said. She was still staring at that last empty chair, like it was going to jump up and eat her.

"Something wrong?" he asked quietly. I froze. Yes, something was wrong. He couldn't remember anything. He was sitting in Amanda's chair. Amanda wasn't there. He didn't give us a brand new factoid. Jamie was falling apart. I was falling apart.

"No." My answer was automatic, fast, wrong. But Cole didn't know that. He couldn't read my mind the way he used to. He smiled and leaned back in his chair. Rae looked at me. I could feel her stare, like a laser on my face. She knew I was lying, anyway. I looked again at the empty chair across from me, and then back to the one Cole sat in. I glanced back at Rae. Her eyes were fixed on the wall behind Cole's head.

"May I take your order?" One of the robotic waiters stood behind me.

"Yeah. Caesar salad and French fries," Rae said. She held out her hand, and the robot passed her a fork, a napkin, and a bottle of ketchup.

"Macaroni and cheese," Cole added. He stared at the robot, confused. Rae grabbed his hand and stuck it toward the robot. It passed him a fork and a napkin.

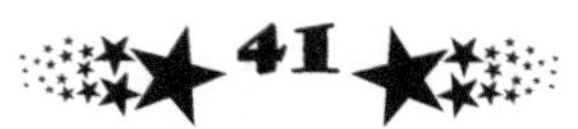

"Um, spaghetti? Thanks," I said. The waiter passed me a fork, a knife, and a napkin. It zoomed off towards the kitchen.

"You guys are acting weird." Cole glared at Rae and me.

"Maybe it's you," I retorted. He blinked. Rae tore her eyes from the fascinating wall and scowled at me.

"He's right," she hissed.

"Whatever. Maybe we all are," I said.

Cole opened his mouth and shut it again.

"Come on, Maddie. He can't help acting different. You can at least try to be normal!" Rae shouted.

I narrowed my eyes.

"You've been staring at the wall like a brick for ten minutes! It's not like you're normal either!" I shot back.

"Guys! Stop fighting! You are being ridiculous!" Cole yelled. I slumped down. Rae put her head in her hands.

"Sorry. I'm a little touchy right now," she muttered.

"Me too. We're all stressed out. Let's agree that none of us is quite right, and move on," I suggested. They both nodded, and then our food came. I stared at the plate of spaghetti in front of me and felt like I might throw up. Rae ate slowly, swallowing each bite with great effort. Cole scarfed down his macaroni and cheese, and then watched Rae glare at the chair next to her. I poked at my food, unable to eat.

"I have to go. Cole, are you still going to meet me on the pier tonight?" I stood and leaned against my chair.

"Yeah, I guess. See you then," he replied. I heaved a sigh and left. I ran through the camp, leaving everyone behind. I

threw open the door to my cabin, slammed it behind me, and fell to the floor.

Hot tears poured out of my eyes, hiccups rattled my chest. Ever since I had left camp the first time, to go on that awful quest, I'd been losing it. Now I was at the breaking point. One more thing going wrong would send me over the edge. I sat on the floor and cried, cried for the life I had lost, cried for the sanity that was leaving me, cried for the boy I loved and the boy who had forgotten me.

 # Cole

After Maddie left, Rae pushed the rest of her salad away and tore her gaze from the last chair. She traced circles on the table with her fingernail.

"You have to tell me what's wrong. I don't want to push Maddie, she seems a little out of it, but I need you to tell me," I said. Rae's eyes shot to mine.

"You're in Amanda's seat. Amanda isn't here. You-"

"Wait. Who's Amanda?" I interrupted.

"The last girl who came with us on the mission we did. She, um, is dead."

"Oh." That explained all the tension surrounding that empty chair.

"Anyway. Back to 'what's wrong.' You told that poor ten-year-old to wipe your memory, and it almost killed you. You don't remember any of us," she said, her eyes locked on mine.

"Why does anyone care?" I muttered.

"I used to be your best friend, Cole. Until Maddie came, I was the most important person in your life. I really care about you, but all of us know that you brought this upon yourself. You know it's killing Maddie. She can't take this too much longer," Rae babbled. She stifled a sob, pinched the bridge of her nose, and took a deep breath.

"Why does she care so much? I know we used to be really close, but she's acting really weird around me," I asked. Rae glanced quickly back at the chair that Amanda should have been occupying.

"Cole? Maddie loves you. A lot. You used to love her, too. But now you don't, and she blames herself," she explained. Her eyes were shiny with tears.

"She loves me?" I asked, stunned.

Rae nodded. "I have to go. I want to check on Maddie." She pushed away from the table, hid her face in her hands, and stumbled out of the dining hall. I was left alone at the table, wondering where to go and what to do. Maddie loved me? That explained her craziness. I felt horrible for not liking her back now, but she was kind of annoying. Not an endearing annoying, but a straitjacket-mental hospital annoying. Someone I sure didn't want to be with. I grabbed a saltshaker off the table and started fiddling with it.

Girls were too complicated for me.

# Rae

I paused at the door to Maddie's cabin. The sound of awful sobs echoed inside. I wanted to cry myself. Telling Cole how Maddie felt, how he was supposed to feel, it hurt. Cole was my best friend. Before Maddie came along, I had been his. I had been at camp longer than anyone. I could barely even remember my old home or my family. I had introduced Cole to camp, helped him with his powers, been his only friend. For a while I thought we had something real together. But then Maddie showed up. Pretty, pretty Maddie, with her blonde hair and blue eyes. She had ripped Cole's affection away, let him fall for her. And then she let him down.

"No. Stop it," I told myself.
It wasn't Maddie's fault. I mean, it was, but she loved him. She didn't mean to hurt him. But I loved him, too. Enough that his confusion hurt me. Enough that I felt his pain more acutely than he did. I touched my hair, twisted it around my finger. I was about to knock on the door when something shattered inside. I threw open the door and raced inside.

Maddie was sitting against the doorframe to the bathroom. A bottle of bright orange nail polish was broken and spilled on the tile near her right foot. She had her forehead against her knees, her arms around her legs. She was shaking with sobs. I stepped back and closed the door, and then went over and sat next to her. Unsure whether she knew I was there

or not, I bumped her elbow with mine.

"Go away." Her voice was small and shaky.

"No. I need you to talk to me," I replied in my best convincing voice. Using my power was like singing would be for a normal person. It was different from talking, but still simple. I could adjust the strength, like changing the pitch of a tune, but I couldn't always control it. Not yet, anyway.

"I don't want to. I know you're mad at me, Rae. I know you blame me. Everyone does. Cole wouldn't have done this to himself if I hadn't done what I did," Maddie replied. She didn't look up.

"That's not true. I'm not angry. Nobody blames you."

"That's a lie. I don't care what you say; I know it's my fault. I know you know that. I know you can't stand to see him like this. I can't either. It hurts, Rae. It hurts so badly. He never would have done this to himself if it weren't for me. Every time he does something differently, asks a question he should know the answer to, looks around like he doesn't recognize a thing, it stabs a little deeper. I'm not going to be able to go on like this. I don't know what to do," she said quietly. Her voice was cracking, fresh tears streamed down her face.

"Maddie. Calm down. We can fix him. I promise. Believe me, I want him back as much as you do." The tears were coming. I knew that I wasn't going to be able to hold on to my composure.

"You love him too, don't you?" Maddie looked up at me with red-rimmed eyes. I nodded, and started sobbing.

"Oh, Rae. I am so sorry. I must have … how long … Oh, Rae. I am so sorry," she cried.

I shrugged.

"It makes no difference. He never liked me that way anyway. But he loved you. I know he did. You two are my best friends. I want you guys to be happy. Until he gets his mind back, neither of you will be. As your best friend, it's my job to help. I swear to you I will," I said through the sobs that rattled my chest. I hated saying it. I hated admitting that I didn't have a chance. But she needed to hear me say it.

"But that means you won't be happy. I feel so bad, I never realized." She leaned over and wrapped her arms around me. I hugged her back, hard.

"It's okay. I promise. But I will do anything to help you two work this out," I assured her. She hugged me tighter, and we cried together over the shattered lives we were trying to live.

"Um, Rae? I'm supposed to meet Cole at the dock in a few minutes. To watch the sunset. And I need help. I don't want to cry," she moaned. Her eyes were red and puffy from crying, and her voice was crackly. I smiled sadly.

"I'll tell him you feel sick and want to do it tomorrow. Does that work?" I asked. She shook her head, sniffed, and wiped tears from her eyes.

"No, I want to do it tonight. Please. But can you talk to me? If you can tell me not to be upset, or cry, I think I can do it." She sounded as if she was trying to convince both of us.

"You need to stay calm," I began. I cleared my throat, and

turned on that power I had. My voice rang out like a melody.

"Don't cry, don't be sad. You and Cole are meant to be. If you can make it through this night, you can do anything. Be strong. Be brave. Don't cry." It felt like the best convincing I had ever done. Maddie's eyes brightened.

I couldn't look at her.

"Yeah. Okay. I'm going to go get ready. Tell Cole to meet me in fifteen minutes? Thank you so much, Rae. Really. So much," she said with a small smile.

I nodded and left the room. I closed the cabin door behind me, and then leaned back against it. What was I doing? I was helping Maddie get together with Cole. I loved Cole. Why was I doing this? Now was the perfect time to go for it myself. And I was wasting it, giving it to Maddie. I clenched the doorknob, closed my eyes, tilted my head back. I was letting friendship get in my way. Why, why, why?

"Rae. Is Maddie in there?" My eyes flicked open, and landed on Cole. He was standing so close. Close enough to touch, close enough to smell. Close enough to kiss.

"Yeah. She wants to meet you at the dock in fifteen minutes. I gotta go." I dropped my head and walked away. I swallowed back the lump in my throat, struggling to keep my emotions collected. I was always there for everyone, but no one ever seemed to return the favor. I sacrificed everything that meant anything to me to help other people, and never got the slightest bit of acknowledgement.

CHAPTER FOUR

Maddie

I couldn't tell Cole how I felt.

I couldn't tell anyone.

I took a deep breath and walked towards the dock. Rae and Cole were both out of sight. The sun was getting low, the light beginning to fade. I kicked off my flip-flops and sat on the end of the dock. My toes dangled in the water. Ripples moved slowly across the placid lake. Everyone was either in his or her cabins or in the dining hall still. The lake was still, calm, smooth. I resisted the urge to jump in and swim, swim until I couldn't anymore. But I didn't. Instead I watched those ripples, spreading farther and farther and farther until they finally melted into the lake.

Footsteps made the deck vibrate beneath me. I turned, and saw Cole. Tall, thin, with hazel-green eyes that made me

want to melt into a puddle. Wavy, pale brown hair hung to his eyebrows. He smiled.

"Hey. How are you?" he asked. I smiled back, but it felt forced. Rae's words were fading a little, and tears were threatening to spill. I wiped under my eyes and shrugged.

"Fine. How about you? Anything coming back?" Now it was his turn hide the emotions spilling across his face.

"No," he replied quietly. He pulled off his sneakers and socks, and sat next to me. The awkward distance between us was unsettling. I hated the way he leaned away from me, the way he refused to be close.

I looked up at the beautiful colors painted across the sky. The sun was nothing but a crescent of unbelievable light around the tip of the mountain range beyond, and the thin layers of clouds around the mountaintop were a wonderful palette of pinks and oranges and yellows. The light was fading around us, and the coming dark only added to the effect of déjà vu crowding this scene. Weeks ago, when I first came to Camp Magic, Cole and I had sat here and watched the stars. As the colors of the sunset faded, and the stars began to appear, my head began to ache.

"Maddie, can I tell you something? Something you may not like?" Cole asked, breaking the silence. I shrugged.

"Yeah, sure." This tense, awkward discomfort was making me cranky.

"Nothing you're doing is helping. Nothing you can do will help. I don't know if there's anything anyone can do. But I

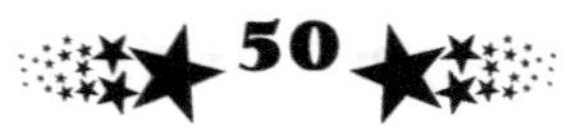

want you to stop trying."

"Cole, stop it. There has to be—"

"No. I don't think there is. Maddie, Rae told me about everything. How I felt. How you still feel. And I'm sorry. But I've given up, and you should too. We can't keep chasing something that doesn't exist anymore, Maddie. We have to start fresh. And you need to let go of me. I know you love me. But I don't love you. I'm sorry. I wish it wasn't true. But it is," he finished. I sucked in a breath.

"Cole. I love you. I screwed up, and I let you go. I shouldn't have. I'm sorry. But that doesn't mean I'm going to give up now. I am going to find a way to get you back. I am going to figure this out. I don't care if you hate me. But I need to fix this. I need to," I said. He looked at me with one eyebrow raised. I could tell that he knew it was a lie, and it was almost a relief to know that he could recognize it.

"Yes, you do. You'd care if I hated you. I can tell. Maddie, I know it's hard. But you have to give up."

I turned away, so that he wouldn't see me cry. I pulled my feet out of the water and tucked them in underneath me. The sun was gone now, and the sky a deep midnight blue. Stars were littered across the night sky, and the Milky Way stretched across the middle. A shooting star flashed by, trailing over the stripe of the Milky Way. It was bright, orange and glowing. It left a thick, bright trail behind it. I gasped, a smile lighting up my face.

"That was amazing!" I cried, reaching out for Cole.

"Maddie." He was frowning, and so far away.

"What? Why are you being like this? Why can't you be yourself?"

"Stop. I don't like you anymore. Accept it. I'm not the same. You need to stop trying," he said.

My mouth dropped open. He got up, grabbed his shoes, and walked away. No goodbye. I collapsed against the cold wood deck, covered my face with my hands, and bawled.

# Cole

I stumbled through camp, fighting to push the emotions back down. Why did she make everything so hard? I didn't like her. I accepted that now. She wasn't even nice to me. She was obsessed with the past, obsessed with what used to be. And then there was Rae. Rae was cool, and she kept her feelings inside. She had been through as much as Maddie, maybe even more. Yet she kept it together, and wasn't trying to bring back the past. She seemed like a better option than Maddie, anyway.

I stumbled into my cabin. Jamie had moved people around so that Rae, Maddie and I would all have some privacy. She knew how messed up we were. I sat on the bed and stared at my hands. I pictured Maddie, probably still out on the pier. Probably crying again. I pictured Rae, probably alone in her cabin. I wondered, if I asked her out, if she would say yes. She was so good at hiding her feelings that it was hard to tell. I

recalled her face, when she had told me to meet Maddie at the dock. I looked up at the ceiling and kicked off my shoes.

I had to choose between two things. Maddie, and the past, or Rae, and the possibility of a new future. At this point, the future seemed to be a much better investment. I hugged my head with my arms and groaned. This was ridiculous.

I had to get out. Trying to be a part of Camp Magic again was impossible. Maddie and Rae were too close, too focused on me. I felt awkward with everyone watching me. Maybe I could convince Jamie to let me go on another mission. Maybe one not so ill fated as the last.

If I was able to go, then I could have a purpose again. Instead of wandering, useless, around Camp Magic, I could be doing something.

I disentangled myself from the blankets on the bed and walked across the messy floor to the door. Crickets chirped outside, and the faint lights from people's cabins barely lit the dark. As I tiptoed through the camp towards Jamie's place, I peered through the dim light toward the pier. A small black shape was curled up on the end of it. Maddie still hadn't moved.

Jamie's door was a pale wood. It almost seemed to glow in the faded dark. I knocked.

"Jamie? Are you in there?" I called out in a half-whisper. I heard footsteps from inside.

"Cole, you're supposed to be in your cabin. It's late," she muttered, rubbing sleep from her eyes.

"I know. I'm sorry. But I really need to talk to you."

She blinked sleep from her eyes, turned, and waved me in behind her. I shut the door and followed.

"What is so desperate that you need to talk to me about it at ten o' clock? Some of us go to bed early so we can keep this place running." She sat on a couch in the living room, and gestured towards a small, cozy chair across from it. Jamie's cabin was huge, with a little kitchen, a den, a living room, a bedroom, and a bathroom. The rest had the main room and the bathroom. Still better than any other campground you'd find, but come on. She put her feet up on the armrest of the couch and looked at me.

"I asked you a question," she said gently.

"Oh. Right. Yeah. It's about Maddie. And Rae, I guess," I paused, and averted my eyes to the leather chair, the tweed pillow, deliberately not looking at Jamie.

"Go on," she prompted.

"Yeah. So, um, something happened with Maddie earlier. That thing we were doing earlier, looking for the trigger thing? Apparently a while ago, before all of this stuff, we watched a sunset or whatever. Maddie thought that if we did that again, it might work." I paused, wondering if I should continue. It was awkward. My pulse was racing in my throat, and I didn't know how to explain what happened. I 100-percent regretted coming here; talking to this woman I didn't know like she was a therapist. I didn't feel comfortable saying anything else, and the right words weren't there anyway.

"And?"

"Um. I guess we kind of had a fight. And I guess I told her that I didn't want to be with her. And she started crying. And I don't know what to do. I don't even know if I actually want my memories back, how am I supposed to know if I want to date this girl?" I blurted.

"What can I do to help? I don't really understand how there's anything I can do here," she said carefully.

"I need something to do. Like a mission, but not necessarily dangerous. I need a purpose. I need a distraction."

"I might be able to handle that. There actually isn't a whole lot of drama right now. The older supers are handling the Others, for now, so we don't have to worry about them. I could have you zip around tracking new kids, though. Does that sound reasonable?" she suggested.

I shrugged. At this point, anything sounded reasonable. I told her that. She was about to say something else, but a knock on the door interrupted us. Jamie stood up, muttering about "those darn crazy sleepless kids." I suppressed a smile and absently rubbed the arm of the leather chair.

Voices echoed down the hallway from the door.

"I can't take it, Jamie. It's like he hates me. I know, I'm sorry, but … Rae? Are you serious! He never… She knows how much …" After a few seconds, I realized that it was Maddie at the door.

"Come on in, sweetie," Jamie said. Footsteps came closer and closer down the hallway. I braced myself for the look on her

face.

Her reaction to my presence was worse than I thought it would be. She stumbled back, her mouth open. She covered her tear-streaked face with one hand while she started to turn and leave the house. Jamie caught her arm and pulled her in, sat her down in a chair next to mine. I tried not to look at Maddie. She was prettier than Rae. That didn't matter, though. Especially when her face was red and puffy from crying. Instead of looking at her, I stared at the fleecy, yellowed rug in the middle of the room. It probably used to be white.

"You two need to pull it together. Maddie, I know this has been hard, but you need to not lose your mind every time life happens. And Cole, you need to figure out how to make decisions without your memory." She didn't elaborate. She didn't need to.

"Jamie, I can't. I try. Every time he gives me that blank stare, or tells me he can't remember a thing, or says that he doesn't feel anything like he used to, it stings a little more. You don't understand!" Maddie cried. I opened my mouth to argue, but Jamie put her hand up in my face, like a stop sign.

"Maddie. I'm not going to tell you that it's not bad. But you need to understand that falling apart is not the answer," Jamie told her. Maddie locked her jaw, let her eyes go up into the corner of the room, and back to Jamie, accompanied with a great sigh.

"I. Can't. Help. It. Stop telling me I don't have an excuse! I did this to him. You want to know what happened? He told me

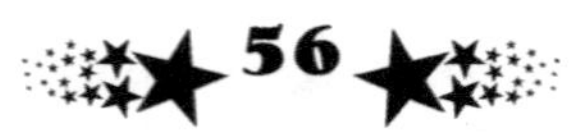

he loved me, and I said I hated him. I growled at him, and then ran away to live in the woods the rest of my life. He told me he loved me. And I rejected him, even though I loved him back. I still do. I told him I hated him, because I hated myself. I hate myself. Don't tell me I need to pull it together. I've been falling apart for fourteen years. I can't stop now." My jaw fell open. I hadn't heard this part of the story before. Rae had only told me the outcome, not the reasoning. No wonder I'd wanted to forget everything.

"That's what happened?" Jamie whispered. Maddie's face contorted, and she hid her face in the sleeve of her black sweatshirt as the tears started to pour again. Jamie turned to me, back to Maddie. Like she wanted me to do something.

"Don't look at me. I don't know her anymore," I said defensively.

Maddie looked up at me, her eyes shining with tears.

"It's my fault you don't. I wish I could fix you. Even Rae wants to help. Did you know that she used to be your best friend? You forgot her, too. It's driving her mad. Not as bad as me, I guess. But enough," she said. She wiped her eyes and tried to smile. I could see that there was something she was holding back.

"I ruin everything. My older sister, Brittney, told me so. Every second of my stupid life proves it a little more." When I heard the name Brittney, I blinked. That name had meant something, before Jezzie and the amnesia.

"Brittney. Did you tell me something about her before?"

I knew it was a bad idea to ask, somehow, but that made me even more curious.

"Yes. Why? Do you remember?" Maddie asked, suddenly excited. I shook my head, and she deflated quickly.

"No. But something about the name seems familiar," I explained in a small voice. Maddie snorted.

"I guess that story would leave an impression, wouldn't it?"

"What story?" Jamie asked. She was interested, had abandoned her reclining position and was now sitting up, leaning on her elbows, rapt.

"Hah. My happy childhood." With that, Maddie wove a tapestry of horror as thick as the one we lived in now. A liar for a father, a pretty yet useless woman for a mother. A sister who told her things she shouldn't have been forced to know.

"Her last words to me were 'it was you who ruined my life.' I can't get them out of my head. Every time I make a mistake, I hear her say it again. Louder, clearer. Sometime it's like a constant roar."

When she finished, Jamie practically had to pick her jaw up off the ground. I found myself staring at my feet, listening to that horror story again and again and again in my mind. How did Maddie live with that? The look on the girl's face answered for me. She didn't.

I'd thought Maddie was messed up because of what I did. I never thought that there could be other things behind her stress. Her family had destroyed her, and when she finally

found someone else to love her, me and Rae and Amanda, she lost it all. If I thought being in my own head was a form of torture, then being in hers would be worse than hell.

"Oh, Maddie. Why didn't you ever tell me this?" Jamie whispered. Her eyes were wide.

"I didn't tell anyone. Until the end of the mission, I had almost forgot about it myself. But then I remembered, and I couldn't forget again. I told Cole, and Jezzie knows. I don't think Rae knows about it. I haven't told anyone else. Until now, I guess," Maddie said. Her eyes were full of tears again. Jamie took a deep breath.

"Maddie, I don't know what to say."

"I do," I said. Maddie's eyes finally met mine.

"Maddie, I'm sorry. I was getting really tired of you crying, and I ended up hating you a little. I thought it was because of me forgetting, and I thought you were overreacting. I didn't know about the rest, about you mom and dad and sister. I feel so bad," I said.

Maddie's eyes flashed to mine. I saw hope there, plain and simple. A hope that infected her entire being. She believed that this confession meant that there was a chance for us. And, truth be told, there probably was.

"You mean you don't actually hate me? It was because you thought I didn't have a real excuse?" she asked, almost excited. When I hesitated, her joy faded. I blinked, unsure what I could say that wouldn't make this worse than it already was.

"I don't know. I don't hate you anymore, but I still don't

know you enough to say if I like you," I said carefully. She nodded, looked away. It was enough for her. Meanwhile, Jamie had recovered from her shock.

"I think you two need a mission. I don't know what you could do, but both of you need something to do other than mourn the past. I'll brainstorm, and you two go and get some sleep. Okay? I'll see you in the morning." Maddie and I nodded, and stiffly rose from the chairs. Jamie waved goodbye to us, and shuffled to her bedroom. When Maddie and I were outside again, she looked at me sheepishly.

"I'm sorry for all the crying. I didn't know it was annoying you. It's been really hard not to, I guess. I'll try to stop though, for you."

"Don't worry about it. I understand now."
She ran her fingers through her hair and focused on something in the distance, blue eyes shining in the faint moonlight. I tried not to stare. She really was gorgeous.

"Thanks for that. I'm going to go back to my cabin, but I'll see you tomorrow," she said. Slowly, carefully, like she didn't want to scare me away, she came up and hugged me tight. I buried my face in her hair and hugged her back. She pulled away, looked up at me through her eyelashes, and smiled. Then she turned and disappeared into the dark. I went the other way, through the camp, and back to the dock. I sat on the edge and stared off into the reflection of the sky above. Stars littered the surface of the lake like someone spilled a jar of glitter. Maddie's explanation had only made things worse for me. I'd thought

I had things figured out, but it was so clear that I didn't. The whole situation made me want to punch something.

I decided to let things happen and roll with it. I was more likely to make things worse by trying to fix it. This decision made, I went back to my cabin and fell asleep.

My dream was hard to follow. I was in a blank, lightless landscape. The ground was smooth and cold, like metal. After a few minutes of this featureless, creepy nothingness, there was a light in the distance. I ran to it, my legs blurring together in that exhilarating rush of speed. When I got close enough to the light, I saw that it wasn't a lamp, but a girl with golden hair. When she turned towards me, though, she didn't have Maddie's blue eyes. Her face matched Rae's. I skittered backwards, away from the combined features of Maddie and Rae. I ran away, as fast as I could, until that terrifying glow of hair was gone. A different, more reddish glow came from the other direction. I began to move towards it, my feet sliding on the smooth floor. When I reached the new point of light, I recognized the figure as another girl. This time, she had bright red hair and glowing green eyes. She stared at me like she could see into my soul. She didn't open her mouth, but I somehow knew it was her voice speaking.

"Cole Quinn, you'll never remember." My knees buckled and light flooded the area. Smooth, pale glass went on for miles on the ground. I spun around, looking for Rae or Maddie or the painfully familiar redhead.

I started running, searching for some way out of the

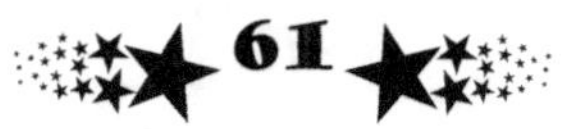

barren landscape, when the glassy floor began to crack, like thin ice over a pond. I scrambled back, but the floor shattered, and I fell through.

I jolted awake, panting and scared. There was more insight to my old life in that dream than I thought I had. A last name, a familiar face, a green man who knew me. There was a message behind that dream.

"Cole? Are you awake? They're about to close the dining hall for breakfast, if you want to eat you have to come out now," Rae called from outside, rapping on the door. I pulled an old sweatshirt over my head and opened the door.

"Hey. Come on, Maddie is waiting there. Jamie wants to talk to us, too."

She grabbed my hand and led me to the dining hall. We walked inside and straight to our table. I could already tell that the bitter awkwardness from last time would be gone. First of all, there was a sense of purpose in the air. Second, the mysterious empty chair was no longer empty. Maddie and Jamie were talking very animatedly when Rae and I sat down.

"Are you serious? They can't do that!" Maddie hissed. Jamie shrugged.

"Mr. Weston is my boss, Maddie. He has a right," Jamie replied.

"Whoa. What's going on?" Rae cut in.

Jamie bit her lip, and Maddie explained in her place.

"The other people with superpowers, you know, like adults, have like, a secret organization all set up over on the East

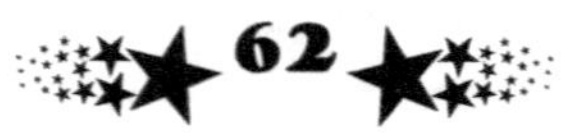

Coast. This dude, Mr. Weston, is going to fire Jamie, send in a different super to fill her place, wipe her memory, and send her back into the normal person world. Meanwhile, they want to take the three of us in for special training, so that we can go and get rid of the Others once and for all," she spat.

Jamie smiled sadly.

"They're coming within the next few days. They told me that a man with the power of mind reading is coming in to take my place. Since I don't have powers myself, they can send me back to the mortal world. If I did have powers, I would probably be imprisoned. They say that I indirectly murdered Amanda. I'm going to have to leave. I'm not going to remember anything about Camp Magic or superpowers."

"No! That's not fair! Come on, Jamie, say no! Camp Magic needs you, not some annoying old man who can hack into our heads!"

"I know, Rae. I have no say in this. Neither do you three, for that matter. You have to go with them. Camp will be okay. You have to listen to them, though. Some of them are a little crazy."

"Jamie, stop. We need you," Maddie said.

"No, you don't. You three especially have grown up so much in the past few weeks. There's nothing more I can do. This is something you need to work out yourselves. Hopefully, I'll see you again. Don't be offended if I don't remember you. I have to go pack up. Goodbye, kids. Good luck." With that, Jamie stood up and walked out of the room. Rae's eyes began to water.

"They can't do this. Stealing her away from us? That should be illegal," Maddie whispered. Rae nodded, then shook her head.

"None of us has a choice. These people are way stronger than us. We have no say. We are going to have to go along with them and say our goodbyes, and hope it all works out in the end."

I didn't know what to say. Maddie and Rae both had strong memories of Jamie. All I knew was that she was supposed to be important to me. They were both adamant, steaming. I felt nothing.

"There has to be a way," Maddie muttered, but her expression betrayed her. She had been defeated.

"We should probably pack. These other people with powers are coming soon, and they're going to take us with them. We should get ready," Rae said. Maddie smiled sadly.

"We have to say our goodbyes to camp. Who knows when we'll get back," she said. Rae wiped a tear from her eye.

"Yeah. You want to do that now? While we have a chance?"

"Yeah. Jamie said they were coming really soon," Maddie replied anxiously.

"Can I come?" I asked. They were so wrapped up in saying goodbye. I didn't really feel a reason to, but I wanted to be with them.

"Of course, Cole," Rae said.

Maddie smiled and reached for my hand under the

table. The three of us stood up and started towards the door. We walked out into the sunlight together, squinting against the brightness. Jezzie, the little blonde girl, came flying out of the hedge spiral and almost ran into us.

"Guys? You have to come with me," she panted, grabbing Maddie's arm and towing her along.

"Jezzie! Jezzie, hold on, what's happening?" Maddie protested. She pulled her arm free and stopped moving. Jezzie stomped back towards her.

"There's a bunch of people here. They put Jamie in a car, and they're asking for you. We don't have time! They're really super duper cranky!" she said, exasperated.

"They're here already?" Rae said, stunned. Jezzie spun to look at her.

"You know who they are?" she yelped.

"Jamie said they were coming. But not yet! We need to pack!" Maddie objected.

A man in a black suit and sunglasses walked toward us through the spiral.

"Are you Rachelle Levine, Madison Thomas, and Cole Quinn?" the man asked in a low growl of a voice, glancing at messy, smudged names written on his palm. Maddie made a squeaking sound, her mouth hanging open. Rae didn't move.

"Yes. But we need a little more time," I said.

"Not going to happen, kids. We need to get this process started ASAP. Hey, blondie? Scram. Gather all your little camper friends and keep them away from the cars. Mr. Riveria will be unloading his stuff, and then he's going to start repairing this place. Okay, kids. Come with me."

Jezzie ran off to follow the man's instructions, and Maddie, Rae and I meekly followed him to the driveway. He opened the back door of a long, black car with tinted windows. We climbed in and sat down. It was set up like a limo, with seats ringing the interior. We were the only ones there. A black sheet of glass separated us from the driver. I buckled my seat belt, and the car's engine roared to life beneath us.

"So much for preparing," Rae muttered.

Maddie's face was glued to the back window, watching Camp Magic fade behind a cloud of dust as the car roared down the driveway. Another car like the one we were in was close behind, presumably with Jamie inside. A third car was left behind, probably Mr. Riveria's. I wondered briefly what Mr. Riveria was like. Jamie said he could read minds. I hoped he would be good to Camp Magic.

"Hey, Maddie. It's gone. Stop staring out the window," Rae said. Maddie shot her a dirty look, and continued to glare at the wall of swirling gray dust that concealed our home. The cars cut through the gates, sped onto the freeway, and began weaving through traffic. A speaker near the black glass crackled.

"Hello, Madison, Rachelle, and Cole. This is your driver, Gregory Vaun. It's going to be a long drive. We won't be stopping often, but there is food and water in a cooler back there. We are heading to a valley in Massachusetts, near Boston. It's been shielded from mortal interference by one of our staff.

Please, do not be difficult. It will make this process easier for us all." The speaker clicked off.

"Boston. That's completely across the country from our home. Oh god, Cole, what are we going to do?" Maddie whimpered. Rae touched her shoulder.

"Maddie, stop. It's going to be okay, calm down." I recognized the faint touch of her power in the words. Maddie's face cleared.

"Yeah. Going to be okay."

Rae smiled, proud of herself.

"I wonder what they want from us," I said. Rae shot me a look. Maddie's eyes flashed to mine.

"They're all adults. Their powers are probably stronger. Why can't they do whatever needs to be done?" she asked.

"I don't know, but I'm a little scared to ask. So let's say that they can't and move on," I backtracked. Maddie blinked.

"Okay. I need some sleep. I'm a little dizzy," she said Rae smiled a little, and Maddie lay down on the seat and closed her eyes. Her breathing slowed, and she relaxed.

"She's having a rough time. I feel so bad for her," Rae said, with a slight condescension in her voice. "Cole? You should probably get some sleep too. Looks like we have a long couple of days ahead of us," Rae said, looking into my eyes. In the low light of the car, her eyes looked black.

"Yeah. Okay. See you in a little while," I said. The seat was plasticky and uncomfortable, but I ended up passing out almost instantly anyway.

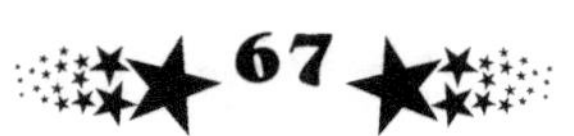

CHAPTER FIVE

Rae

I watched Cole's muscles relax, heard his breathing steady out. Both of them, Maddie and Cole, were sleeping like rocks. I couldn't even think about sleeping. The three of us might never return to Camp Magic. What was I supposed to do? I couldn't be with the two of them if they were together. Now that I had let myself, I loved Cole too much. Looking at him, I wanted to scream. When he was asleep, that little wrinkle between his eyebrows, the one that indicated how hard it was for him to not remember himself, was gone. My shoulders tensed. I couldn't have Cole, or Camp Magic, or even Jamie anymore. It wasn't fair. Stealing another glance at the boy of my dreams, I knocked on the black glass between the driver and us. It slid sideways, and a woman in the passenger seat turned and looked back at me.

"What do you want, Rachelle?" she asked with a heavy Boston accent.

"It's Rae. I was wondering if there's an iPod or a movie player or something here? Cole and Maddie are both asleep, and I'm a little bored."

The woman handed me a laptop and a small DVD case. The glass slid closed again. I flipped through the DVDs, not seeing any familiar titles. I hadn't been a part of the normal world for years. I wondered if this new place would be as isolated as Camp Magic. I watched a couple of movies, but after a while my eyes started watering, so I closed the laptop and put it down on the seat. Cole was starting to wake up.

"How long was I out?" he asked groggily.

"Couple of hours. I was watching movies," I replied uneasily. I looked at Maddie again. She had turned so that her face was turned into the seat. My eyes returned to Cole.

"You okay?" His hazel eyes narrowed.

"Yeah. Yeah, I'm fine. I, um, feel a little—I don't know. Haven't lived anywhere but Camp Magic for a long time."

One of his eyebrows lifted a little. He could tell I was lying. I couldn't tell him the real problem, though. With Maddie asleep, and Cole so close, the temptation to kiss him was impossible to resist.

"Yeah. Me too. It's the only place I remember," he said. I pushed my hair back.

"About that. Are you remembering anything?" I asked. He shrugged.

"I get these feelings. When I see something I must have known before, I get this achy feeling, right here." He pointed to the middle of his forehead.

"When I see you, or Maddie, or Jamie, or my room, it hurts more. Stuff that would have been more meaningful to me," he continued. My stomach twisted when he mentioned me. Pathetic.

"But no actual memories?" I pressed.

He looked at the floor. "Nothing."

The pained expression on his face stung. I crossed the car and sat on the fake leather seat next to him. His eyes met mine as I twisted my fingers together with his.

"Rae, I can't." He slid away. "I don't even know who I am. I don't want to hurt you or Maddie. I need a little space. I'm sorry," he said. His expression contradicted his words. His eyes met mine, the green in them glowing. I closed the distance between us, and our lips met. After a few seconds, he pulled away.

"Rae, please."

I scooted away.

"I'm so sorry, Cole," I said, my cheeks burning. At the same time, all I wanted to do was kiss him again.

He swallowed hard.

"It's okay," he replied. We both looked at Maddie. She was snoring slightly. He looked back at me.

"I don't want to hurt her anymore," he admitted.

"Same. That's the last thing she needs," I agreed, even though

I didn't want to. She had hurt him, and as far as I could tell she deserved this. He took a deep breath.

"We won't tell her," he said. I faked a smile.

"So, what movies do they have?" he asked. I grabbed the DVD case and the laptop. He picked a movie, and we watched it together. I was all too aware of his closeness, the memory of the kiss playing itself over and over in my mind.

Maddie woke up halfway through the movie. She sat up, blinking sleep out of her eyes, and pulled her hair out of its messy ponytail. She shook it out, raked her fingers through it, and looked up at us.

"Hey there, sleepyhead," Cole said. She smiled.

"How long was I asleep?"

"A few hours," I said.

"Did I miss anything?" she asked.

Cole and I both jumped in, saying no so fast and so loudly and so nervously that the computer dropped to the floor. Maddie looked at us suspiciously.

"Are you sure? Seems like something happened."
I cleared my throat and switched on my power. "Nothing happened. I promise."

She looked confused. "Okay," she said slowly. My cheeks flushed.

"Wait. You're blushing. Something happened!" Maddie insisted.

I stammered through another sentence, but my powers betrayed me.

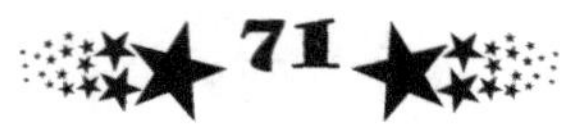

71

Chapter Five

"Guys. Calm down. We don't need to get mad at each other this early into the drive. Who wants to watch a movie?" Cole cut in.

I glanced at him, relieved. Maddie shook her head a little and looked at the ground.

"Right. Of course. Do they have any Disney movies? I feel like watching a kid show," she said. She crossed the car and sat on Cole's other side. Cole twitched, looked at her out of the corner of his eye, and then turned on the laptop. The three of us flipped through the DVD case, and Maddie chose a Disney movie titled Mulan. I had never seen it. Even before I was at Camp Magic, my family hadn't really been into TV or movies. It was a good movie, I guess. But, instead of Cole being so close to me, he seemed increasingly distant. He was leaning towards Maddie, laughing whenever she did, touching her hand every so often. It was like he was trying to make the kiss up to her, even though she didn't even know. It made me a little angry. He didn't owe her anything.

If anything, she owed it to him.

"What next?" Maddie asked when the movie ended.

"I don't know. This car ride is gonna take forever."

Especially long with this new awkwardness between the three of us that hung in the air like smog. We sprawled across seats, sleeping or talking or thinking. After a few more hours, the glass separating us from the driver slides back.

"We're stopping for gas soon. Anything you guys want?" the woman asked.

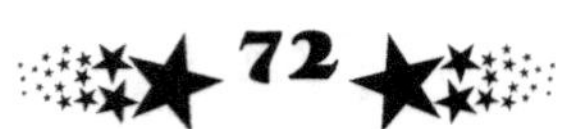

"Candy," Maddie grumbled.

Cole smiled a little.

"Nice, Maddie," he laughed.

Maddie's eyes lit up, and my heart broke a little. I hated her for stealing Cole from me, but I couldn't hate her. She was the closest friend I had left. But I hated her.

"Where are we?" I asked.

"Middle of Utah."

"Okay, kids. I'll grab some candy for you when we stop. Thank you for being good," the woman said. The divider slid back into place. A few minutes later the car stopped, and a few minutes after that the divider slid aside and the woman dropped a plastic bag full of candy onto the seat.

"I got a bunch of different things. I hope there's something you like," she said. Maddie dug through the bag and found some gummy worms.

"What now?" Cole asked.

"I guess we chill for another couple hours," I replied.

"We should play a game," Maddie volunteered, a gummy worm dangling between her teeth.

"Like what?"

She pursed her lips.

"The alphabet game? Or 20 questions? I Spy? Truth or dare?" she offered.

"The alphabet game," Cole decided.

We all scooted over to the nearest window, and it soon became clear that the alphabet game would be impossible. We

were in a half-deserted area, and there weren't any road signs in sight. Groaning, we returned to our old positions. I pondered Maddie's options.

"Do you want to play truth or dare?" I asked. Maddie shrugged.

"Sure."

"I'm down," Cole said.

"Okay, sounds good." I said. "Maddie, truth or dare?"

"Dare."

"I dare you to turn into a monkey."

Maddie grinned, not even hesitating. Her eyes closed. Her skin shivered, blurred, and changed. There was a moment when it felt like my eyes weren't functioning, and then there was a monkey on the seat across from me.

"Very nice," I said with a laugh. Maddie screeched once, and shimmered before turning back to herself.

"I didn't realize you changed. It looked just like you," Cole joked. Maddie playfully punched his arm.

"Rae, truth or dare?" she asked.

"Truth."

"What actually happened while I was asleep?"

I cursed under my breath. There was a sense of satisfaction in her voice. I glanced at Cole. He looked worried.

"Um, we broke the computer. It doesn't really work right anymore. Playing movies is the only thing it can do without shutting off," I lied. I could see the doubt written clearly on Maddie's face. My spine tingled as I turned on my power.

"No, really. I dropped it on the floor, and the hard drive fell out. Cole tried to fix it, but it still isn't working." My lies even worked on Cole. He was nodding, a blank look in his eyes as he replayed the scene that hadn't happened in his head. Power tickled in my stomach, and I couldn't hold back a devilish smile.

"Okay, so, Cole. Truth or dare?" I asked to distract them. "Truth."

"What's your biggest fear?" Maddie interrupted. I shot her a glare.

"It's my turn to ask!" I said. Maddie stuck her tongue out at me. Neither of us noticed the worried set of Cole's eyebrows, the slight downward twist of his lips.

"Never remembering," he whispered.

"What?" I asked, distracted.

"My biggest fear is never remembering who I was," he repeated.

Maddie looked confused. "I thought you said you had given up on it?"

"I want to give up on it. I hate how much I depend on who I was. But I can't. It's impossible to let go of almost fifteen years of experiences like it's nothing. I wish I could let go, really I do. But no matter how much I try, my biggest fear is that I'll never find out who Cole Quinn used to be," Cole said. There was a sad, faraway, pitiful look in his eyes. Usually he didn't let his emotions show like this. It was indescribably cute.

"I'm sorry," Maddie said. There was a weight to her

words that made me feel like there was a deeper meaning to the overused, meaningless phrase.

"Maybe we should do something else," I said.

Cole held up his hand. "Not yet. Maddie should do a truth."

I saw a faint flicker of fear register on Maddie's face, but it was gone before it was really there.

"Fine."

"If you could have dinner with any dead person, who would it be? I mean, they'd be alive. You know what I mean," Cole asked.

Maddie blurted something out, obviously not thinking at all. My jaw dropped.

Was she serious?

Maddie

"The old Cole," I said. Immediately I clamped my mouth shut, wishing I could reel the response back in. Rae's eyes hardened, anger tightening her features. Cole blinked, frozen.

"Sorry. Um, Elvis?" I amended.

"Cole isn't dead, Maddie." Rae sounded really mad.

"I didn't say he was. I said he might as well be," I retorted, then cursed myself again. "No, sorry. It's just that he's not the same." Cole's face twisted into a thoughtful grimace.

"She's right. It's like I don't exist anymore."

"Um, no. That's not right. I, um, miss how you used to be," I stammered.

"That's because you were the only girl he looked at. You're jealous now, because he likes other people. You don't want the competition!" Rae's voice was shrill.

My mouth turned sour. Looking at Rae, my heart stung. Did she hate me? If she didn't, then why on earth was she treating me like this?

"Whoa, Rae. Easy," Cole said. I was frozen, unable to move. Unable to defend myself. But it was true, wasn't it? I wanted that poor boy all to myself. And now that Rae was trying to pull him away, I was starting to hate her. I couldn't make the words come out of my mouth. Rae, you're wrong. That's not it. I'm not jealous. Why are you accusing me like this? But I couldn't make myself move. I couldn't speak the lie. Apparently, Rae knew exactly what was happening in my head.

"That's what I thought," she sneered, turning away.

"Rae. Go easy on her. You said yourself that the last thing she needed was another way to hurt," Cole said. All I could move was my eyes. I watched Rae through a hazy fog of pain. She still looked angry.

"That was before she decided to bring up this painful topic. Again. You say you don't want to hurt her anymore, but she seems to think it's fine to go around reminding everyone that you can't remember one stupid thing!" Rae screamed.

I finally broke free. "Rachelle. You are being ridiculous! I

don't try to bring it up. It hurts me just as much as you or Cole!"

Rae rolled her eyes, a sarcastic and stony grimace twisting her face into something I didn't want to see.

"Then why the hell do you keep doing it?" she said, her voice calm but unbearably hostile.

"It's funny that you think I try to," I muttered. I turned away from her, into the black leather seat. Cole glared at Rae, and scooted closer to me. I waved him away.

"Not now, Cole." He left again. I felt tears coming, hot and messy. I couldn't let them see me cry again. Rae had enough reasons to hate me right now.

"How can you stand her?" I heard Rae whisper to Cole. I waited longer than I should have had to for his answer.

"Because it would hurt all of us too much if I didn't."

I stewed over this, trying to understand what he meant. I couldn't decide if he meant it in a bad way or not. While I tried to understand, my brain slowed down. After a few more minutes, I fell asleep again.

Cole

I tried not to look at Rae. I could practically smell the smoke pouring out of her ears. Instead, I focused on Maddie's face. She looked so calm, so peaceful. All the worry was gone from her face, all those little wrinkles that had developed on her forehead and around her eyes disappeared. As there always was when I looked at her, there was a certain degree of pain in my skull. But there was also something warm and nice at seeing her without the giant weight she'd been carrying.

Before, I'd always shied away from the idea of love. It seemed stupid and girly and silly and mushy and gooshy and absolutely coated in cooties. But I knew from the past week that Maddie's arrival at Camp Magic had changed all that. Obviously I had loved Maddie. Now, I wasn't so sure. But I felt more open to the idea of it. Rae and Maddie both seemed set on convincing me that I loved them, but I couldn't take it much longer. How was I supposed to love someone else, and truly know them, when I didn't even know if I had any siblings? Or where I had lived? Or even if I loved someone else before?

"Cole. Stop staring at her," Rae snapped.

"Why should I?" I retorted angrily. Rae was getting really cranky, and I was kind of sick of it.

"Because you don't like her. You keep saying that you can't stand her incessant crying and ridiculous obsession with you. You are supposed to be sick of her, and yet you keep staring at her and being nice to her and pretending that you don't want to punch something!" she snapped.

"Because I don't. I still feel something there, Rae. I wasn't sure at first, but now I am. And for a while, I thought I might like you. But your attitude right now is kind of pissing me off. Soon I'm going to start hating you, and I don't think you want that."

"Cole! What is wrong with you?" she hissed.

"I'm trying to figure everything out. First impressions

count, Rae. Just because you've known me for forever, doesn't mean I've known you. This is all new, and I'm not sure I like who I'm meeting," I replied. Rae's face turned a violent shade of purple, and then she burst into tears. I groaned internally, wishing I could escape these overemotional girls and their crying and their feelings and their infatuation with me and their insistence on sharing all of these things with me.

"I don't know what's happening to me. I don't want to be mean, I really don't. I can't stop." She wiped her tears off on the blue sleeve of her sweatshirt.

"Go to sleep, Rae. Maybe things will be better when you wake up," I said soothingly. Not the way she could, but it was enough. She sniffled and nodded, curling up with her face to the back of the seat. Within minutes her breathing steadied. I studied them both, feeling waves of guilt rock me. I had hurt them both in ways I couldn't fix, and whatever I chose to do would hurt them again. I had nowhere to turn.

The air in the car was getting colder, and I crossed to car to peek out the window. Snow laced the ground, fluffy white filling the view. Fat, icy flakes swirled through the air, turning the air into a freezing, glittering mass of nothingness. Faint red taillights lit up the blizzard, lining the road ahead. What month was it? At Camp Magic, the seasons didn't change. It was always summer. So I'd heard, anyway. But it had to be winter everywhere else.

I knocked on the glass between the driver and us. It slid back.

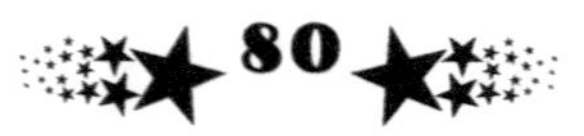

"Yes?"

"What's the date?" I asked, glancing at the thick flurries of white outside the window.

"November 28," the woman in the passenger seat replied. I sucked in a breath as an ache sliced through my brain. The date was important.

"How much longer are we on the road?"

"Only nine hours more. We're making really good time," she replied.

"Tim's helping," said the man in the driver's seat.

"Who's Tim?" I asked, sensing an opportunity to talk to someone.

"A man with the power to make time move quickly," the driver explained. His voice was deep enough that I could feel it rumble through my chest.

"Yep. He's not really powerful, though. None of us pre-generations are. You guys are lucky," the woman said.

"Laura, stop. Christie wanted to explain everything when we got to the town. We don't want to freak the kids out," the driver scolded.

"Right. Sorry, Cole," she said, frowning.

"What are Madison and Rachelle doing?" the driver asked.

"Sleeping," I replied.

"They should. They need it," he said. I leaned back into the seat with a frown.

"I guess. It's a little lonely, though. Even though they're

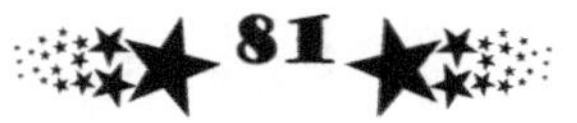

both being kind of — never mind," I said, backtracking quickly. "I needed someone to talk to,"

"Cole. Life's going to suck for a while, but things will get better," Laura said with a sympathetic smile.

"Yeah. Okay. Yeah." I backed away from the two adults. The glass slid closed. There was so much that didn't make sense in my life right now. Too many secrets, too many mysteries. Too much missing from my mind. I could feel that I didn't react to things the way I should have. Life wasn't the same. I decided to go to sleep, so that I wouldn't have to think about any of these things. Otherwise, I was sure I'd go completely insane. I sprawled across the seat, peeking once at the girls before I closed my eyes. They were both asleep. And not fighting, which was super cool. I closed my eyes, and felt comfortable darkness sweep my mind.

* * *

I woke up when Maddie started shaking my shoulder and Rae stared shaking my foot.

"Wake up, dude! We're here," Maddie said.

"Finally. Maddie and I have been up for like, an hour. We were getting bored of watching you sit there like a brick," Rae said.

"A brick that snores," Maddie giggled. They laughed together.

"Okay, what did I miss? You guys were ready to punch each other earlier," I reminded them. Maddie looked confused for a second, but then her face brightened again.

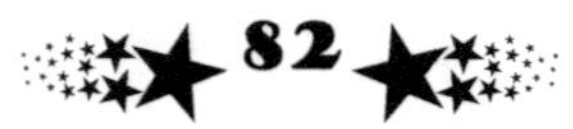

"We talked it out. We're good," she said. Rae winked at me. I blinked and shook my head.

"Okay. So where exactly is here, then?" I asked.

"The whatever old-person super power camp-town thing. I don't know what they call it," Rae said. She tugged her sweatshirt sleeves over her hands.

"We're going through, like, a scan or something right now," Maddie added.

"Mmkay. Sounds good. So, are you guys excited?" I asked. Maddie wrinkled her nose.

"Eew. I'm going to miss Camp Magic. And Jamie. I don't know, but this seems like it's going to suck," she grumbled.

"Yeah, agreed. We are going to be, like, the youngest people there," Rae said.

"The only delinquents," I corrected. "There might be some controlled kids there."

"That sounds really boring," Maddie said with a laugh.

"Okay, kids. Hop out here. There'll be a man there, his name's Ricardo. He'll show you where to go," the driver called to us. Rae flung open the door and leaped out. Maddie followed, leaving me to scramble and tumble after them, my feet automatically speeding up as I tried to catch up.

"What was the guy's name we were supposed to look for?" Rae asked, looking around her in confusion. There were a hundred people milling around. We were on a wide paved street, lined with small shops with names that betrayed magical qualities. Snow was piled in thick drifts next to the road. Rae,

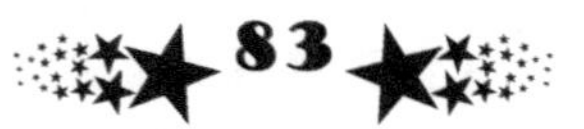

Maddie and I stood in a close huddle, confused and lost. We hadn't been out in the real world, with other people we didn't know, for months or even years. This was crazy.

"Madison Thomas! Rachelle Levine! Cole Quinn!" A strong, booming voice cut through the crowds. We searched for the source.

"Ricardo?" Maddie called, quiet and shy.

"Hey, kids! Come on, I have to show you around!" a man said. He was pretty average size, with a Spanish accent. His black hair was short and combed into a stiff Mohawk.

"Come on, come on! There's not much time to lose! I'm going to take you to your apartment, let you get settled a bit, and then show you to the labs. Until then, I'm going to show you around town a little," he said. He led us down a crowded street, filled with people and taxis. The sidewalks were icy, and snow was piled in thick drifts around the corners. A sweet smell hung in the air, and purple-tinted fog drifted overhead. Ricardo pointed out important stores and buildings. Maddie was looking around in dazed wonder, but Rae was staring intently at something else. Me.

She grabbed my hand and held me back until Ricardo and Maddie pulled forward a little bit.

"Cole? I didn't tell her anything," she said.

"I know, Rae. I don't get how you guys are so happy now," I replied uneasily.

Girls were so confusing.

"I apologized. She doesn't want to be mad. I don't either,

truthfully. I couldn't take it anymore. So we talked and now we're good. I didn't say anything about … the kiss," she said.

My eyes darted to Maddie. Rae squeezed my hand, and when I didn't look at her, she placed her other hand on my cheek and turned my face towards her.

"Don't worry, Cole. We'll all be okay," she said, her warm brown eyes melting into mine. Of course, Maddie chose that instant to turn and look at us. I pictured what she saw, how that image would affect her. Rae and I, holding hands, eyes locked, her fingers still touching my cheek. I suddenly felt like I was betraying her, somehow. I pulled away from Rae and caught up with Maddie and Ricardo. Maddie refused to look at me.

"We're at your apartment. I'll give you an hour, then take you to the labs. There's stuff up there you can use, since you didn't get to pack back in California," Ricardo said.

We were stopped in front of a huge, towering building. After six floors, the brick walls vanished into the purple fog.

"Um, how do we know where to go inside?" Maddie asked, staring at the plethora of windows.

"Say your names at the desk. Lindy will tell you where to go," Ricardo said. He shooed us into the building and disappeared back into the town. Rae stepped fearlessly up to the giant wooden desk and knocked on it. The lobby we were in was dominated by the desk, but a few chairs and card tables were scattered around. A few seconds after Rae knocked, a tiny, fat woman waddled out of an office behind the desk and hopped onto a swivel chair.

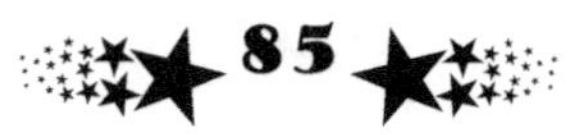

Chapter Five

"How can I help you?" she asked in a harsh and screechy voice.

"Rae, Maddie, Cole," Rae began, pointing to indicate who she was talking about. "Ricardo said that someone named Lindy would help us get checked in and show us our room."

"I'm Lindy," the woman said. She plucked a key off the hook on the wall behind her and waved us after her. A hallway led around the desk and to a set of elevators. Lindy consulted the key and tapped the "up" button. The doors dinged open, and the four of us piled inside.

"I hate elevators," Rae muttered as Lindy pressed the button next to number sixteen. The elevator shot upwards, leaving my stomach on the ground floor. Rae looked dizzy. The doors opened, and Lindy marched out and turned left. Maddie brushed past me to follow her.

We followed Lindy down the halls, turning right and left and left and left and right again, and finally stopped in front a brown wooden door. Lindy handed me the key, so I stuck it into the lock and twisted. The door creaked open, and we walked inside.

"Most people thought you should have separate apartments, but we didn't have enough vacancies. So there are two bedrooms, one for the girls and one for Mr. Quinn. I'll send Ricardo up here when it's time," Lindy said. She left, closing the door behind her. The apartment was massive, with a big living room directly ahead and a kitchenette to our left. There were four rooms leading off this one: two bedrooms, a bathroom, and a closet. It was all decorated in varying shades of hotel blue and green.

"This one is ours, Rae. It has two beds," Maddie called from the bedroom on the right. Rae disappeared into it, and I went into my own. There was one twin-sized bed with a blue quilt. Big, hotel-like windows spanned one wall. It was a perfectly decent room, sure, but I missed my cabin at Camp Magic.

I opened the closet and looked inside. None of the clothes were anything I usually wore. I glanced down at my wrinkled camp T-shirt, basketball shorts, and running shoes. I couldn't remember exactly what my style was supposed to be, but the only kind of clothing in my closet at Camp Magic was like what I was wearing. Not the gray, polyester, oversized lumps of fabric that hung in the closet.

"Hey, Cole. Come here," Maddie called. I left the room and stood near the couch, while Maddie and Rae, giggling, tumbled out of theirs.

"Look at this! How old do they think we are? Seven?" Rae demanded. The sweatpants and sweatshirts looked like something out of a prison ad. All the same vibrant shade of gray. Maddie rubbed the slimy fabric on her arm, laughing.

"Why haven't you changed, Cole?" she asked.

"It's the same stuff in my room," I replied with a shrug.

"We should order other clothes," Maddie said. I nodded, staring skeptically at the gray fabric. Rae headed straight for

the wall phone, and searched the laminated card next to it for a number. She dialed it in and waited for an answer.

"Hello, this is Rachelle Levine. I'm one of the three kids from Camp Magic. My friends and I were getting ready to clean up and change, but we can't wear any of the clothes here. Is there any way we could … oh, of course. Yes. Should I call, or is there a … Oh, okay. Sorry! Jeez, I said sorry, calm down!" Rae slammed the phone down.

"People are so cranky sometimes," she muttered as she dialed another number. I went and fell over the back of the couch, sprawling across the cushions. Maddie found the TV remote and flopped into the blue armchair. She pulled her knees up to her chest, and for a second, I saw through the convincing mask she was wearing. She wasn't okay. Her blue eyes flicked to Rae, and then that vulnerable expression was gone. For a moment, she had looked scared. She'd looked lost, alone, and depressed. But now she was smiling and cheerful smiling Maddie again, searching for a movie while Rae talked to whoever was on the phone. I blinked, wondering if I'd imagined it.

"Seriously. We need them delivered in fifteen minutes. I am not, I assure you. Please? Okay, I guess that's all right," she said. Maddie turned on an obnoxious action movie, and sunk into the chair until her eyes barely peeked over her knees.

"I explained what we want. They said they would be here as soon as they could," Rae said. She sat on the couch.

"Cool," Maddie muttered.

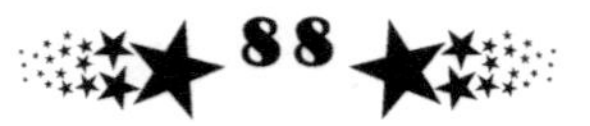

Rae glanced at me, an eyebrow raised, a question in her eyes. I shrugged, unsure how to answer.

"What movie?" Rae asked, her feet on the coffee table.

"Something my dad used to watch a lot. I don't know, felt like home," Maddie replied. She was the only person who wanted to watch it, but didn't make any move to change it.

"Cool. What time did Ricardo say he was coming back?" Rae asked. She glanced at me again, and then at Maddie. A trace of that awful sadness was creeping into Maddie's features, and I knew Rae saw it.

"He was giving us an hour. We've been here around half," Maddie's voice was more apathetic than I had ever heard it. Rae flicked my leg. I shrugged again.

"I'm going downstairs to meet the guy with the clothes. Cole, can you come with me?" she said, tossing her hair. Maddie blinked twice, as if waking herself up, and moved her feet to the floor.

"Not me?"

"I don't think we all need to go. I was thinking Cole could help carry stuff back up. But if you want to come—"

"No, it's okay. Go ahead. See you later," Maddie said. Suspicion and a sad acceptance put wrinkles on her forehead.

"Okay. Cole, come on." Rae put on her old flip-flops and stood by the door. I shrugged apologetically to Maddie and followed Rae out the door. As the thick panel was closing, the sound of muffled crying hit me like a gunshot.

Rae was already pulling me away.

CHAPTER SIX

 Maddie

I was exhausted.

The tenuous façade of happiness I was trying to hold on to was getting heavier and heavier. Pretending that the dark gray fog wasn't overwhelming my consciousness and smothering all emotion and threatening to swallow me alive was like holding the world on my shoulders. If I stopped resisting for even a second, it would crush me.

Rae had made her attempt to apologize. I could tell she was at least a little bit sorry. And I knew that she was right. So I forgave her, at least on the outside.

Those comments still stung, though. And knowing that she loved Cole, and that something happened between them in the car, and they were together out there, while I was here … I couldn't help but cry. Cole obviously didn't know what was really happening. He still had come no closer to any sort

of decision between Rae and me. And his quality time with Rae was making my heart ache.

So I watched the movie and raided the kitchenette and cried. Cole and Rae didn't come back, and Ricardo didn't come to pick me up, and neither did Lindy. After 45 minutes, I started to worry. I changed back into my old Camp Magic clothes and left the eerily quiet apartment. Hallways blurred together as I wove through them, walls and numbers shifting before my eyes. Finally I found the elevators, and blearily stabbed the button for the lobby. I felt sick. The floor rolled under my feet as I stumbled to the front desk. Lindy sat in her swivel chair, furiously typing on her computer.

"Lindy? Do you know where Cole and Rae are? They came down here like an hour ago," I said. The words slurred together in a jumbled mess, but Lindy understood.

"Ricardo took them out to the labs. Rachelle said you weren't feeling well and didn't want to go. She and Cole left this box to send up to your room," she replied, lifting a huge box from under the counter.

My knees wobbled.

Rae lied.

They left without me because Rae used her honey-sweet words to convince them that I didn't even want to go. As I took the box from Lindy, ice crept through my veins. How could she do that to me? Didn't she understand that I hated this as much as she did? Nausea churned in my stomach. My knees shook with a new intensity. Lindy stood behind her desk, her mouth

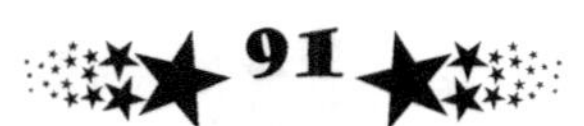

moving frantically. It sounded like echoes in a cave, like screams underwater. The words were unintelligible. Colors turned sepia, faded and brown and crumbling. I clutched the box in my arms, and stumbled forward until I was leaning on the counter.

Rae betrayed me again. Cole wouldn't have done this. It was Rae.

"Madison …" like a thin scream from the end of a tunnel, a weak voice finally penetrated the dizziness that made my body sway against the cool surface of the desk. The box fell to the floor. A reaction like this was completely unprecedented. What was happening to me?

"I don't know, Chris! She's pale as a ghost, leaning on the desk, looking like she's going to pass out and die!" Lindy shrieked.

I couldn't see anything but swirling brown shapes, and my limbs were feeling fuzzy. This was no emotion anymore. It was serious and I couldn't stop it.

"The Dansamine? No way! She's been getting in for days! She shouldn't have a reaction now. Oh, my! Chris, you couldn't have mentioned that sooner? I'll rush her over, okay?" Lindy slammed to phone down. Huge tremors exploded through me. Cold hands touched the tops of my shoulders. My knees collapsed. My head hit the floor in an explosion of white, and my eyes fluttered shut. Or maybe open. I couldn't tell anymore.

"Somebody help me!" Lindy screamed. Her voice pierced my ears, and it hurt. Voices battered my ears, until they faded into distant echoes. A hundred hands touched me, each one so

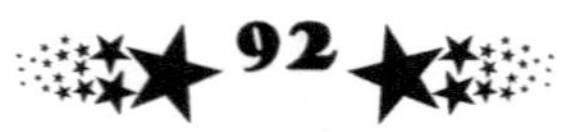

frigid and hard that it burned. I needed someone familiar. The pain, the raw stinging burning frozen pain, was too terrible to endure without someone I knew. Someone who knew me.

"Cole!" The primal scream lifted my back off the floor. One word, one name, loaded with so much agony and memory and meaning.

"Cole!"

"Shh, sweetie. Come on, Maddie, quiet now. We are going to help you," something said soothingly.
What was happening to me?

* * *

"Maddie, honey, come on, wake up," a sweet voice crooned. I tried to open my eyes, but my lids wouldn't respond.

"She's waking up. I can feel it. Maddie? Can you hear me?" This voice was all too familiar. The only voice I had wanted to hear through the whole nightmare, blackness heavy as a mountain.

"Give her a moment, Cole. Madison, sweetie, wake up," the first voice said.

Cole.

I forced my eyes to open, blinking rapidly to try and clear my vision. I was lying on a narrow bed, cold and stiff. Blank white walls surrounded me, but the ceiling was a comforting shade of pale green.

Two faces leaned over me, eyebrows worriedly pushed together. One was a woman, with a huge beaky nose and frizzy

black hair. Her skin was the creamy color of milk chocolate. The other face was the one I most desperately wanted to see. Caramel colored wavy hair falling haphazardly over his forehead. Hazel green eyes boring into mine. A hint of a smile touched his mouth. Cole. Cole!

"Maddie, you're okay," he breathed.

The nurse tapped his shoulder and gave him a stern look. He nodded and left the room. I stared wistfully at the door he had left through as the nurse began bustling around the room, attaching things to the IV in my arm and checking my temperature.

"You definitely scared us, hon. Usually we don't see reactions like that to Dansamine," she said as she scribbled on a clipboard.

"What is Dansamine?" I asked. It sounded suspiciously like a drug.

"It's a drug. You were given it to help steady your emotions. Jamie thought that you might need it. Rachelle, too. You've been on it since before you left Camp Magic. Your emotional reaction two days ago triggered a dangerous hormonal response. You're under control now. The Dansamine is out of your system. You can leave soon, once the last of the anesthesia wears off," she explained.

Jamie and Rae drugged me. Fantastic.

"Have I missed anything important?" I asked.

"I'll let Cole tell you. I'm done for now. I'm going to send him in," she replied.

I let my eyes close for a few seconds until a hand twisted into mine.

"Hey, Maddie." Cole stood next to me, a small smile on his face.

"Cole. I'm so glad you're here," I said. Careful not to upset the needle in my arm, I sat up and leaned on one elbow.

"I came as soon as I heard. I know you sat with me while I was out, so I thought I'd return the favor."

"How long have you been here?"

"Two days. Rae's been touring and training and sleeping. She was here a few hours in the beginning, but didn't stay," he said.

There was an uneasiness to his words that told me loud and clear that something else happened, but he didn't tell me.

"Where are we?"

"The hospital-slash-testing facility of the labs." Cole wrinkled his nose and glared at a Band-Aid on his arm.

"Testing facility?" I asked fearfully.

"Yeah. They needed to test our power levels and some other stuff. They took blood."

"That's terrible."

Cole looked to the door as raised voices rattled the doorframe.

"We can't send them back there! Are you crazy?"

"No, Georgia. You don't get it. This trend is still continuing. Those kids have more knowledge and power. They are better equipped than we are!"

"They're children!"

"Rachelle is sixteen. Both Cole and Madison turned fifteen recently. They aren't children. They've done this before." The door burst open, and the nurse before stormed in, followed by an unfamiliar man.

"Georgia," the man begged, touching the nurse's arm.

"No. It's a death sentence. Go away, Doctor. I'll take care of these two." The nurse, Georgia, plucked the needle out of my arm and unfolded a Band-Aid over the red spot. The doctor grumbled and exited.

"What was that about?" Cole asked.

"A lot of people want you to go back to destroy the Others' lair. Soon. Alone. You and Maddie and Rae," Georgia said. Her face clouded, and she twisted her fingers into her blue uniform.

"They want us to go back? Even after we ruined the whole thing before?" I squeaked.

"Yes. They believe that—"

"We have more information," I interrupted.

"And power. But I'll let someone else explain that," Georgia added. She scribbled something onto her clipboard.

"But I don't have any information," Cole complained.

"I don't know, kids. You are free to go, though, Madison. I'll call Ricardo to pick you up."

Georgia gave me my clothes to change into, and directed Cole and I to the front of the labs, which opened up onto the main street. Ricardo was there, and led us back to the

apartment, constantly jabbering in his cheerful accent. He left us in Lindy's care, who helped us find our room again. Rae sat on the couch, a family sized bag of chips tucked under one arm. A sappy romance movie was playing on the TV.

"Hi, Rae," Cole said, poison in his voice.

"Oh, hi. How are you, Maddie?" Rae asked. She flicked off the TV and rolled the bag of potato chips shut.

"Fine, no thanks to you," I growled. The anger from earlier still burned.

"What do you mean?" Rae was definitely focused now. Cole awkwardly passed us and closed the door to his room behind him.

"Have you ever heard of Dansamine, Rachelle?" I asked. Recognition flickered in her eyes, but she quickly blinked it away.

"Maybe. Why?"

"Because apparently someone has been slipping it to me since before we left Camp Magic. Someone I really, really trusted," I hissed.

"That's c-crazy," Rae stammered. Her face was red. She picked at her fingernails.

"The nurse told me everything. Why, Rae? I mean, I trusted you more than anyone, and the whole time you were drugging me? And lying to my face? What was your goal? "

"No, Maddie. Jamie wouldn't let me."

"Bull. It was all you, wasn't it?" I accused. Rae winced as she ripped off a hangnail.

"It would have freaked you out."

"It freaks me out that you were drugging me and I didn't know! That reaction could have killed me, Rae. And you weren't even there while I was recovering. No, you were off having fun in this god-awful place while Cole stayed with me!"

"You know what? It's not worth my time to sit and watch you sleep!" Rae yelled. She stood up and clenched her fists. Her eyes glowed with anger.

"Maybe it's not worth my time to know you!" I screamed back. I didn't remember moving, but the next thing I knew I was in her face, screaming obscenities at her and clawing at her face. She fought back, fingernails sharp despite her picking at them, and a shallow scrape stung my cheek as I screamed and hit and cried. Cole burst out of his room and grabbed Rae's arms. He pulled hard, tearing her away from me and sending her sprawling on the dark green carpet. He shoved me, and I collapsed onto the couch.

"What the hell, guys! You used to be best friends! Can you calm down and spend five minutes not trying to kill each other?"

Rae glared at me from her spot on the floor.

"Why do you suddenly hate each other? I may not remember a lot, but when Rae came back, you were so happy you cried," Cole said to me. He turned to Rae.

"You were perfectly happy with the rest of us until we got in that stupid car. Why can't the two of you be nice?"

Rae looked at me again.

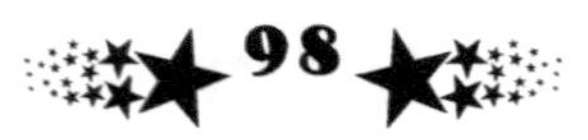

Cole. Cole was the reason. We both loved him. Rae was jealous, I was confused and an emotional mess. But we both loved him, and we knew that both of us couldn't. So we hated each other, and Cole was caught in the middle of it. Like a giant spider web, we were all stuck. The web getting stickier and more complicated as we struggled, suffocating us all.

But it wasn't Cole's fault. So, through all the resentment and jealousy and hate, we silently agreed to keep this from him.

"I don't know, Cole. I can't stand her. Can we move on? I need to get out. Take a walk."

Rae stood up and wrapped her arms around Cole. He shrugged her off, but not before she whispered something in his ear. He nodded, and she left the apartment. I couldn't meet his eyes. Shame sat in my stomach like a rock. I was dragging everyone else. Without saying another word, I got up and left the apartment.

Rae was long gone by the time I made it outside. With no plan in mind, my directionless wandering led me away from the apartment building, into an alley. I sat down on the cool, damp pavement and pulled my knees into my chest. Now would be the time to cry. Rae couldn't mock me for it here. But the tears wouldn't come for once, for whatever reason. The sun was high overhead, but the air was frigid. I wished I had thought to grab a jacket before I left the apartment. Goosebumps crawled on my skin.

"Rachelle!" I heard. My head snapped up. Cole's voice.

"There you are! You could have told me where to meet

you," he said. I scrambled towards the entrance of the alley, slipping on patches of ice. I stopped short of the sidewalk and peeked around the corner. Cole, a sweatshirt draped over his arm, stood in front of Rae. He held out the sweatshirt and smiled.

"Thanks. And I'm sorry. I was a little frazzled," she apologized, taking the sweatshirt. She looked short next to him. Her dark hair tumbled down past her shoulders. I wanted to rip it out of her head.

"It's okay." He looked nervous as she stared at him. I flattened against the wall and took a deep breath. I wasn't supposed to know they were here. Anything could happen.

"Cole, you should like me." That, for instance. That could happen.

"You're supposed to. You have to feel it! You used to. You can again. Forget Maddie. Please. Love me," she said. Her words washed over me. I didn't matter. Rae deserved better. We could be close again.

Then I realized.

She was using her power. She was convincing him to like her. I could practically see the smoke coming out of my ears as I turned and looked around the corner again. Rae had her arms looped around Cole's neck. His hands were in her waist. Horrified, I ducked away. But not before I saw her reaching up, him bending down. Kissing. He looked almost confused, but she was euphoric. I sank to the ground. She'd hypnotized him.

"Rae, no," Cole said.

"Come on, Cole," she said. He didn't protest more. I stood and walked out of the alley, back the way I came. I hid my face as I passed my "friends." I made my way back to the apartment building, trying not to cry.

"Are you okay, Madison?" Lindy asked as I hurried through the lobby.

"No. See you later," I grumbled.

"Hey. I can help." Her shrill voice cut through my mood and made me turn around.

"How. My life is falling apart. Everything keeps getting worse. How can you make things better?" I growled.

"My power. I could help you into a better mood. For a while, at least."

"Sure. Go ahead," I said. Anything was better than this black mood.

"Okay." Lindy closed her eyes. A dense, warm breeze drifted over me, loaded with the scent of cotton candy. My anger and frustration and jealousy melted away, leaving a warm, sweet sensation in their place. I still remembered why I had been angry, but the feelings themselves were gone.

"Better?" Lindy asked. She looked a little strained.

"Yeah. Thank you," I said. I continued to the elevators, and wandered through the hallways to my apartment. I went into the bedroom and leaned on the door. Without quite realizing what I was doing, I sank to the carpet. I suddenly wished I hadn't accepted Lindy's help. Emotions battled within me, the happiness from Lindy smothering the hate and rage and fury. But I wanted to feel those emotions. The image of Rae and Cole kissing was branded into my brain. I wanted to feel infuriated about it, but I was happy. It made my head hurt.

I rolled onto my stomach and sprawled across the thick green carpet, pressing my forehead into the floor. I didn't move for what felt like hours, doing multiplication and counting fat fluffy sheep to distract myself from my emotional turmoil. I heard the apartment door open, and voices drifted in, but I ignored them and continued to solve 53 times 739. Carry the four. Add the 27.

"I hope she's okay."

"I don't care."

"Come on, Rae. You know you do."

"How can you even think of her right now? After…"

"Rae."

Ignore the voices, ignore the voices.

The door handle rattled, the wood trembling two feet from my fingertips. My eyes flicked open, my hand twitched. Numbers flew out of my mind.

"It's locked." The door rattled again.

"Do you think she's in there?"

"Yes. Don't think about it. Come on, let's watch TV." The springs of the couch creaked.

Ignore, ignore, ignore.

"Cole, sit next to me."

"No."

"Are you guilty?"

"Yes."

"Don't be."

"Too late."

Ignore. Count the sheep. Cute, fluffy little sheep. Running past me with their little woolly coats and little black faces.

"Come on."

"Stop with the voice!"

"Have you forgotten the last hour already? Let me remind you. It was amazing."

Sheep. How many sheep? Twenty-seven? Restart. One sheep. Two sheep. Red sheep. Blue sheep.

"Stop!" A door slammed across the apartment. The one next to me shook.

"Madison! Let me in!" The handle rattled. I slowly picked my head up.

"Madison!" I got up and turned the handle. Rae barged in. Her hair was disheveled, her clothes wrinkled, but her eyes glowed with fury.

"You. You need to stop distracting him."

"I do? Excuse me, but you're the one that strips his will away with your stupid powers!" I shot back at her.

Her hands curled into fists.

"He likes me. I didn't convince him to — do anything." Her voice failed her.

"Yeah, right. I saw everything, Rachelle. I heard everything."

Chapter Six

"You saw?" She looked horrified.

"Yes. Admit it, Rae." I sat on the bed, tired and angry and sick to my stomach with Lindy's power.

"Fine. But he does like me," Rae said stubbornly.

"Give it up. This stupid fight is ruining everything."

"Whatever." Rae stomped out of the room and rapped on Cole's door. Cole replied with a string of profanity.

"Jeez, Cole. Calm down." Silence. Rae sat on the couch and pulled her knees up to her chest. At least she understood that she wasn't wanted.

Finally.

CHAPTER SEVEN

Rae

The apartment was painfully silent. Maddie, still sitting on her bed, picked at the fringe on her blanket, her lips forming silent words. Cole remained in his room. I shifted, uncomfortable on the stiff decorative pillows of the couch.

I had screwed up. I got that. I'd pushed Cole too far, and nagged Maddie halfway to insanity. I couldn't blame either of them for hating me, as much as I wanted to.

Hours passed; the sun slid behind the violet clouds. Not one of us made a sound.

When the stars were beginning to glow, a knock sounded at the door. Maddie got up, her eyes trained on the front door.

"Who is it?" Cole called from his room. Maddie ran to the peephole.

"It's Ricardo." I stood up, ran my fingers through my tangled hair. Cole's door creaked open.

"Let him in," he said. Maddie turned and opened the door, allowing Ricardo to come in.

"We need to talk. Get dressed, meet me in the lobby in fifteen minutes. I'll be taking you to Town Hall." He left.

"Well then. Better hurry." Cole went back into his room and closed the door. Maddie walked into our room, and I sheepishly followed. She pulled a pale gray sweatshirt out of the closet. As I dug around for a second sweatshirt, she tied her ratty purple Converse on and ran a brush through her hair. I tugged on a pair of dark brown Uggs and turned to face her.

"I'm sorry." She froze, and then her eyes met mine.

"Why do you want to ruin my life?" she asked, her voice a frail challenge.

All I could do was blink.

"You know I'm a little fragile right now, yet you insist on making me miserable. Can we go back to that easy friendship? Do you not realize that you're taking advantage of his memory loss? I'm not trying to be mean, but he would be with me if he hadn't forgotten who he was," she continued.

"Which, by the way, was your fault," I reminded her. I instantly regretted it.

"Thank you. I do remember. But do you remember that he chose me over you? Back when he was himself? I remember that. Do you?" Her voice was getting louder. She stood by the door, a hand clenched around the knob.

"Yes, I did the wrong thing. Many times. I don't know what I'm doing. But Cole has been the only thing keeping me

sane. I need him. Knowing that he would be right there, no matter what I did, made me strong enough to save us. Knowing that he wouldn't blame me for mistakes made me brave enough to take risks that saved us. If I don't have that, if I don't have that anchor, I'm nothing. I can't do this without him. What don't you understand about that?" she said, her voice almost too quiet to her by the end. My resolve, my outrage and my loathing, crumbled. I didn't rely on Cole the way she did. I'd made my peace with losing him before. She never had.

"Oh, God, Maddie. I'm so sorry."

It wasn't enough. No simple sorry would ever be enough to describe the apology I needed to say. But I was too stunned to add to it.

"For what, exactly?" she asked. Her lack of emotion was unsettling, like she'd expended everything she had explaining herself.

"For not understanding. Not trying to understand. I'm supposed to be your friend, but instead I'm making things worse," I replied. To hide my face, I pulled my sweatshirt over my head.

"I forgive you. I can't say it's okay, but I'm willing to move on if you are."

"Of course I am. So, are we good?" Maddie nodded, half a smile breaking the wrinkles in her forehead. She closed the distance between us and hugged me.

"I missed you," she whispered.

"You have no idea," I replied. Cole knocked on the door.

Chapter Seven

"Come on ladies, we're late," he called. I opened the door, still smiling.

"Um, what's going on?" Cole asked, eyes narrowed.

"We made up. Now we'd better head down to the lobby. We've been longer than fifteen minutes already," I said. I marched out the door, tugging Maddie behind me. She caught Cole's hand and pulled him after us. Once we were in the elevator, Cole finally pulled his hand free.

"I'm going to say it: are you actually friends again or doing that fake giggly girl thing??" he asked. I met Maddie's gaze. She arched a blonde eyebrow, the challenge tangible in the air.

"Actually friends." Both of them slouched in relief.

"Good. Good," Cole said. The elevator doors glided open, and we walked out apprehensively, looking for Ricardo. He was leaned over Lindy's desk, talking to her quietly and intently. When he saw us, he nodded to her and waved us forward. He didn't wait before he flung open the door and waved us outside. Cole disappeared, only to vibrate to a stop by the door. At least he was running again. Maddie and I jogged to catch up.

"What's happening?" Maddie asked Ricardo.

"The Others. We need to get rid of them, and that means you need training and information."

"Why now?" I said. I was half running to keep up with him. My breath froze in midair.

"Because the Others have a new plot. They're planning

to destroy all humans with powers and have Others take their places, slowly undermining all the government systems on the planet. They're more organized this time. They've got battle plans for destroying this town, Camp Magic, and others like them across the world."

I wanted to say something, reply in some way, but I was shocked. I could barely keep my feet shuffling forward.

"How do you know this?" Cole asked. His eyes looked shattered. He'd lost as much because of the Others as any of us.

"A few weeks ago, we planted a drive in the Others' computer system. They haven't noticed it yet, and until they do, we can record most of their communications," Ricardo explained. As we rushed down the sidewalk, snow began to fall. Ricardo cursed.

"Come on. We're almost there. The plane won't be able to fly in this weather!" He pulled his hood up and led us into an enormous, ancient looking building. It soared up into the violet clouds, dark brown stone laced with ivy. The stained glass windows were an architectural miracle, taking up most of the walls. Ricardo led us through the dramatic, heavy wooden doors. Inside, there was a huge round table surrounded by hundreds of chairs. Only four were full. Thick, carved pillars soared up five stories to the painted ceiling. The stained glass windows, the carvings, and the paintings all depicted people using powers. I stared, awestruck by the centuries of history. Maddie tugged on my shirt. I looked at her, and then to what she was staring at. When I finally focused on the four people at

the table, I stumbled. Cole looked at us, confused.

Thompson and Barker, the heads of the Others. The two women next to them were dimly familiar, too. I'd probably seen them in the Other's lair at some point.

"Ricardo, we have to get out of here. Ricardo, those are Others," I hissed. Our guide only laughed.

"You forget! The people there match the people here. I'm sure I have an Other there too. This is the real Thompson, and the real Barker."

"Rachelle, Cole, Madison. Sit, please," Thompson called. We sat, four chairs to their right along the huge expanse of table. Still suspicious, I didn't take my eyes off of the two men.

"You are going back to the lair of the Others," Barker said. The woman closest to him swatted his arm.

"Hey, Gabriel. Let's introduce ourselves first," she said. The man rolled his eyes, but agreed.

Barker introduced himself first. Co-president of the "American Powers," he was partly in charge of everyone with powers in America. He had the power to force people into things, through some telepathic magic. His power was a bit like Rae's, but harder to block out. The woman next to him was his wife, Ella Lora. She could make small objects appear out of nowhere in seconds. To show us, she pressed her palms together, paused, and slowly pulled them apart. A pencil grew out of thin air between her hands, shimmering and wiggling like an earthworm before solidifying into wood. She tapped it against her palm to make sure it was sturdy and handed it to

Cole. He stared at it like it was about to disappear again, like it was an illusion. But it could even write normally.

Next to her was Alan Thompson, the other co-president of American Powers. He could locate any object, as long as it was intact and he had some connection to it. He said it was like reading a map in his brain, but less difficult. The last person, Thompson's sister, was named Christie. She could mimic backdrops to become nearly invisible, which she said was extremely useful in embarrassing situations.

"We are the Council of Power, and the four of us are the country's most powerful people," Thompson said.

"Technically, we are five. Mr. Weston couldn't be here tonight," Christie said. I recognized the name of the man who fired Jamie, and felt a flash of heat through my body. Ricardo timidly raised his hand.

"We don't have a lot of time. I need them to be at training in half an hour so they can be ready to go by tomorrow afternoon. The plane can't leave until then because of the storm," he said.

"Alright then, everyone shush. You three. What do you know of our society?" Thompson asked us.

"Um, not much. Mostly that all of us have powers," I said. Christie raised an eyebrow, and Barker snickered.

"Jamie is slacking. Do you know why you were sent to destroy the Others rather than an experienced adult?" Thompson asked.

"No. We were wondering why, actually," Maddie said.

Chapter Seven

"If Jamie told you anything, you would know. Your generation, anyone from approximately seventeen years old to none, is the most powerful we've ever experienced. We noticed your expressions while we described our powers. Because you have spent so much time in the presence of the new generation, you were skeptical. You didn't think we sounded very powerful at all. Indeed, we all have extreme limits. Look at Ricardo, here. All he can do is make his hair an inch longer or change the color of his eyes. I'll bet there is a person at your camp that can completely change their appearance at the drop of a hat," Thompson continued.

"Now we have learned of a new plot. You three are incredibly powerful, and know the lair of the Others better than any of us. We wish for you to return, to save us all a second time. Now, we are in even more danger. We need your help. Will you do it?" he finished.

Maddie's jaw fell. I leaned back away from the table, fear churning in my stomach. Cole met my eyes, then Maddie's. We were all terrified. Last time we tried to destroy the Others, we got possessed, shot, went insane, or died. Maddie lived in the woods for a week, Cole asked a little girl to erase his life, and I crawled from god knows where to California. Why on Earth would we accept a quest that would likely end the same way, or even worse?

One look at my friends and I knew the answer. We would do it because we had no other option. Everyone needed us, and so there we were.

"We'll do it," Cole said. He sounded calmer than even I could have managed. All four members of the Council relaxed into their chairs. I hadn't realized how tense they'd been.

"Thank you. Now, please, go with Ricardo to the training center, and prepare for your journey," Christie said. The four of us stood up and left, nodding to the four people that made up the Council of Power as we went.

The snow was falling heavily outside, already a thick layer on the street. Lights glowed ominously through the fat, fluffy flakes. The sky was dark, but still tinted by that purple fog, drifting listless across the horizon. As we raced down the street, I replayed the Council meeting in my head. Adults, fully grown adults, with superpowers no less, had begged us to go on this quest. We were fifteen-year-old kids who had almost died doing the same thing less than a month ago. The amount of trust and pressure and hope on our shoulders was crushing. Completely crushing.

"This snow is crazy. What day is it?" Maddie asked as she shook snow out of her hair. More replaced it in seconds.

"December 2nd," Ricardo replied. He pulled the hood of his jacket over his head.

"Really? That means I turned fifteen yesterday," Maddie said. She looked a little disappointed.

"Birthdays aren't such a big deal when everyone is in danger of dying," I said. "Cole's birthday was, like, two weeks ago. You're both 15, congratulations."

November 21. I remembered his birthday, even if he

didn't. And Maddie hadn't said anything either, so I was probably the only one who knew.

"Okay, guys. We're here." Ricardo opened the door to the building in front of us and waved us in. It was a tiny, bare room, empty but for a door on the left. Ricardo opened it, revealing a set of stairs. Cole led the way down, followed closely by Ricardo and Maddie. I watched them descend, worry making my stomach cramp. This whole mess was getting more and more real. Training was our last step, and then we would go back.

"Rae?"

"Coming." We went deeper and deeper, almost four stories. After the stairs, there was a long hallway, lined with photographs and newspaper articles. Faces smiled down at us, generations of powers sitting forgotten on the walls.

"Here we go, the training bunker," Ricardo finally said.

A huge room opened up in front of us, the ceiling at least two stories high. The walls were cement and metal, and boxes of props sat in disorganized piles in the corners.

"Who wants to start?" Ricardo asked. Cole raised his hand slightly.

"Me, I guess. I don't even know what I'm doing."

The perpetual look of confusion was haunting. Ricardo led Cole across the room to discuss. Maddie and I stood by the door, watching them talk. As Cole explained his situation, Ricardo scratched his head. I couldn't hear the words, but the desperation and frustration in Cole's body language was enough.

"You have snow in your hair," Maddie said to me, swatting half-melted piles of snow off my head and back and shoulders. Freezing water was soaking through the sweater and my shoes and my jeans, and I wished I had brought better clothes.

"Thanks," I said. As I watched Cole, I recognized a black mass of resentment still boiling in my stomach. Maddie and I weren't fighting anymore, sure, but I was still jealous. And I knew it wouldn't go away, even if I had promised to leave both of them alone.

Ricardo waved me over. I shot a slightly smug smile at Maddie before joining them in the corner.

"You know what Jamie was having Cole do to train. I don't know how to help him. Can you try to talk to him, figure it out? I'll be back in a second, I want to check in with Madison." With that, Ricardo walked away.

"What do you want me to say?" I asked. Ice water was creeping through my clothes, and I shivered.

"I don't know. I remember how to do some things, like run without breaking my legs, but other things I can't figure out. Like stopping, steering, or controlling my speed. I don't remember how."

"Okay. So, you need me to remind you?" I asked.

"Yeah, I guess." I opened my mouth to start talking, words already lining up in perfectly neat rows for me to use, when Cole pointed across the room. I frowned, insulted, but turned to look where he stared in slack-jawed awe.

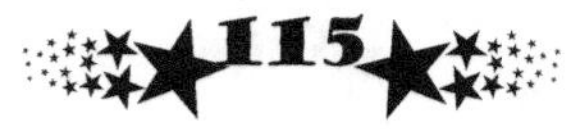

Ricardo was standing next to a massive grizzly bear. And then it shimmered and became a chair. And then a moose. And then Maddie, flushed and still slightly blurry from changing, who looked at Ricardo's stunned face and doubled over laughing. Her face was bright, and she looked so effortlessly beautiful that I wanted to tear her hair out.

Ricardo encouraged her to keep going, and she did. I'd never seen anything like it. She would transform into something, and seconds later, the form would begin to shiver and something new would take its place. When she was Maddie again, Ricardo asked her something I couldn't make out, and they began to discuss it in hushed voices.

"I had no idea she could do that," Cole murmured. He rubbed his chin in a gesture that seemed too old for him.

"Neither did I," I replied. The fact that he was so impressed by her powers rubbed me the wrong way, though it shouldn't have.

"She looks so happy," he said in a tiny voice. I tried to read the emotions in his voice, but all I could come up with was shock. This new Cole had never seen Maddie happy.

A huge crashing sound echoed around the bunker. I slapped my hands over my ears. Cole's eyes widened. A rush of air and dust and scraps of concrete blasted by, like bits of hail.

"What is it?" I squawked.

"Maddie," he mouthed. Or maybe he said it. I couldn't tell over the noise of the crumpling bunker. I spun, and couldn't breathe. My heart stopped.

The entire far end of the bunker was collapsed. Dust and smoke and flames filled the air. Maddie was on the floor, crumpled, facing away from us. Ricardo had been flung back from the explosion, and was holding his fingers against a cut on his forehead.

"What happened?" I screamed. Ricardo shakily stood up, and Cole helped support him as I went to make sure Maddie was okay.

"She was doing really well. She did all kinds of transformations. I asked her if she could do something a little more… conceptual, like fire, or air, or water. She closed her eyes, and like, combusted. She disappeared, and a giant shockwave sent everything flying. Then she popped back into existence on the floor there."

I dropped to my knees next to Maddie, and gently shook her shoulder. She coughed, blinked, and sat up.

"Whoa. What happened in here?" she asked, eyes widening.

"You," Cole said.
Ricardo explained what he knew.

"I don't remember any of that. I seriously did all of this?"

"I guess. There's no other way it could have happened," Cole answered. He was focused totally on her, on right now, and that haunted and perplexed expression faded. Seeing him happy, or at least the way he used to be, was like seeing the sun come out after winter.

"We can't stay down here now. It's too dangerous. The

whole place could collapse on us. Especially this side. The roof is weakened," Ricardo said.

Maddie frowned. "Where can we go?"

"It'll be cold. But there's an outdoor training facility across town, away from the residential area. We'll go there," Ricardo said.

"I'm so sorry. I wish I hadn't done it," Maddie said.

"Come on, before it collapses," I said.

The walls shuddered, and clouds of dirt rained down on us. Maddie scrambled to her feet and we ran for the stairs. Once we made it outside, I finally felt my heartbeat returning to normal. There was a massive sinkhole behind the building, with a few trees and a tool shed lying shattered at the bottom, but nothing else was affected.

"Come. There isn't much time," Ricardo said.

It was pitch black out, and the snow was falling more heavily. Maddie looked up at the sky, an eyebrow arched.

"An outdoor place?" she asked skeptically.
"You're the one you demolished the indoor one. We don't have anywhere else to train, and you need it before the Council will let you leave," Ricardo said.

"Let's get this over with," I said, swatting snow off my sweatshirt. Already the damp fabric was freezing stiff. I thought wistfully of the constant summer weather of Camp Magic. We marched back through town, trying to stay under awnings and overhangs. I lost feeling in my hands and feet. After another fifteen minutes of walking (or slipping and sliding on the ice)

we arrived at a big circular plaza. Concrete walls surrounded most of the space, and crumbling pillars were arranged in neat concentric circles throughout. There were scorch marks and cracks all over the walls. Snow was almost three feet deep on the ground, piled heavily around the pillars.

"I can't run through this," Cole said. He shook snow out of his hair.

"How can we melt it?" I asked. Maddie frowned.

"I could turn into something. I can do nonliving things, but not for long. Otherwise I freeze up and can't change back. So if I turn into a snowplow or something, you have to work fast," she suggested. Ricardo nodded. Maddie closed her eyes and clenched her fists. A few seconds later, she dropped to the ground as a snow blower. Ricardo spent five minutes clearing a path about three feet wide up against the wall. When he got back to the entrance, he told Maddie to switch back. The snow continued to fall for an agonizing few seconds. Maddie didn't move.

"Maddie" I said. The engine of the machine revved, a pattern…

"That's Morse code! Maddie, start over," Cole exclaimed. He knelt down next to Maddie and closed his eyes in concentration. His fingers traced letters in the snow.

"Did I take too long? Is it that?" Ricardo asked frantically. Cole held up his hand for a few seconds until the engine went silent.

"No, it isn't that. She didn't anticipate how tired she

would be. She's done more transformations in the last hour than she has in weeks. She can't pull herself together enough for a change," Cole explained. The snow blower made a whining sound, and another shorter message.

"She says she can feel herself starting to stick," he translated. Ricardo cursed and ran his hand over his spiky hair.

"Can I help? Would talking make a difference?" I asked. The air was Arctic, the snow fell in thick drifts. Already the path they had carved was gone. The engine roared again.

"No, it wouldn't help," Cole said. I reached down and dusted the snow off of the icy metal of the snow blower. "What can we do?" Ricardo asked. The engine sputtered, a brief message, and died.

"She has no idea," Cole said, quietly enough that his voice blended into the sound of falling snow. The streetlights behind us, our only source of light at this practically-morning hour, flickered and went dark. In the pale gray almost-light, with snow swarming my lungs with every breath, panic swelled in my stomach and forced tears to my eyes. Could it be possible that Maddie wouldn't make it?

Maddie

I could barely remember where I was.

Or what.

Or who.

I could no longer hear the voices of my friends. I didn't

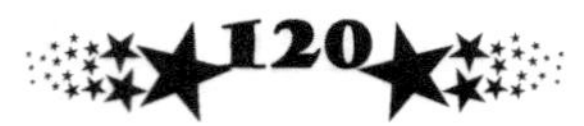

have the power to make the engine turn again. My mind was going cold. The longer I stayed there, in the snow, as a stupid snow blower of all things, the less I felt. The less I knew. The less I remembered.

Was this the end? There certainly wasn't anything left I could do. Would I see my life flash before my eyes, or see light at the end of a tunnel?

The dark and the cold and the nothingness slid deeper into my mind. I was too tired. My thoughts spasmed, unable to stay connected, and I stopped struggling.

I was over.

Cole

The machine gave one last hissing sound. Ricardo fumbled with a flashlight and switched it on. The colors of the object had turned to dark gray, the dim indicator lights completely dark. All the sharp edges melted.

"No! Maddie! No!" Rae shrieked. I was frozen. I couldn't move, couldn't breathe. My hands and feet were numb with cold, but the rest of my body was frozen with shock. Total, complete shock.

The snow blower flickered and disappeared. Maddie, in her human form, took its place. But she still didn't move.

"Maddie!" Rae wailed. She shook her shoulders, slapped her face. Nothing. Nothing.

"Her heart isn't beating! Do either of you know CPR or

something?" Rae said. Ricardo looked shattered.

"There's nothing we can do. She's gone. We killed her," he murmured. Rae spun, fury lighting a fire behind her eyes.

"Yes there is. Do something!" she screamed. The heat in her words made both of us jump, and Ricardo began what must have been CPR. I didn't recognize it, but that meant nothing. The flashlight fell into the snow, and I picked it up and held it over the grim scene. He tossed a cell phone over his shoulder, gasping out a string of numbers I assumed to be an emergency line. I punched them in and listened impatiently to the ringing.

"What's your emergency?" the dispatcher finally asked.

"My best friend is dying, we need help!" I replied anxiously.

"Where?" The voice was brisk now.

"Ricardo?" I called, away from the phone. "What's the address?"

"Say … practice … plaza," he said, in time with the compressions he was doing.

"Practice plaza," I repeated into the phone.

"We'll be there right away. Does someone there know CPR?" the dispatcher said.

"Yes," I replied. Sirens wailed out across town, loud and obnoxious in the quiet. They shut off quickly, probably because they weren't needed at this hour and everyone was asleep. But at least I knew they were coming.

Rae was stroking Maddie's hair, saying, "Wake up, open your eyes, wake up," over and over and over again. Ricardo

was still doing CPR. I felt useless, simply holding the flashlight. The snow stripped me of any power, of any usefulness. I didn't know CPR and I couldn't sit there and talk like Rae. I had no way to help, except for holding the flashlight. So I continued to grip it, making sure that the one small thing I could do was done right. I wouldn't let them down, even if it only meant holding a flashlight. Another thirty seconds passed, each one an eon. The sirens went off once, briefly, close enough to touch. But they weren't here yet, and Ricardo was getting tired.

"I'm sorry, I can't do anymore," he apologized, his accent thick. He sat back on his heels and plunged his arms into the snow, up to his elbows. His eyes shut against the blizzard.

"Come on, Madison! Wake up!" Rae screeched. The force of her voice sent adrenaline shooting through me, and Ricardo jolted upright. We were awake, for sure. But Maddie still wasn't.

Paramedics flooded the plaza. Headlights from their van illuminated the scene, making my one job futile. Rae, Ricardo and I were shoved out of the way, deeper into the snow. I couldn't see her. I was panicked. The hushed and nervous voices from the mob of medics scared me to death. What was happening in there? After a few seconds of frantic activity, they carried her to the ambulance on a stretcher and drove away. I started to follow, but Rae snatched up my hand.

"Do you think she'll be okay?" she asked in a tiny voice.

"I don't know. The fact that they're still trying is hopeful," Ricardo said.

"Where are they taking her?" I asked, not recognizing my

own voice. The ambulance disappeared around a corner, and we were left in the dark again.

"The hospital, probably. So, the labs," Ricardo said uneasily.

"What are we waiting for? Let's go!" I shouted. I was still freezing cold and half numb, and probably frostbitten, but I didn't care anymore. I wanted to be with Maddie. Rae clumsily got to her feet and followed me. Ricardo got up, but didn't follow us.

"Maybe we shouldn't," he said.

"What are you talking about?" I hissed. "She's in trouble, and we're her friends. She needs us!"

"But if the doctors can't save her, you don't want to be there. Trust me," Ricardo insisted.

"Yes, we do. We have to be," Rae argued.

"I won't go with you. I can't agree with you on this," Ricardo said.

"Fine. Goodbye, then," Rae said. She grabbed my wrist with icy fingers and dragged me away. I glanced back only once, to see Ricardo watching us go through the thick curtain of falling snow. The two of us marched through the streets, trying to hide from the storm.

"Do you know where we're going?" I asked after a few minutes.

"Sort of. I know the labs are on this street, in this direction. Keep your eyes open," Rae replied. We continued. Five minutes later, we still weren't there.

"Are you sure this is—"

"No! I'm not, okay? I've been here no longer than you. I'm guessing. This street is right, and we started on the far side, so I'm guessing that this is right. Satisfied?" she snapped, her nose bright red from cold.

"Sorry. Come on, let's hurry. The snow's falling even faster now," I said. Another ten minutes passed before we found the labs. We ducked inside, and the warm air made me stumble. Rae marched right up to the desk to ask for directions.

"Left elevator, floor six. Room 17. Oh, you two look positively frozen! Take these. Tell the doctors up there that you need a little attention," the woman said, filling up two cups from a jug of hot apple cider behind the desk. I thanked her quickly and bolted after Rae. She was repeatedly pressing the "up" button. When the doors finally opened with a ding, she stepped inside and hit the close door button almost before I could catch up. We zoomed up to the sixth floor, and she looked queasy.

"I hate elevators," she moaned. But her nausea disappeared when the doors opened again, and she was off down the hallway like a bullet. My hands, feet, and nose were burning and stinging as warmth slowly bled into them, and each slight movement sent pins and needles through every limb.

"What room number was it?" Rae called over her shoulder as she waited for me to catch up.

"Seventeen."

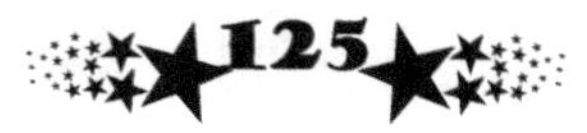

She nodded, finished off her cider, and took off again. I struggled to keep up, the pain in my feet stabbing up through my legs with every step.

When we found Room 17, we found all five members of the Council standing outside the door, fury turning all their faces to stone. I assumed the last person to be Mr. Weston, with deep-set eyes and bushy eyebrows, the one who fired Jamie. Rae stared daggers. When Thompson caught sight of us, his expression turned murderous.

"How did you allow this to happen?" he growled. Barker tried to placate him, to no avail.

"We had no idea. She was fine until she had to turn back!" Rae said.

"It doesn't matter. You, of all people, should know her limits. You pushed her too far! It's hopeless!" Thompson screamed. A doctor down the hallway shushed us. Christie, Thompson's sister, stepped in front of him.

"We aren't angry—"

"Shut up, Christie," Thompson growled. "We are definitely angry."

"Whatever. Is Maddie going to be okay?" I asked, frustrated.

"That depends," Barker said.

"On what, exactly?" Rae stood next to me, her voice smooth and confident.

"Whether we vote to allow her to on your journey or not."

A low growl buzzed in the back of my throat.

"She has to come," I said.

"If she lives," Mr. Weston interjected. Rae shot him a look so savage that he actually flinched. I scowled at Barker and knocked on the door to Room 17. A doctor poked his head out.

"What do you need?" he asked.

"Can we see Maddie? We're her friends," Rae said.

"I suppose. She should wake up soon, and it'll be good to see familiar faces," he said. Thompson pushed between us.

"Me, too. I should be there," he said. The doctor shook his head.

"You won't be familiar." He beckoned Rae and I inside and shut the door in the Council's face.

Inside the hospital room, the air itself was buzzing with frantic energy. In the tiny space, there were a total of six people. Three doctors, Rae and I, and, of course, Maddie. She was in a pale green hospital gown on the narrow white bed, an IV needle pumping anesthesia into her system and one of those strange tubes spilling air into her nose. When the doctors saw us, they backed up so we could see Maddie better. I stood next to the bed, staring. Rae squeezed my hand.

"Okay, kids. She's sleeping now. She'll be fine, but press this button when she wakes up." The doctor pointed to a red button by the light switch, and they all filed out. I heard Thompson and Barker arguing with them through the thin door.

"What do we do now?" Rae asked. I gazed at Maddie, picturing stunning silver-blue eyes behind the closed lids.

Chapter Seven

"We wait."

"I guess there's nothing else we can do, is there." Rae touched Maddie's still shoulder. I could only watch.

As Rae and I waited, I wondered. Was this how Maddie felt when I was unconscious in the beginning? This horrible suspense, wondering when I would wake up? Imagining the color of my eyes, wishing I could smile one more time? Was this moment karma for all I had put her through recently?

I gripped the flimsy railing of the hospital bed and pictured Maddie's eyes again. A blue so silvery and icy and deep that it sucked you in and didn't let you go. Mesmerizing in their brilliance, so bright they looked unreal. For the gazillionth time since I woke up I wished that I could remember her. That I could remember the way we were.

"She's starting to move! I think she's waking up!"

I focused on Maddie's face again. She was moving a little bit. Her eyes flashed open, focused on mine. An instant later, she was gone again.

"Should we call the doctors? Do you think she's awake?" She sounded far away. I was remembering my time in the dark, buried in the first moments I could remember. Thick, dreamy blackness, interrupted by sudden flashes of light. A pair of remarkable blue eyes. Darkness again. Was Maddie doing the same thing I did? Not truly awake, but able to open her eyes to taunt me? Was this another cruel trick of Fate?

"Cole. Dude. Snap out of it. What are you thinking about?" Rae waved her hand in front of my face.

"Her. How I did the same thing she's doing now when I was out?"

"Don't be blaming yourself. None of us could have known," Rae said. How did she know what I was thinking? Did she really know me that well?

My life was one big question to which I had no answer. Each moment there was a new thing to consider, a new problem I could solve if only I had my life back. If only.

"Hey. Stop it. Don't go to that place. You're going to figure it out. We all are." Rae squeezed my hand again.

"Yeah. Mm-hm." I was distracted, not paying attention. My fingers and toes stung like crazy as warmth seeped into them. Water dripped out of my soggy clothing.

A knock at the door made us both jump. Rae slumped when she saw that it was only a doctor.

"Is she awake?" he said gruffly.

"Not yet. But she'll be fine. Right?" Rae said.

"Maybe. We can't be sure until she wakes up."

"I guess. But still, it can't be that bad. Right?"

"Most likely. We'll see. I'll be back to check on her in a bit." With that, the doctor left again.

"She'll wake up soon. That's what they said. It's fine," Rae said, talking more to herself than to me.

"Yeah, but her heart wasn't beating for a solid few minutes. That can't be good in any circumstances," I added.

Rae glared at me. "Think positively. She'll be fine."

Fine didn't seem that positive, nor particularly likely.

CHAPTER EIGHT

 Maddie

I knew I'd seen her.

Sand stung my face, powerful winds tore at my skin. I saw that flash of red again, an unusually bright, gleaming river the color of sunset. Only one person I knew had hair like that. Stumbling through hot desert sand, it took me ages to reach her. I reached for her, cautiously called her name. She turned, and I met her stare for only an instant before the wind began dragging me away. Sand bit my cheeks, hot wind shoved me to the ground. As flaming hot sand buried me, I heard Amanda's voice.

"Beware. We're not who you expect. Don't trust."

My head went under, and the dream dissipated. Instead of waking up, though, I floated through a biting blackness. Hours passed, and I saw light. Two faces, one overwhelmed by hazel eyes and the other by brown, crowded my vision. I fought

the darkness, not wanting to part with the light. But I was too weak. The dark was all that ever existed and all that ever would. Another eternity later, I saw light again. Those striking sets of eyes. Instead of slipping back into the darkness, though, I drifted into a dream.

The room was white.

Whiter than anything I'd ever seen.

Blinding.

From the colorless walls, eyes formed and floated through the air. Hazel-green. Rich brown. Icy blue. Green. Framed by dark lashes, pale ones, thick and beautiful. Around the four sets of eyes, faces began to form. From the faces, bodies. It was an appalling sight.

A tall, thin, strong-looking boy with honey-brown hair formed around the hazel eyes. A smaller, stunning girl with thick, wavy tresses the shade of a midnight sky around the brown eyes. Blonde hair and an expression of self-doubt surrounded the blue eyes. The last person, with the green eyes, lay crumpled on the ground. A hand over her stomach, a pool of blood around her. Hair the color of a flame.

I stumbled away from the bodies, away from the unnerving eyes. My head was aching from the glowing white, my fingers and toes stung like they were cold, for no discernible reason. My veins turned to ice as the figures turned on me. They stalked closer and closer, barely able to control awkward limbs. The blonde girl shuffled right up to me.

"You've destroyed lives. A hundred of them." The voice

was crackly, rough, like it hadn't been used in ages. With a bone-chilling horror, I felt my own lips forming the same words. I knew that face. I knew it as well as I knew the voice. It was my own.

"There is no excuse for what you've done." My mouth continued to form the words, a silent mirror of the body in front of me. The two others, the boy and the girl, each pointed an uncoordinated finger at the dead girl on the floor. The other me pointed directly at my nose.

"You have ruined everything. Life dealt you a fair hand, an unusually good one, really, and yet you still managed to destroy any chances you had at goodness." I clapped a hand over my mouth to keep it from mimicking the ghastly girl. But I couldn't stop it.

"You've done nothing but hurt people since the beginning of your time. Your father. Lindsay. Brittney. Amanda. Rachelle. Cole. Jamie. Jezzie. Thompson. Barker. Christie. Ella. Ricardo. Lindy." With each name, her finger inched closer to my nose. When she stopped, she paused. Her skin melted, her bones crackled to dust. Her body disintegrated, layer by layer, until all that was left was an oily black cloud, with eyes like daggers. I tried to scream, but nothing happened.

"I am you. A soul blacker than a raven's wing. A girl so vile she caused every life she touched to perish." The black ghost drifted closer. I pinched myself, trying to wake up, trying to get away. The white floor was slippery as I stumbled back.

"We are one and the same. Do not hide. You cannot

escape me." The cloud disappeared, and I almost felt relieved before I started to feel cold. As I looked down at myself, my skin began to bubble. It dripped away, along with muscle and tissue and bone. I was the blackness. I was … me.

"One and the same," said the voice.

One and the same.

I looked back to the other three people. They were on the ground, unmoving.

"It was you," the voice said.

"It was me," I repeated.

And then I started to scream.

Rae

"Something's happening," Cole said, nudging my shoulder with his.

"It's been two hours, Cole. Nothing is happening," I muttered. I was sitting on the cool floor, knees pulled up to my chest. As much as I wanted to leave, I couldn't bring myself to. But that didn't mean I still had hope. Because I didn't.

"Rae? She's sitting up." The quiet tone of his voice was so off that I scrambled to my feet to look.

Sure enough, Maddie was sitting up. Her eyes were open, but flat, somehow, and I was almost positive that she wasn't actually completely awake.

Cole leaned forward to shake her awake, but I stopped him. I had heard something somewhere about it being bad to

wake people when they were sleepwalking, and I wasn't sure if that applied here or even if it was true, but I didn't want to risk it.

"You've destroyed lives. Hundreds of them." Maddie's mouth moved, matching the words, but somehow it didn't sound like the sentence was coming from her.

Cole looked over at me. So he heard it too.

Maddie kept talking, but neither of us was able to discern the words. It sounded like someone was talking to her, through her. She listed off several names, mine among them. I wished I could see inside her head, to know what this dream was.

As soon as this wish came true, I regretted wishing it.

A black cloud swirled in the air in front of Maddie's face, looking like the oily smoke that comes from a melting candle. Lightning flashed like eyes, and I felt deep in my stomach that this was what had been speaking through Maddie. Cole gripped my hand, pulling me back against the wall, as far as possible from the thing.

It swirled closer to her, and then it was in her, creeping in through her nose and mouth, and then it was gone.

"It was me," she said.

And then a bloodcurdling scream ripped through the room.

Maddie doubled over with the force of the noise she was making. Cole was by her side in an instant, holding her down against the pillows.

"What's happening?" he called over the screaming. I

shrugged and helped him pin Maddie down. It was a long few seconds before she went silent. Her eyes opened, and she blinked. Her hands curled into fists.

"Was it real?" she asked hoarsely.

"What?" Cole asked.

"I thought it was a dream. But at the same time, I don't feel like it was."

"What happened?" I asked. Did she see what we saw?

"I saw myself. Or something like me. It was talking, and then I was talking with it, and then it melted, and turned into this creepy cloud, and then it was a part of me, eating who I am. I couldn't stop it," she murmured. She sounded broken. It seemed to match what Cole and I saw, and that made the whole thing even more terrifying.

"Oh," was all I could say. Cole glared at me. His eyes said something along the lines of, "Aren't you supposed to be the articulate one?"

"What does it mean?" she whispered. Her eyes were wide with fear.

"Probably nothing. We do need to tell the doctors that you're awake, though. They'll want to make sure you're okay," Cole said. I couldn't fathom how he could possibly be acting so normal. He tapped a rhythm on the frail railing of the bed.

"I'm okay. What we really need to do is get out of here. The Others are getting more and more dangerous every day," she said. "We should get out of here, go and destroy them before they destroy us."

"You need time to recover," Cole said.

"I'm fine. This isn't about me."

"It is until you're better," I said.

"I'll be fine! We have to go before something bad happens. You heard what the Others are planning. We can't risk that. Let's go," Maddie insisted.

"We can't. No way," I said. She glared at me, and then turned to Cole.

"Cole?" You think we should go, right?" she asked him, her voice turning plaintive. She blinked, looking pathetic, exactly how she needed to in order to get him on her side.

"No." His answer shocked us both. He agreed with her every time she made that face.

"What?" Maddie said. She flopped back onto the pillows of the hospital bed.

"No. You're crazy," Cole said.

"I am not!" Maddie squeaked.

"You want to go back to the most dangerous place you've ever been when you practically died three hours ago."

"The world is at stake again! We don't have time to be sitting here!"

I hit the button that would summon the doctor.

"Relax, Maddie. Everything with work itself out," I said. She rolled her eyes.

"If we go now, then yes. If not? No way. Not a chance." The door banged open and the doctor came in. He pushed Cole and I aside and began taking her blood pressure, temperature,

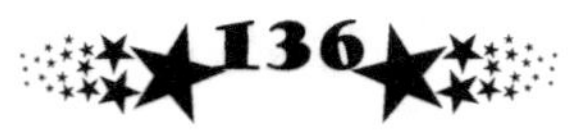

etc. Finally he decided that she was healthy enough to go back to the apartment.

"Make sure you avoid strenuous activity and especially shape shifting for at least a week, maybe two. I'll send someone by to check on you in a few days. Make sure you stay hydrated and get lots of rest." With that, the doctor left.

"You'll be okay," Cole said softly.

"But no shifting," I added.

"We have to risk it. Come on, guys! Look at the bigger picture! I'm one person, and the whole super community and the entire world is in jeopardy!" Maddie protested.

"No, Madison. Final answer," I spat.

"What gives you the right to say that?" Maddie asked. "Why do you get to make these decisions?"

"I'm older than you," I said, unable to come up with anything else. She rolled her eyes.

"By, like, a year."

"But I didn't just almost die. So I win," I said. She was acting like a six-year-old. Why couldn't she accept that she was being ridiculous?

# Cole

I helped Rae and Maddie get back to the apartment, then changed out of my still-damp clothes and left again. I needed to clear my head, and that meant getting away from those two. Every moment I spent with them was a stinging reminder that I

didn't know them at all. They were people from another world, one I'd never been to. The longer I went without my memories, the worse the headaches got. The more distant I felt. Things I should have known, things I should have understood, left empty pockets in my brain, and those spaces hurt. Like knives in my brain, stabbing deeper every time I thought of them.

"Hey, Cole. What's up? Didn't you just go up there?" Lindy called from behind her desk.

"I'm going for a walk," I said. She didn't answer, absorbed in some paperwork she'd found.

The snow was done falling outside, though clouds still darkened the sky. A group of chilly people scurried down the sidewalk, chatting and laughing. I gazed down the main road, lined with shops and businesses and other buildings. The whole place was layered with snow. A snowplow labored forward down the street, shoving the uneven drifts aside. An airplane zoomed by overhead. I swiped a thin sheet of snow off of a bench and sat down. An awning covered most of it, but the wind must have tossed a few flakes inside. I stuffed my hands in the pockets of my sweatshirt and watched the snowplow slowly inch its way down the road. The pavement glistened wet and dark behind it.

"Boo!"

I tried to pretend I hadn't jumped as I turned to face Rae.

"Ha, ha, you're hilarious," I said sarcastically.

"You know it," she laughed and plopped down next to me.

"Where's Maddie? Why are you here?"

"Back at the apartment. Lindy promised to make sure she stays there. Are you ready to go?" she answered. I flipped my hair out of my eyes.

"Where?"

"The lair. I was thinking-"

I cut her off.

"Are you nuts? We explained to Maddie exactly how stupid that idea was, and now you want to do it, too?"

She cleared her throat. "It's stupid for Maddie. Not us! She was right. Someone has to go!"

"We can't do it without her, Rachelle," I said. Rae picked up a chunk of ice and examined it.

"Yes, we can. We're both powerful, Cole."

"Not the way she is."

Rae dropped the ice. Her expression turned stony, and I cringed a little.

"We're leaving. Now." She stood up, and waved me after her. I knew there was no convincing her otherwise. Women are always right, after all.

"How are we getting there?"

Rae flashed me a white envelope. "Lindy said she'd get us a car. We won't have a problem."

"Fine. Let's get this over with," I grumbled.

We walked down the street to a car rental. She gave our names and Lindy's, and the man at the desk didn't ask any questions before handing us a set of keys.

Chapter Eight

"I'm impressed," Rae whispered as we pounded down the stairs to the garage.

"Does she know that you don't have your license?" I asked.

"I don't know. Either way, we have a ride."

We followed signs through the massive garage to a brand new BMW.

Rae slipped into the drivers seat, running her hands over the leather and the steering wheel. I buckled my seat belt as she warily pulled out of the parking space.

"It's a much shorter drive this time. A few hours southwest, instead of days southeast," Rae said brightly, driving out into the open. I helped her navigate out of the town, and through the purple bubble that shielded it. Finally we made it to the freeway.

"What happened to Maddie, in the hospital. The black thing. What do you think that was?" I asked. The cloud was still haunting me, and the thought that it could be something evil was extremely concerning.

"I don't know. The only idea I have that makes any sense is that she shape-shifted part of herself into it. Like sleepwalking, but sleep shape-shifting. Only problem is, I don't think she can just change parts of herself. And I don't know what you could turn into a black evil cloud. Maybe a kidney?" Her weak attempt at a joke fell flat.

"Do you think it's dangerous?"

"Well, considering how our lives have been going the last

few weeks, I would say it probably is. But we don't really have time to worry about it now. She's safe with Lindy. The council will take care of her."

"I still can't believe we're leaving her," I murmured while adjusting the radio. The entire situation reeked of déjà vu. One man down, left behind.

"I know. I feel awful, honestly." Her fingers shifted on the steering wheel, and she opened her mouth like she wanted to say more.

"Then why?" I asked. I knew she knew what I meant.

"We have to. Think about it," she replied. There was a familiarity to the timid way she sat in the seat.

"That isn't an answer," I said. Rae took two seconds to search my face.

"Maddie and Amanda and I did the same thing to you, once, too, you know," she said, settling deeper into the leather seat. I fiddled with the radio and the temperature dials while she continued.

"We got into a car crash on our first trip out there. You and Maddie ended up in the hospital. Her parents showed up, and she had to get out, but you were hurt really badly. We had to leave you." Her knuckles paled around the wheel, and she discreetly rubbed her eyes. I still said nothing, not wanting to upset her further.

"So we left. It was horrible, but you couldn't come with us. Afterwards, hundreds of miles later, you showed up. You ran halfway across the country at top speed, while injured, to

stay with us. With her."

"Maddie? Rae, I'm not—"

"Shut up. I don't think you know how much you mean to her. I didn't. You're everything to her, Cole. Everything." Her voice faltered, and she rubbed her hand over her face.

"What about you?" I asked. Both of us kept our eyes straight forward. This was uncertain territory, unsteady and dangerous beneath us. I hate asking the question, hated diving into this nuclear pit of emotions, but I wanted to know.

"I don't know. I can't keep you apart. Not now that I know how she feels." I could tell she wanted to say more, but I didn't know how to ask. After all, I was a 15-year-old boy. I was supposed to be allergic to feelings.

"But how do you feel?" I asked cautiously. I braced my arm against the window.

"Like the world is going to crumble if I don't have you to help me hold it up. Like a life without you is a life without purpose. I need you, Cole. But Maddie wouldn't last a second without you." She changed lanes to break the awkwardness.

"As a couple, we never existed. But you and Maddie did. I can't take that from her now," she finished.

"Rae …"

"What?" Her voice was harsh, grating. I didn't continue, afraid of saying the wrong thing.

"What?"

"Never mind." I quickly changed the subject. Do you know where you're going?"

"What were you going to say?" she growled.

"You're saying a lot about how Maddie feels. How do you feel?" Rae stiffened. I winced, regretting saying it.

"I said already." I thought about Jamie, and Rae, and Maddie, and based my next words on what I hoped they would have said.

"But that wasn't real. Forget Maddie. Forget what I think. Let it out, Rae." She sniffed and bit her lip.

"Watching her try to win you back is tearing my heart in half. I have loved you since you came to Camp Magic close to two years ago. I thought for a while that you were starting to feel that same. Then she showed up and you fell for her, and she fell for you. I was happy for you guys at first. But then she started losing it, and you both went crazy. When I finally made it home and she wasn't able to keep it together at all, I thought I saw a chance. I let my heart believe that I had a chance. Then Maddie told me I was hurting everyone, and I tried to stop, but I can't turn those feelings off again. I know I should stop, because it's making everything more confusing and complicated than it needs to be. But I can't. I'm torn. That's how I feel. I feel like there's a war going on inside me that won't stop," she said. She smeared tears from her eyes and let her hair fall between us. I had no idea how to reply, so I didn't. I allowed the loaded silence between us to thicken and congeal as we waited impatiently for the other to speak. I changed the radio station again.

"I'm sorry. I should have kept my mouth shut," Rae

Chapter Eight

finally admitted.

I tapped a rhythm on the dashboard with my fingers, a Morse code series of taps. I believe. I believe. I believe. It was familiar, like everything was. It meant something.

"No. I'm glad you did. It was good to hear it."

I believe. I believe.

"That's not the point. It was too much," she said.

"But it wasn't. So stop kicking yourself," I insisted.

"Fine," she said. It wasn't sincere. She still wanted to take it all back.

The silence was tangible after that. Neither of us was willing to say more, to push deeper into the bottomless cavern of feelings. The drive was too long, the awkwardness too opaque. So we stewed in our own thoughts for hours, hoping that something would break the ice between us.

When the sun began to set, Rae pulled into the parking lot of a Motel 6.

"I hate driving in the dark," she explained as she opened the door.

"How far away are we?" I asked.

"Maybe three hours of driving tomorrow." She started towards the door of the motel, locking the car door behind her.

"Did you bring any stuff?" I asked.

"I couldn't be packing in front of Maddie. But Lindy gave me this," she flashed an envelope, "so that we can get through the next couple days."

"What is it?"

"Two hundred dollars. Lindy raided the cash register at the apartment building. She told me no one would miss it." The door jangled with bells when I yanked it open. The dour, unkempt man behind the desk frowned at us.

"What do you need?" he grumbled.

"One room for the night. Two beds," Rae said.

"Yeah. Do I know you kids?" he mumbled as he pulled a small metal key off the wall.

"People always ask that. We starred in a commercial last year," Rae said with a giggle. Her power coated the walls in honey. The man only grinned like a shark.

"I don't watch TV." Rae had an answer ready right away.

"We were on billboards."

"What company?"

"Macy's."

"Can I look it up?"

"Maybe. It was a really long time ago, they might not be online."

"You two are related?"

"Step-siblings."

I don't know how she did it, but Rae had an answer to every question the man asked. She seemed to be having a lot of fun with it too. Finally, the Motel 6 man gave up. He took our money and told us how to get to our room. Rae smiled and practically skipped out.

"You're sister's annoying," he said before I could close the door between us.

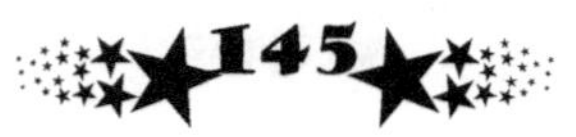

"You have no idea," I said. The door jingled again as it clicked shut.

"Come on, slowpoke," Rae called over her shoulder. I didn't want to risk running out in the open, so I speed-walked down the narrow line of cheap motel rooms. Rae was already unlocking the door when I caught up. She pulled on the handle and immediately started coughing. A cloud of stink wafted out of the room, cigarette smoke and bleach and puke and cheap air freshener.

"Fifty dollars for this?" Rae choked.

"Should we ask for a different room? We can't stay here," I said.

"We have to. Besides, I don't want to draw extra attention to us. We were lucky he was distracted enough not to ask for ID or something the first time. We stay at Motel Sucks tonight," Rae said glumly.

"Yay." To let to room air out, we opened all the windows and even the door as far as they would. We sat next to the windows and craned our necks, gasping somewhat fresh air. Despite the stench, the room was clean enough. The sheets on the two twin beds were good. So we stayed, panting in fresh air from the windows. Looking out over the dilapidated neighborhood, from the dim neon lights to the rusty street signs, I thought of Maddie. What was she doing? Had she been upset when she found out that we were gone? Had she tried to follow us?

"She's going to be okay. Lindy and Ricardo and the

Council will take good care of her. Besides, we don't need her. Our powers will be enough. You'll see," she said, bumping my shoulder with hers.

"I know. Think about it, though. She was trying so hard to convince us to come here, and we said no. Now we're here and she's there. What is she going to think?" I said. Rae shrugged.

"It's going to be okay. She won't hate you. Promise," she said. Her voice washed over me like a cool breeze. Maddie wouldn't hate me. No way.

"How are we going to do this? The Others are going to be ready for us."

"I know. We'll have to talk our way in and hide from there. I have no idea how, but I know we can. We have the power," she insisted.

Underneath the sharp intensity of her voice, there was a quaver of uncertainty that convinced me that she didn't think we had the power. As sad as it was, we needed Madison Thomas.

"Cole?" Rae's voice was different than I'd ever heard it. Small, plaintive, and terrified.

"What?" I responded.

"Do you think she'll catch up with us?"

"I don't know. I really don't," I said.

The words that defined my life.

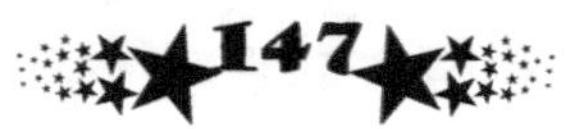

Maddie

I slammed the door in Lindy's face and slid down the wall to the green carpet. Tears welled in my eyes before I could stop them.

Cole and Rae left without me.

After everything I tried, after all the things I said, they ditched me. I was alone. At the mercy of the Council and Thompson. The carpet was itchy and unforgiving beneath me, but I didn't move. I was too stunned.

I would have gotten up to race after them hours ago, but the Lindy had me trapped. The windows were covered over with thick sheets of plywood. The front door was locked tightly and guarded. Lindy had obtained some special anti-magic spray from the hospital, similar to the stuff the Others used on Cole and I in their prison. The entire apartment was flooded with it. The place smelled sick. Every escape route I possibly could have taken was blocked. Rae had made sure of that. Unless I managed to break through the heavy plywood over the window, I was doomed. I was an important part of the team. Rae and Cole would need me. I felt vain and self-centered for thinking it, but I was strong and useful and important. And alone.

"Madison? I have breakfast for you," Lindy called. Without standing, I reached up and turned the door handle. Lindy bustled inside with a tray in her hands. Her beaky nose twitched as she caught the cloying smell of the anti-magic spray.

"Maddie? Where are you, sweetie?" She set the tray down in the kitchenette and looked around.

"Here," I muttered.

Lindy spun and appraised my position on the floor.

"Maddie, Maddie, Maddie. Don't be upset. This is for your health, darling. Rae wouldn't have insisted on all of this if you were better. And I certainly wouldn't have helped her. I mean, you really shouldn't even be away from the labs!"

I dropped my gaze to the carpet. I tugged at the shaggy green fabric with my fingernails.

"Don't worry about those two. They can take care of themselves." Obviously irritated by my sour attitude, she sniffed and left. Once the door closed, I stood. It had been a day since they started driving. If they stopped for the night, which Rae would have, they would probably be arriving around noon. If I could get out and change into something fast, I could catch up with them by nightfall. If they stopped outside the lair to plan, I could make it in time to help.

I peered out the peephole of the door. The same tall man was standing there, guarding me. Even if the door wasn't locked, which it was, I would never be able to get past him. Standing, the heavy stink was worse. It swarmed my senses and made me dizzy.

I stumbled through the apartment and into the bedroom. I found a small-ish backpack, and loaded it with a change of clothes and food from the kitchen. I stuffed an extra pair of sneakers inside, and then raided the drawers for supplies.

Chapter Eight

I found a pocket knife, a lighter, a flashlight, and a watch. I struggled to zip the bag and paused to let my head clear. I would need to go through the window. If I had time, I could chip out the wood quietly enough that no one would notice. But I didn't have time, so I would have to break through as fast as possible. I examined it carefully, searching for a weak spot that would be easy to break. Once I found a spot I could probably bust through, I ate the food Lindy had brought and checked the door again. The guard was playing Fruit Ninja on a smartphone, headphones over his ears.

I had a chance.

I picked the cumbersome backpack up off the couch and stood in front of the window. Grunting with the effort, I swung the bag as hard as I could at the plywood. It made a muted, dull thud. The wood didn't even crack. I swung again, and this time a thin split showed between the grains. I continued bashing at the planks, thankful that the guard had music blasting so loudly. Finally there was a legitimate hole, which I yanked at with my fingers to make it bigger, ignoring the sharp sting of splinters digging deep into my skin. As I started to try and squeeze through, I heard a shout.

"Hey! Get away from that window, now!"

The guard had come in, brandishing a stun gun. I wriggled through the hole, kicking out the glass on the other side. I balanced precariously on the window ledge, ready for a change. Warmth twinged in my gut, the ripple—but then I hit a wall. My skin was like stone, inflexible and unchanging. The

spray must have gotten on my skin, and was now stopping me from changing.

Panicked, I thought about crawling back through the window. But the guard was there, and if I went back now, there was no hope whatsoever of escaping. On the other hand, it was a 16-story fall to the bottom.

The guard's rough hand closed around the backpack, pulling it back through the hole I'd made. His other hand grabbed the sleeve of my sweatshirt.

"Come on, kid, don't do anything stupid."

I looked down at the ground, a narrow alley between the apartment building and whatever skyscraper was next to it. Snow was piled five feet deep below, but a measly cushion like that would do nothing for a fall at terminal velocity.

I frantically looked around, hoping to see something helpful. In my hazy panic, I hadn't even noticed the balconies lined up along the building opposite me. Neat columns, all perfectly aligned. I wrestled free from the guard and jumped. He still had a grip on my backpack, so I left it behind. The railing of the balcony was coming up fast, but not fast enough. I wasn't going to land on it, as I'd hoped. Instead, I had to catch the thin ledge of the balcony with my fingers, desperately holding on for dear life. The guard shouted angrily, hanging halfway out of the jagged hole in the boarded up window. My fingers cramped and slipped a little on the concrete ledge. I swung myself towards the building and fell, landing hard on the next balcony down. My palm and left knee were scraped,

but I jumped up and swung down to the next balcony, and the next, and the next. It was slow going, and I kept hearing Lindy's voice in my head. The guard would have plenty of time to tell her and gather reinforcements to meet me at the bottom. But I made it down to the snow-covered ground without hearing their voices. I trudged through the thick snow, the cold stinging the space where my jeans ended and my sneakers began. I made it onto the main road, where pedestrians and traffic made an effective crowd to blend into. I squeezed past people, no real goal in mind. I had to get out of this city, and then I could figure out what to do next.

"Stop that girl!" someone screamed.

"Don't let her leave the city!" This was in Lindy's irritating screech.

A hand wrapped around my arm, and I jerked free. I started running, frenzied, terrified of being stopped.

"Stop her!" Lindy's screechy voice slid through the crowd like a knife.

I was doomed. They could chase me forever. I still couldn't manage a transformation. Even so, I didn't give up. I charged through the thick snow like a bull, hoping that the cold, sharp-edged ice would strip the anti-magic spray from my skin and free me.

"Someone, for God's sake, stop the blonde girl!" Lindy yelled. Faces now lit with recognition when they saw me, instead of mild irritation. Hands reached from all directions. I was stopped, held tightly by a strong woman toting a baby

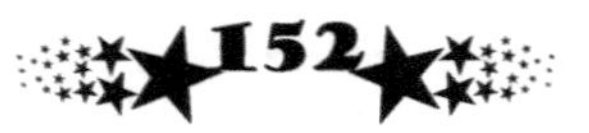

stroller. Lindy puffed up to us, red-faced and sweaty.

"I thought that you were more trustworthy," she said, making the tsk-tsk sound with her tongue, as she approached.

"I thought you were more understanding," I countered as I struggled against the woman's strong grip.

"You're sick. Now, your guard is coming to escort you back. Can you be trusted to stay here if lovely Mrs. Cooper releases you and resumes her day?"

"I won't promise anything," I said with my chin held high.   Lindy waved her hand and Mrs. Cooper let me go. Nodding curtly to Lindy and shooting me a suspicious look, she turned and pushed her baby stroller away down the street. Lindy stared me down, daring me to try something. I sat in a snow bank and discreetly scrubbed my skin and clothes with a snowball.

"You'll freeze," Lindy muttered, but do anything to stop me. As the guard slowly approached, I rubbed my hair and my face. I was shivering and goose-bumpy and damp, but the spray had to be gone. At that point, there was hardly any skin left to cling to.

"Don't let her escape again," Lindy murmured into the guard's ear as he passed her. He snapped a pair of handcuffs onto my wrists and wrapped his meaty fingers around the collar of my shirt.

"You're sure she can't change species right now?" he asked nervously as he prodded me back down the street. Lindy shot him a look over her shoulder.

"Of course. She's been marinating in that spray for hours." Lindy sounded so angry. Like I'd ruined her life by trying to escape. I stumbled in front of the guard, trying to close my eyes and focus my thoughts. Lindy said I'd been stewing in the spray too long for my powers to work, but there was no way I was going to give up and accept that. So I tripped and stumbled my way along with my eyes shut.

I didn't know what to try to turn into. What would work? Probably a bird, but what kind? Something fast, strong, and small. Eagles were too big, hummingbirds to small and weak. As the answer I needed came to me, I heard the animal's screech in my head.

A hawk.

The guard yelped as I shrank out of his grasp. The handcuffs rattled to the icy ground.

"Lindy!" he yelled. I leaped up and beat the air with my wings. The ground fell away, Lindy and the guard and all the people gaping on the street. The buildings spiraled out of sight, and the thick purple fog approached. I was looking down, saying a silent goodbye to the city, when I hit the wall. The wind was knocked out of my lungs. I spiraled sideways, the wind screaming in my ears. Once I had regained control, I went back to figure out what hit me. But it was gone. The whole town was absent, with a dark green forest in its place. I slowly dipped lower, and felt a solid surface below my feet. There was an invisible wall there. I pushed hard on the bubble with my talons, and they poked through. Sounds of the city filtered

though, along with a strange purple glow and rich smells. I pulled away and took off south.

No more procrastination. I had to help my last remaining friends.

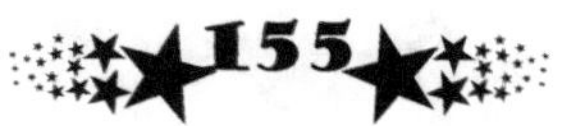

CHAPTER NINE

Cole

I dug the toe of my worn running shoe into the dirt. The warehouse loomed over us, raining dust and creaking with age. Beyond that, though, there was the shrill scream of metal and a fluorescent glow from beneath the ground.

"I'm so scared," Rae whispered.

"I know."

"We should hide a little bit longer. You know, to plan." The last part was hurried, like she wanted to make absolutely sure that I knew truly exactly what she meant. Of course, that convinced me that she was really waiting for Maddie to catch up. As determined as she was to prove that she could do this alone, she knew she really couldn't. So we decided to wait until nightfall to break in, and tried to plan out methods as the sun dipped lower in the sky. Unfortunately, all of our plans included the help of a third person, an object, or an animal. All

three things were found in one girl. Who, of course, was absent. Because we abandoned her.

"This was a horrible idea," Rae finally admitted.

"We are supposed to be a team."

She pulled her hair away from her face with a rubber band. We were in a secluded park a few streets away from the warehouse. Rae hugged herself and rocked back and forth, back and forth, back and forth.

"I know. I've been cocky and immature about all of this. I apologize, honestly. From the bottom of my heart. I thought we could, but we can't. Now we have to hope that Maddie is smart enough to evade Lindy, the guards, and anti-magic spray to escape," she rambled.

I decided not to reply. Any wrong move on my part could send us both spinning down into another toxic conversation. So we waited in stifling silence, watching the shadows lengthen and the light dim. The air was cooling, the unnatural warmth of the winter day faded. The sun was already being swallowed by the horizon. If Maddie didn't show up soon, Rae and I would have to go in alone. And most likely fail.

"She'll be here soon, if she's coming at all," Rae said quietly. Her eyes were trained on the sky, searching the northeastern horizon for any trace of our friend.

"She might not be."

The sun finally disappeared, plunging us into night. Maddie hadn't come. Rae and I were on our own. She looked pleadingly at the stars, tears in her eyes.

"So how are we going to do this?" I asked.

"We wait for Maddie."

"What if she isn't coming?"

Rae shook her head. Her hands trembled. "She has to," she whispered.

"You took so many precautions. It's practically impossible for her to escape, because of you. Now you're relying on her to break out of the prison you built her. Don't you think that's a little unfair of you?" I said.

Rae closed her eyes against the words. In her dark clothes and dark hair and dark shadows, I almost couldn't see her. But she shivered in cold and fear, and her teeth chattered. Unbidden, a memory of our kiss flooded my mind. Feet planted in the snow, but about to drift away. In that brief moment, her mouth had been my lifeline.

I knew it was wrong. I knew it was wrong to choose. I knew it was wrong to draw a line.

But I leaned in and kissed Rachelle.

She stiffened, like she wasn't sure what was happening. Then she relaxed, and inched closer. After a few seconds, she pulled away a little, rested her forehead against mine.

"Are you sure?" she asked quietly.

"Yes." I kissed her again.

"Seriously?"

Rae and I both jumped, skidding on the wet grass. Rae covered her mouth with her hand.

Maddie stood next to one of the trees, her hands on her

hips. Her hair and clothes were disheveled, but her blue eyes glowed with anger and adrenaline.

"Do you people need a chaperone?" she spat.

Rae scooted away from me as Maddie turned and stalked away from us. Towards the warehouse.

"Maddie, wait!" I called.

Rae didn't follow as I jumped up after Maddie.

"Don't follow me," she growled over her shoulder.

"Come on. Don't be like that."

"Don't be like what? Like everything's falling apart?" Maybe it is!"

"Maddie…"

"I love you." A broken, pleading statement. I met her eyes, saw the pain in them.

"What?" I said. I had never heard those words spoken like that. Like it was a curse.

"I love you."

"But—"

"Listen for a minute. I have loved you since the day I walked into camp, I just didn't know it. These last few weeks have only made it stronger. And then everything was happening at once, and everything that went wrong was my fault. Every time I looked at you it hurt, because I knew I would end up hurting you too. So I pushed you away to help you. As it turned out, that only made things worse. Still my fault. I've been pushing you away so that I can't ruin your life any more that I already have. But it still hurts more than I will ever be able

to say. Because I love you."

She turned around and her shoulders shook with sobs. I looked at the ground, only glancing up when I heard gentle footsteps behind me. I violently waved Rae back behind the trees, then stepped around Maddie so she was facing me again. Red from crying, the unreal blue of her eyes seemed brighter than usual.

"Listen. Stop blaming yourself. I don't. Rae doesn't. Why should you?" I said.

She sniffed and wiped tears from her eyes. "Think for a minute. Every single problem that we have run into has been my fault. I know you don't remember, but it's true."

"Maddie, I don't know if that's true or not. But you are more important than any of us, Madison Thomas. Never forget it."

"But you don't—"

"Don't what? Don't understand? I can't say that I do. But I do know that you need some self-confidence."

"Is that why you like Rae?" Maddie accused. "Because she has self-confidence and I don't?"

"I don't like Rae. I don't know any of us well enough to like one of you."

The conversation was rapidly spinning out of control. Rae was starting to creep closer again, and I discreetly gestured for her to stay back.

"Cole, you've kissed her at least twice. You haven't even …" she trailed off, drifting into a flashback. Her hand drifted

faintly to her lips.

"You aren't thinking. Now, please, stop worrying about who I like and worry about our mission. We can work all of this out later," I said.

She blinked at me. I looked down and picked at my fingernail.

"I'm sorry if you feel left out. I'm trying to figure this out. Don't be upset," I added when she still didn't reply.

"No, you're right. I'm sorry. I was being ridiculous," she finally said. Then she brushed past me and walked away. I stood still, watching her sit against a nearby building. She looked searchingly into the sky.

"Cole!" someone whisper-yelled. I turned to see Rae beckoning me crankily. With a glance at Maddie, I zipped over to Rae.

"What?"

"What was happening?" she squeaked. I looked back, but the building concealed Maddie from view.

"We had to work a few things out. We need to get out of here. The Others aren't going to wait for us."

"You had a ten-minute conversation, with tears and screaming and running away, and you consider that 'working something out?'" she spat. Her hair fell into her face, and she angrily whipped it into a messy ponytail.

"It's nothing that matters to you."

Rae sneered. "Whatever. Let's go."

The dark night swallowed her as she strode towards the

shadowy mass of a building where Maddie hid. Reluctantly, dragging my shoes through the gravel as I went, I joined them.

This mission was getting more and more complicated, and through it all I couldn't remember my middle name.

 Rae

"You want me to do what?" Maddie squeaked.

I glanced at Cole before repeating our grand plan. We were all sitting in the same grassy grove of trees as before, and Maddie was tearing up chunks of grass and examining them.

"You turn into something small and sneak inside. Then you trigger some alarm. While everyone's confused and freaking out, Cole and I sneak in and meet you at that control room. We activate the self-destruct, run away, and go home conquering heroes," I repeated. Easy as pie. Maddie stared at the messy green clump in her hand.

"What if I can't?" she asked a particularly long blade of grass.

"Then you carefully come back out and we regroup," Cole said before I could answer. I narrowed my eyes as she smiled at him gratefully.

"But you can, so you will," I added.

" When should I go?" She looked apprehensive, but determined.

"As soon as you're ready. Whenever that is," Cole said. Maddie sighed theatrically, closed her eyes, and wrinkled

her forehead. Within seconds, she was replaced by a delicate butterfly, pale blues and yellows fading into white at the tips of her wings.

"Cole? She'll need help opening the door," I suggested.

He stood up and walked into the inky blackness, slow enough that the clumsy little butterfly could keep up. The buzzing and screeching from inside the warehouse was louder in the silence. Watching the two of them melt into the dark, headed directly towards the most dangerous beings on the planet, fear twitched in my stomach. The two of them were the only two things I had left. I'd lost my family, Camp Magic, Jamie, and Amanda. Cole and Maddie were the only remainder of my old life. And so far, the new one wasn't great.

The next few minutes were agonizing, lasting longer than any ever had. Images of the dungeon and the aliens inside danced threateningly through my mind. If they got captured, I didn't know what I would do.

Finally I heard — and felt — the vibrating buzz of footsteps moving faster than sound. Cole skidded to a clumsy stop in front of me, waving him arms for balance.

"She's in," he said.

* * *

I will probably never know how Maddie managed to set off the alarms she did. What I did know what that she took long enough to do it. Almost two full days.

By the time the alarms started blaring, Cole and I were getting ready to break in and save her. Before we made it in, a

panicky woman blasted out, With her came the noise, screams and the shrill wail of the alarm. Cole and I raced inside, carefully dodging frantic, screaming Others. The brightly lit hallways were packed, the sleek metal floors clanging deafeningly with hundreds of footsteps. I wracked my memory for the way to the control room, knowing that both Maddie and Cole needed me to find it. When the chrome-plated hallways began to look familiar, I pulled Cole to a stop. Others pushed rudely past us, but I gripped his arm tightly against the throngs of aliens.

"Keep your eyes open. She should be close," I said as loudly as I dared. He nodded, and we were off again. The entrance to the control room was like a beehive, Others swarming in and out. The heavy, high-security door had been ripped free, and blocked the hallway that led to the elevators. A flutter of movement too high for a person caught my eye. I looked up and spotted a butterfly with pale wings, almost blending into the silver ceiling. It dove down between Cole and I, rippling and growing into Maddie before lightly landing on the floor.

"You made it," she said. A huge man ran past us, shrieking like a little girl, and she stifled a laugh. She seemed happier, more confident than she had in weeks. Maybe being alone for those two days had been good for her.

"Shall we?" she asked with a smile.

Before we could agree, her eyes focused sharply on something behind my head, down the hall. Her eyes widened.

"Go. Hurry, get inside. Hide your face. Go," she hissed. I peeked back, and saw the dreaded dark sports coats. Thompson and Barker, the leaders of the Others. Not their decent counterparts back at the town, but the actual Others. Unlike the majority of the Other population, they would recognize us in a split second. Even with the clothes we'd bought that blended into the uniforms. The three of us melded into the crowd and pushed our way into the control room.

It was a mob scene.

Unlike the sparse, clean, orderly room we entered the last time, the control room was packed with people, and flames flickered around charred piles of smashed computers. I pulled someone aside and asked what was happening, careful to not meet their eyes.

"The OPS is here. They're going to shut us down. They'll execute all of us for being here!" The woman yanked free and bolted out the door.

"We have to find the self-destruct," I said.

Maddie pointed at the last bank of computers. Guards in silver suits beat people back with heavy metal poles. I pushed through the masses and tried to ignore the confused looks I was getting. Despite the pale clothes, we were conspicuous. I had lived here for weeks. Of course people would recognize me.

"Rachelle!" Maddie called. She and Cole were huddled by the wall. I hurried over.

"I wanted to tell you how the self-destruct works. I figured it out the day you and Amanda were …."

"Tell me," I prodded.

She snapped out of her flashback and pointed at Thompson and Barker stepping in to the room. We were running out of time.

"There's going to be a massive rush to the escape pods, because there aren't enough. Basically a giant fire is going to burn everything in here to a crisp, to make sure all evidence is destroyed, and then the whole thing will explode. There's some bubble thing, though. I can't remember how far it goes, but if we get outside it, we're safe. The explosion and all the debris and the shockwave and that sort of stuff will stop. Everything will turn into a smoking crater. So the second we activate it, we run. Get as far away as we can," Maddie explained. She made certain that we understood before allowing us to continue. By that time, Thompson and Barker were uncomfortably close.

We raced towards the bank of computers. The guards were still whacking people with their metal bats to keep them away. Maddie closed her eyes, but nothing happened.

"Crap. I'm too stressed or something. Rae, is there anything you can do?" she asked. I shrugged.

"I hope so." Suddenly, Maddie yanked up the hood of her sweatshirt and spun.

"Guys. Thompson and Barker are right there." I ducked my head and let my hair fall over my face. Cole pulled up his hood.

Thompson waved the guards aside and sat down at a computer. He typed in the password and opened a file on the

desktop. He turned to look at Barker.

"Are we sure?" he asked. Barker nodded curtly.

Thompson tapped the mouse with a flourish, and the screen turned blood red. The other three remaining monitors did the same.

"Okay, everyone. We have five minutes," he shouted. Screams pounded at my ears and the crowd began to funnel madly out the door.

"Attention, Others. Self-destruct has been activated. You have four minutes and thirty five seconds to get to the escape pods located throughout the hideout. 4:30. 4:29. 4:28," an automated voice said through the speakers. As it continued to count down, the three of us bolted.

Unfortunately for us, six hundred frantic aliens had the exact same idea. We were lost in seconds.

"Three minutes," the robotic speaker said.

"We have to get out," Maddie said.

"No, really? I thought we should stay," I spat.

"Shut up. Does this look familiar to anyone?" Cole asked.

I squinted against the blinding fluorescent lights. "Of course it does. They all do. The all look exactly the same!" I screamed.

"Five seconds," the speaker said ominously. In five seconds, the fires would start to rage. Starting at the bottom, working their way higher and higher until they roasted us alive. We continued to run, and finally, saw the open space of the lobby.

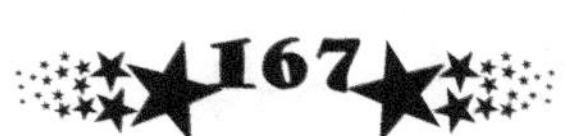

A giant crash and a scream stopped me in my tracks. I turned to see Maddie halfway beneath a collapsed section of the ceiling. Ahead, the lobby called to me. We were so close. Cole and Maddie struggled against the mass of metal and wood and plaster. I hurried back to help.

"Rae, Cole, go. Get out of here. I can save myself. Go," Maddie gasped through clenched teeth.

"No way," Cole said. "I'm helping. I can run if I need to."

"Rae," Maddie pleaded.

"No way. We aren't splitting up now!" I said.

"Rachelle Levine. Get out of this building. Now."

Cole shoved me towards the lobby.

"I'll take care of her," he said.

So I did the only thing I could.

I ran.

 Cole

"Can you change? Maybe you could squeeze out as something smaller," I suggested. Her legs and her right arm were struck under the pile of debris. She was trapped on her stomach.

"No. I tried. I'm too stressed or unfocused or something. I can't change." Terror pinched her voice.

"Then we have to push this stuff off," I said. If only Rae were here to help. As least she was safe. Maddie pressed her forehead to the floor and breathed in deep. Smoke was

starting to scent the air, and there was an uncomfortable heat surrounding us.

And that's when I saw the flames.

They were rocketing down the hallway, prodded on by a hot wind that blew in our faces. Somehow they managed to scorch the metal walls, melting them into liquid silver. A shrieking Other was sucked into the fire.

"Maddie?" Smoke billowed into my face, and I coughed. She twisted to look behind her. Fear froze her body.

I started pulling at the wreckage again, madly heaving at the heavy masses that pinned her.

"Cole, go," she said, eerily calm.

"What?"

"Get out of here. You can make it out. Go with Rae."

"No way. Are you crazy? I'm not leaving you," I insisted. The flames licked at the back of the collapsed mass of ceiling.

"Yes, you are. Can't you see? I'm not getting out. You can." The heat was unbearable, like sitting in an oven. But I shoved at the pile even harder, unwilling to let her go.

"Say goodbye to Rae for me," she said over the roar of the flames. At that moment, the fire sucked up the sheet of metal pinning Maddie. The wood and plaster slipped away easily, and I grabbed Maddie's arm and dragged her to relative safety down the hallway. I helped her stand, and we ran for the exit. In the lobby, there was a mad rush of Others for the few remaining escape pods. The flames licked at our heels.

"Cole, go. I'm only holding you back. Don't die for me,"

Chapter Nine

Maddie insisted. She pushed me.

"Madison, Thomas, I am not leaving you. Get over it and run."

"Attention. There are twenty seconds remaining until the building explodes. Please calmly make your way to the nearest escape pods. Fifteen. Fourteen. Thirteen."

"Run!" Maddie screamed.

"Not a chance," I shot back. The doors were so close. We could make it. But, of course, everything went wrong.

"Madison! Hurry up, girl! We can't hold this pod forever!" Maddie was ripped from my hand, and dragged towards an opening in the wall by a guard.

"Cole, you too. Right there." Both of us struggled, but the guards were too strong. They shoved us into separate escape pods and slammed the doors shut. Through the window on the door, I could see the Other Maddie and Cole being led into the lobby through the last unburned hallway. The guards who closed us in looked shocked, and I could hear Maddie screaming from her escape pod. And then everything went down in flames. Seconds later, the explosion hit. I crumpled to the floor as the rocket shot up, and had to haul myself up to peer through the window at the warehouse below. A hundred silver spheres were sailing upwards; all identical to the one I was in. The building below was gone, replaced by a smoking crater miles deep. Shrapnel and debris flew through the air, hitting a barrier at the edge of the crater. Before the rocket got too high, I saw a dark haired figure crumpled outside the

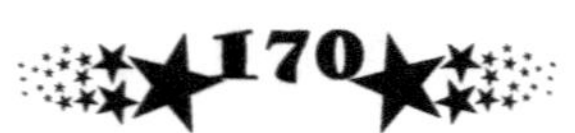

barrier, alone.

At least Rae made it.

It was only a few moments before the herd of rockets blasted out of the atmosphere and into space. I searched the pods I could see for one that could have Maddie in it. I couldn't find her. When Earth started to disappear into the distance, something started beeping behind me.

I turned to locate the source of the sound, and finally looked at the inside of the escape pod. It was about 8x8 feet inside, with a narrow bed on one side. Across from that was a panel of buttons. A screen above that flashed red. Thick, bold blue lettering announced that to move to speed, I had to press the red button. I glanced out to see the rockets leaping one by one into space and disappearing among the stars. I pushed the button.

Nothing seemed to happen, but the stars all blurred together into nothingness outside. The screen flashed again, open to a page of information. I started reading.

The flight would last a week, traveling faster than was possible, by human standards. There was food and water in a closet behind the bed, and a waste disposal system under the computer. The computer could access websites and games from Earth as well as Planet Oppo, along with movies and TV shows. The narrow stretch of floor between the computer and the bed could become a treadmill should exercise be necessary.

My brain swimming with possibilities and Maddie and Rae, I flopped onto the bed to endure the next seven days.

CHAPTER TEN

Rae

The escape pods twinkled to nothingness in the sky. Wood and dirt and melted clumps of metal pinged against the barrier, and the smoke was too thick to see through. I picked gravel out of the scrapes I had gotten after being launched through the barrier by the shockwave. I wondered if Maddie and Cole died from the fire or the explosion. Neither was a good way to die. Hours passed, and day faded to night. Police and reporters flooded the scene, searching for causes, explanations and survivors. There was nothing but ash and the melted remains of metal. The Others had been smart to include the fire. A mere explosion would have left clues.

I should have been in there with them. I should have died with them, instead of running away like the craven idiot I was. My fear of the lair and its inhabitants had frozen me, and now my only friends were dead.

The night was cold and long, spent hiding from the reporters and cops and wondering how long Cole and Maddie suffered before they died.

When morning finally came, I said goodbye to my friends and the lair and found the car. At least I didn't have to hitchhike home this time, and I wasn't injured. Not physically, anyway.

I drove carefully, aware that I didn't have a license. The days passed, only stopping for gas and the occasional nap in the backseat of the car in a parking lot. The sign announcing the California border was a blessing, an ice pack over the scalding wound on my soul. Camp Magic could help me. There would be people to comfort me.

A few short hours later, I turned into the magically concealed driveway and sped under oaks and redwoods into camp. I parked in the narrow dirt lot and got out. I stuffed the key in my pocket and started walking. I saw no one, and it was a little disappointing. Last time I crawled into camp, I was greeted by 60 people and plenty of drama. Now, the place looked like a ghost town.

I walked towards the center of camp, noticing a new ring of freshly built cabins outside the last one. I had been around long enough to witness four new loops being built, over forty people. Campers were coming in faster than they were leaving.

The camp was silent, ghostly. Instead of the usual noise of teenagers and kids enjoying the summer weather, there

was an eerie silence broken only by the occasional chirp from a bird in the trees. Nothing was physically different, but there was a definite change in ambience. The startling screech of a hawk sent me stumbling into one of Amanda's stone statues. I continued through the hedge spiral until I reached the center, where the dining hall and auditorium and training bunker were. The sounds coming from the bunker were unfamiliar, only adding to the strangeness of the situation. How was everything so different?

And then I remembered. Jamie was gone.

No wonder things were messed up.

Slowly, careful not to disturb the quiet, I let myself into the training room. The floors creaked as I crept towards the staircase. A strange cold feeling on the back of my neck made me aware of how wrong the situation was. I touched the doorknob and turned, but it blasted open before I pulled. A sobbing blonde girl ran out and stumbled up the stairs. I shut the door and ran up after her. She was on the grass outside, kneeling on the grass and sobbing into her hands.

"Jezzie?" I called. The girl turned, her eyes widening as she recognized me.

"Rachelle! You're back!" she gasped. She was up and throwing her arms around my waist in an instant, relief wiping away thoughts of whatever had happened before out of her mind.

"Where are Maddie and Cole? Does he remember yet?"

she asked. I shook my head, a fresh wave of grief hitting me. Jezzie's face fell.

"It was stupid to hope. It's awful seeing him so sad," she said.

"It's worse than that," I whispered. "Jezzie, we went back to the lair. We had to destroy it. And, um, Cole and Maddie…"

"What? They went back to that city? They stayed at the lair to make sure all the Others were gone?" Jezzie asked. I almost laughed at her optimism.

"No, Jezzie. There was, um. They…"

"Wait. No. You're wrong. Nononono. No. You're wrong." I looked at the sky to stop the tears.

"Jezzie, Mr. Riveria needs you to come back in, or you get, like, nine detentions," someone called from behind the door. It creaked open, and a familiar face peered out.

"Rebecca," I breathed. She squealed and ran out.

"Rae! You made it home!"

"Yeah. I did," I said. But without my friends.

"Are you okay?" she asked.

"Yeah. Definitely," I replied. She smiled again, and poked Jezzie.

"Jezzie and I have to get back before Mr. R. blows a gasket. You do not want to get on his bad side," she said. Taking my hand, she pulled me back to the bunker. She pushed open the door at the bottom of the stairs and I gasped.

Everyone was in uniform. Dark gray pants, paired with

long sleeved, high-necked shirts in the same color. It looked like a prison. The eighty or so kids were all aligned in organized rows, standing stiff and silent. Mr. Riveria, Jamie's replacement, stood with a grim face at the front. He had dark brown hair streaked with gray, and at least three chins. His eyes were black pits dug into his wrinkled face. He was huge, in height and width, and somehow managed to look comfortable in the uniform. Color was absent, happiness was nonexistent, fun was a memory. It looked like boot camp.

"Ah, Rachelle Levine. I see you've made your way back here," he said. His feet, clod in heavy boots, clomped toward me. Jezzie and Rebecca scurried away to their places in the lines.

"Yeah. Home sweet home," I said. I caught a faint sardonic smile on a boy's face.

"Last I spoke with my friends at the Council, you were in deep trouble. A renegade, off to save the world. Along with Madison and that Cole." Mr. R. looked me up and down. "The Council can go look at the big-ass crater where the Others used to live and tell me again if we're in trouble," I said.

Mr. R. arched an eyebrow. "Right now, I am looking at one disturbed teen when I should see three. You, my dear, are in trouble."

His statement was a hard blow, and I heard confused whispers from the campers as they realized that I was alone.

"In any case, Rachelle, you will need to change into a uniform and join us for drills. No one is exempt. Uniforms are

in the supply cabin."

"Drills for what?" I asked.

"Mastering powers and military training. The Council is thinking of building an army to fight the Others, and I've taken the liberty of training our younger, stronger supers."

Mr. R. waved me towards the door. Regretfully, I turned and walked out. Stares were hot on my back.

I made my way through the ghostly camp to the supply cabin. Inside, most of the usual products were gone. Now, there was only the barest minimum, all boring and generic. No more makeup, jewelry, perfume, or fancy products. Only store-brand soap and shampoo and toothbrushes. Gray uniforms in a range of sizes now dominated the huge section that had housed clothing of all shapes and colors and sizes. I picked through until I found one in my size, and carried it back to my cabin. But it wasn't mine anymore. Clearly, someone else had moved in and been living there recently. So I grabbed the few things of mine that were left and carried them to Maddie and Amanda's cabin.

The door squealed in protest as I pushed it open. I pulled off my sweatshirt and glared distastefully at the thick, scratchy gray material I'd tossed on Amanda's bed. Feeling like a burglar, I went into the bathroom and ran a brush through my hair. The mirror was unforgiving. The last few weeks had etched their sadness deeply into my expression. I couldn't recognize my own face.

I left the bathroom with a sense of abandonment, like I'd lost the last bit of myself I had. I donned the awful gray uniform and sat on Amanda's bed, hearing both their voices drift through the room. They were both here, and their presence would drive me crazy if I didn't learn to ignore it. I kicked one of Maddie's favorite shirts out of the way and left the cabin, headed back through the spiral to the bunker. Mr. R. assigned me a place in the rows and began drills. Military training. One by one we went to the front to show our powers. To show our lack of control. Despite her talent, Jamie had a hard time really helping to train some of the campers. Mr. R. was vicious with criticism, barely ever offering assistance. I could tell that there would be no time for fun anymore.

I had moved from Camp Magic to boot camp.

 Maddie

The sky was filled with stars, but still seemed empty. There were still a few of the silver escape pods in sight, but most had disappeared either in front or behind. After only a day, I was bored and stir-crazy in the tiny escape pod. On my way to an alien planet, where people would certainly know I wasn't like them.

I flopped onto the narrow mattress, and opened the food cabinet. There was a big tub full of packets of dehydrated food, and a huge palette of canned water. A machine built into the cabinet had slot for both, and a cup underneath for the food to

go once it was rehydrated. I pushed a first-aid kit out of the way and sifted through the packets, selecting a packet of noodles. I dumped them into the machine and added a can of water. I ate the tasteless, gooey pasta quickly, gagging and gasping as the heat burned my tongue.

I still had several days to suffer through. This particular journey was not a fast one. At least the pods had gravity. Bored out of my mind, I logged onto the computer and opened the web browser. I found a website with free episodes of TV shows and movies and flopped onto the bed. The movie I had chosen was bright, happy, and full of singing. The contrast from my own mood was so extreme it was almost funny.

I personally felt like the world was crashing down. Hopefully Rae had escaped, but I knew Cole hadn't. He had stayed with me, made sure I wasn't alone, and had paid the price. There was no way to tell who was safe and who wasn't anymore.

After three more movies and another five hours of gloomy thoughts, I switched off the computer. Lazy and unmotivated, I dragged myself up and turned on the treadmill. I tried to run for a bit, to stretch my cramped legs, but quickly got bored and laid down again. I rolled the empty can from my earlier meal around in my palms, and then dropped it onto the spinning treadmill. It skidded and was launched into the far wall.

It was going to be an atrociously long week.

SIX DAYS LATER

I was terrified.

The escape pods had entered a small solar system, identical to the one I knew. After shooting past four huge planets, and one smaller one, I saw Earth. At least, its identical twin. I wondered if nature itself was flipped around, like the personalities of the Others.

As the familiar planet got closer, I began to sweat. How was landing supposed to work? Would we crash to the ground? Would we actually survive?

The rocket tumbled and rocked and twisted when it hit the atmosphere. I was tossed all over the place, until I finally caught the edge of the bed and pulled myself down. Orange flames licked at the window, My heart pounded as the rocket continued to spin and shudder, like it would fly apart. I made a tiny whimpering noise in the back of my throat that somehow made it to my ears despite the rattling of the pod.

The ground was approaching rapidly. A small city came into view. I wasn't slowing down. At the speed I was going, the ground would liquefy me and anything else that happened to be in a mile wide radius. When I had given up hope of slowing and ultimately surviving, a huge tremor sent me sprawling across the floor. When I managed to drag myself back to the window, my view was partially obscured by a white sheet stretching above and around me. Finally, a parachute had come out.

The reduction in speed actually made me nauseous, it was so extreme. The thousand feet remaining drifted by slowly, safely. The escape pod settled gently on a paved road between a candy shop and a nail salon. Cars honked, and a huge pileup of traffic built on either side of me. The door of the escape pod hissed and glided open. I tasted the air, so fresh and clean and sweet compared to the week-old air in the rocket. The sun, so similar to the one I knew, was warm and friendly on my skin. A crowd of people emerged from their cars, cursing and yelling at me. Two other escape pods landed roughly down the road, one on a building and one on a parked car. There was confusion and screaming, and I used the distraction to duck out of the street and into the doorway of the candy shop. Sirens blared, and a helicopter beat the air as it landed right next to my rocket. Six people tumbled out, helmets and thick suits completely concealing them. They pointed at spots in the crowd, and split into pairs. One pair came straight for me. I turned to run, but grippy rubber gloves wrapped around my arms. Cold, sharp-edged metal handcuffs clicked onto my wrists.

"You are under arrest for defying the government and attempted genocide. You and your group of deviates are hereby-decreed outlaws. Come with me."

I was dragged toward the helicopter, the words like ice in my brain. These people—aliens—thought I was an Other. I wondered whether telling them I was human would make my situation better or worse. I decided probably worse, and meekly

followed the police into the helicopter. Two other Others were thrown in with me. I recognized one as Nicco, one of the guards.

"Madison! Everyone said you died in there! There was this huge rumor that you and Cole Quinn got tricked. But you're here, at least. Going to jail, like the rest of us, but finally home," he said cheerfully.

Panicked, I made a sorry attempt to mimic Other Madison's disdainful expression. I had no idea how to act around this person. He would see right through me. I thought of the things I was least likely to say, hopefully the things Other Madison would be most likely to say.

"I'd rather be dead. At least then I wouldn't be stuck in jail with this lot of idiots."

"Easy, Madison. You don't need to get like that. I'm sure Thompson and Barker have some ideas," Nicco said. He turned and fled to the other corner of the helicopter, talking quietly to the other man. I was stunned. He believed I was Other Madison. I was safe.

The helicopter lifted off and flew away. An hour passed, Nicco and the other man respectfully keeping their distance. A huge gray-brick prison came into view, razor wire glistening in deadly loops atop the twenty-foot walls. The helicopter descended onto a yellow landing pad on the flat roof of the building. The police ushered us off and into the waiting arms of more guards. We were hustled into cells, separated by thick concrete walls.

I was left there for forever. It could have been hours, or days, or weeks. Without a window, or any particular schedule for meals, I had no way to tell. I spent my time using rocks to chip at the lock on the door. It probably did less than nothing, but it gave me something to think about aside from my predicament. And Cole.

After a long enough time to make my legs stiff and my mind crazy, the door opened. Three guards carried me out of the cell, despite my struggles, and into another stupid helicopter. I waited for close to an hour in the cold metal box, until a pile of guards climbed into the front of the machine and started it.

The helicopter took off again. I was too scared to try to figure out where we were. From the suspenseful looks on the guards' faces, I could discern only that something major was happening.

The flight was much longer this time, split by a stop for fuel. I spent the hours we were flying surveying my surroundings. The inside of the helicopter was spacious, and surprisingly quiet. There were two separate sections, one for me and one for the cops. Benches lined the smooth metal walls. Narrow windows framed the doors. Outside, the landscape was harder to recognize. Dense forests and long, sloping hills made an unrecognizable carpet over the ground. We could be anywhere.

"Madison. We will be landing again soon. Be prepared."

I peered out the window, searching for a place where the

promised landing could occur.

A thin plume of smoke rose out of the forest less than a mile in front of us. A tiny space, barely big enough for the helicopter, was cleared there. The machine descended, carefully avoiding the crater left by a smashed silver rocket. The six men climbed out. Two held my arms and led me to the crater. I shut my eyes against the sting of smoke.

"The boy couldn't have survived. The crash would have killed him," one said.

"You'd be surprised how tough these things are. It may look crushed on the outside, but I'll bet the inside is intact, along with the kid. Have her make some noise," replied the other. My body went cold, and I understood why I was there. They needed me to lure Cole here.

One of the men holding me growled, "Scream. Scream his name like you're terrified." At the last second I remembered that I was supposed to be Other Madison. Not me.

"Why should I? I hate him and he hates me." It was a wild guess, but we were opposites, right? So wouldn't we hate each other? All I knew was that it felt so wrong to say it.

"We know you aren't Opposite. You and Cole are human. The Opposite Cole and Maddie died in the lair. So scream, girl, or I'll give you a reason to," the guard spat.

I stammered, protesting incomprehensibly. The man yanked my arm back, bending it in a direction it was not supposed to. I screamed.

"Say his name." My arm twisted back farther, and I lost my voice. A low whimper escaped me, until the man wrenched my shoulder again.

"Cole! Cole, please!" I screamed. Tears streaked down my face. My shoulder and elbow were on fire, bones grinding and muscles straining. I screamed again, and my arm was released. I rubbed my strained joints, gasping for breath. A shadow fluttered in the corner of my eye. I turned, and saw Cole half-hidden behind a tree. Frantic, I glared at him, willing him to run. But he'd been spotted. Before he could take a step, the four extra cops had him surrounded.

"Put her in the helicopter. We take care of this one now," one said. The two people holding my arms nodded, and dragged me towards the helicopter. I struggled, tearing my arms free only to have him catch my waist and lift me off the ground. I kicked and squealed and wriggled, all the while keeping my eyes on Cole. He slowly raised his hands, trying to placate the angry mob creeping in on him from all sides.

"We are the Oppo Protection Services. You are a human and therefore cannot be on this planet. You are a danger to our people and must be exterminated." The guard drew a dagger out of his sleeve. I screamed until my guard punched my in the stomach, knocking my breath away.

Cole could have run, but he tried reasoning with the man instead.

He didn't stand a chance.

Chapter Ten

The dagger was driven hilt-deep in his stomach. His face went white. He gasped like a fish, eyes and mouth wide. Cole Quinn, the only person in my life that really meant anything, collapsed into a lake of red on the forest floor. I ripped my way free of the guard, clawing his face with my fingernails. My vision was tunneled, tinted red. A scream like no other snarled through me, and I stumbled over to him. I threw my arms over him, tears blurring my vision. The guards began the process of dragging me away, and I resisted with all I had. But there were six of them, and one of me. They pulled me towards the helicopter.

"No! Cole! Cole! No!" I shrieked. I was hysterical. My mind was in a million pieces. Cole was gone.

The OPS threw me in the helicopter and slammed the door. I beat at the window, staring at the pale, crumpled shape across the clearing. The helicopter rose, propellers beating the air. Dust rose up, and I lost sight of him. I screamed again, punching so hard at the glass that my knuckles bled. I slid down the cold metal wall, finally able to stop crying. Unfortunately, that meant I wasn't able to do anything. I shivered on the floor, hugging my knees to my chest and breathing raggedly.

It was you. Brittney's voice was loud inside my head. It was you. I huddled into myself, trying to block her out. It was you. It was me. Cole wouldn't have come back if I hadn't screamed. Yet again, I was stuck knowing that I killed my

friends. First Rae and Amanda. Now Cole. I was a destructive force, a bomb set to blow and kill the people I loved the most.

It was you.

It was me.

The metal door was icy against my back, but I didn't feel the cold. My mind was somewhere else. With Cole, the first night we'd met. Lying on the dock on the lake at Camp Magic, under the stars. Already starting to feel something extra warm and fuzzy.

Another memory, one of his triumphant face as he told us he'd run halfway across the country to get back to us.

Another, of his lips against mine outside the Other's lair.

Another, of his face as he tried to help me when I was possessed.

Another, of him telling me about his family and listening in horror as I told him about mine.

Another, of the look of hurt and betrayal when I said I hated him, and again when I growled at him as a coyote.

Watching him watch me walk away.

Watching him at the camp, not knowing who he was or who I was.

It was you.

"Shut up, Brittney," I mumbled. Voices from the front of the helicopter drifted back to me.

"We can't murder Oppos!"

"They aren't Opposite, Anastasia! They're human."

"They're children. You've killed the boy already, can you not be satisfied? Spare the girl."

"Anastasia, stop. They don't belong here!" The people lowered their voices again.

So they planned to kill me. I deserved it, honestly. I was a horrible person. But if I was going to die, it needed to be on my own planet.

I shakily stood, using the door to balance. We were passing over a small town, with a bigger city off in the distance. It reminded me strangely of my hometown. I glanced at the wall separating me from the others, and sent my fist sailing at the glass of the window. Cracks webbed the pane, but it wasn't broken yet. My hand, though, probably was. After beating the door and the windows, it was swollen and bleeding and aching. I turned and kicked at the pane with my foot. Glass rained on the forest below.

Shouts echoed from the next room, but before they could stop me, I jumped. As the treetops blurred together, I shut my eyes. The warm, rippling feeling spread through me, and I flapped my new wings and flew towards the town. I was in the body of a bluebird, something common where I came from. The helicopter droned on above, having given up on me. I landed on a building, looking out over the town.

The resemblance to the place I grew up in was uncanny. Short, fat buildings painted in abstract colors, with fancy signs depicting the businesses within on the doors. Cars darted

up and down the narrow streets. People milled around on clean sidewalks. Disconcerted, I looked closer. I knew these people. Teachers, neighbors, friends, relatives. I was dizzy with recognition. This was my home.

I leaped off the building and zipped down the road to where Aspen Street dove into the woods. I flew along the road, counting mailboxes as I went, until I reached the familiar driveway. A car was pulling out. My heart stopped. The man in the drivers seat glanced right, then left. He pulled out and drove way too fast down the narrow street towards town. The brown hair edged with gray. The nose a little too big for the face. The eyes sunken deep into the skull.

The man was my father.

I watched as the car disappeared around a blind turn, and followed the driveway to my house. Seeing the big gray place again gave me déjà vu powerful enough that I staggered. The front door had been painted midnight blue, and a flimsy wooden railing had been added to the wrap-around porch, but the house looked exactly the same otherwise. I changed back into myself and crept toward the door. The stairs creaked under my feet. Feeling like a lie, I swatted dirt and wrinkles out of my clothes and rapped on the door.

"Coming, coming," someone called. I sucked in a breath. The voice was my mother's. The door was yanked open, and a familiar face appeared. Platinum blonde hair tied into a messy yet glamorous knot, blue eyes lined expertly in mascara and

eyeliner, expensive clothes draped on a perfect model's frame.

"Holy …" Rosalie muttered.

I blinked, and hid my bleeding hand behind my back. I was sure I smelled horrible, and my clothes were torn and filthy. I looked like I'd been through hell, and I honestly had no idea if I was welcome here or if Other Madison had destroyed any links to her family the way I had mine.

"M-Madison? I thought … but …" my Opposite mother stammered. I had seconds to come up with a plan.

"Excuse me. I was … dropped off here. By some … cops. They said you were family. I … can't remember much. They said they erased my memory. I have nowhere else to go," I said. I could fake memory loss. I could mimic Cole's expressions. This way, I had an excuse for not understanding anything about the Oppos.

But when I thought of Cole, grief streaked through my like an earthquake. My knees buckled under the weight. Rosalie caught me and dragged me inside.

"Brittney! Help me!" Rosalie called up the spiral staircase. A young woman with black hair and green eyes, so different from Rosalie's features and mine, skipped down the stairs. All the blood rushed out of my head, leaving black spots dancing across my vision.

"Madison? Oh, Rosalie! Come on, let's get her to the couch," Brittney trilled. The voice that had repeated it's condemning words in my head for weeks now. Half-paralyzed

by all the homesickness and misery, all I would do was sob and gasp for breath.

"Madison! Madison, calm down! Rose, do you know why she's like this?"

"They erased her memory," Rosalie said.

"How? The only way the OPS has really developed is still experimental!" Brittney said. Rosalie only nodded. I cursed to myself. I'd assumed that Oppos, in all their high-tech glory, would have access to amnesia-causing machines. What if they really didn't?

"Wow. It's four already? I need to head back south. I told my boyfriend I'd be home by dinner tonight. I'll try to come up again next weekend. Tell Dad I say bye," Brittney said. She went upstairs again, returning with a suitcase bouncing behind her. She touched Rosalie's right cheek with two fingers, smiled, and left.

"Okay, Madison. Let's get you to bed. You can rest until dinner," Rosalie said. She helped me stand and guided my up the stairs.

"Brittney's been sleeping in your room when she comes up, because we had to turn hers into a home office when she left. But it's still the same." My knees almost gave out again when I saw the room. My room. The pale blue walls, the white shelves covered in books, the antique white desk covered in neat stacks of papers and notebooks, organized cups of pens and pencils. The door to the closet, covered in a thick layer of

posters, certificates, and photos. The white wooden bed with a thick featherbed and piles of pillows with blue, cloud-covered cases. Rosalie gave me a change of clothes, tucked me in, and went back downstairs. Again, I was left alone with my thoughts.

It was you.

I was so confused. Brittney had been so amiable, so friendly with Rosalie. She hated Rosalie. And she hated me, too.

It was you.

How did this crazy planet even work?

To add to my misery, without distractions, the crushing weight of heartache stomped onto my chest again. I had watched the Oppos murder my best friend. I had done nothing to stop it.

It was you.

I let him die.

The minutes passed slowly, each one bringing another memory of Cole. And then Amanda. Both my fault. Both my responsibility. I let them both down. I would never see either of them again because I had been too stupid to figure out how to protect them. If anyone deserved to be dead, it was me.
Any sleep I might have gotten was haunted by nightmares, the very worst kind. Monsters, murderers, me on their side. Cole being stabbed, over and over and over. When Rosalie finally came to wake me, I was behind the knife. I was the one driving it into his stomach. I was the one listening to the screams of a useless damsel in distress in the background, crying about Cole

without doing a thing to save him.

"Maddie, you're sweating. Is everything alright?" Rosalie asked nervously when I sat up. My palms were clammy, my head spun.

"Yeah."

"Alright then. I made you dinner. Come on down when you're ready." She left me again, and I hugged a pillow to my chest and waited until I heard her clanging around in the kitchen again before I followed. I numbly stumbled down the spiral staircase, my socks sliding on the slippery wood.

"Your father will be home soon. I wanted to make sure you got some food," Rosalie said. I had never seen her maternal side. My dad had always been the one taking care of me. Rosalie was a model. Young, irresponsible, and not super smart. She was (duh) the opposite of the woman standing in front of me.

"Thanks," I said. She placed a blue bowl full of macaroni and cheese in front of me. I inhaled the creamy, rich, delicious stuff in seconds. I hadn't realized how hungry I was, how much I craved a decent meal that didn't come from a little packet.

"Rosalie? I know this sounds like a stupid question, but can you explain how things work here? I mean, on this planet? And how it all relates to Earth? I honestly can't remember a thing," I said as she spooned more pasta into my bowl.

"Aw, honey. We all look the same as a person on Earth, but our personalities are opposite. Since Oppo follows Earth, though, we all have to hold their jobs and responsibilities. Any

person on Earth that loves or likes their job has an Opposite here that loathes every second of it. And think- the smart people there are the dumb people here. Our doctors are often total idiots, for example. Tell me, how do you think that works?" Rosalie began.

"I'd say it probably doesn't." Rosalie nodded. "It doesn't. Most of the time, the janitors and delivery people end up doing the jobs that require a genius. It's impossible."

"So why do you — we continue to follow Earth? If we have to compensate by having homeless people help lawyers and doctors, then why don't they all switch?" I asked.

"We have to stay in sync with Earth. If a man has a job here, but doesn't have it on Earth, then he may meet someone he isn't supposed to. If, say, they have a child, then that kid can't exist. It becomes something like a glitch, and begins tearing apart our systems simply by being alive. The last time something like this happened, was almost two hundred years ago, and we're still trying to clean up the imbroglio. The government is on strict lockdown, making sure that everything stays as close to Earth as it can. Anything else, and it all comes crashing down." Rosalie paused, gazing out the big kitchen windows.

"But how did you end up with all of the advanced technology you have if you have to follow Earth?"

"Think. Earth is mostly idiots, so Oppo is mostly geniuses. Even within strict guidelines, we can still develop a higher level of strength and knowledge. But most of us are

trapped in a position we hate."

"That sounds pretty miserable," I said. Rosalie only smiled sardonically. Headlights cast a glare on the windows.

"Your dad is home," Rosalie said. I stood up, staring apprehensively at the door. It banged open, and my father barged in. When he saw me, he staggered.

"Hi, Dad," I said.

"You're supposed to be dead," he replied.

# Rae

"Attention! A bus is coming today with four new recruits. I want you to debrief—"

"We aren't recruits. We're people," I spat at Mr. R. He glared at me like I was the biggest curse on his existence he could ever dream up. He slapped a sheet of paper with names and numbers down on the table.

"You're all going to be soldiers. Debrief the new kids and get them prepped for training. Ignorance won't be tolerated, so for your friends' sakes make sure they're prepared." Mr. R. stormed out of the dining hall. Rebecca and Jezzie stared at me from across the table.

"You need to stop aggravating him. One of these days he's going to do something drastic. And it won't be pretty," Jezzie said. For an eleven-year-old, she was impossibly sagacious.

Chapter Ten

"Rae, what you're doing is dangerous. You don't want a man like that to hate you as much as he does," Rebecca added. I shrugged. They were right. It was stupid to play games with someone so sadistic and psychopathic. But I couldn't let him win without fighting back.

"Are you done? We should be there when the bus arrives," I said. Rebecca pushed her plate of gray, overcooked pasta away from her.

"Let's go."

We marched through the gray, sad-looking camp to the parking lot. The bus hadn't come yet, so we sat on the dusty ground and listened for the sounds of birds in the trees. In the weeks that Mr. R. had been in charge, all life seemed to have left Camp Magic. It was as boring and gray and monotonous as the uniforms we were forced to wear.

"Here it comes," Jezzie said. I spotted the narrow plume of dust quickly.

"I wonder what they're like," Rebecca mused.

"They'll be amazing. Like Maddie," Jezzie said, in a rare moment of naiveté.

"Let's hope," I said.

"The bus rattled into the parking lot. The driver got out, opened the luggage hatch, and nodded to us. He got in his black sedan and peeled out with a squeal of protest from the tires.

"No one wants to stick around here anymore," Rebecca said darkly.

I didn't reply, only watched the people walking off the bus.

The first was a boy about twelve, scared and confused.

The second was a girl a little older than me. Or maybe it was her dark makeup and glittery jewelry. And the fact that she was wearing heels.

The last two were the most interesting of the bunch. A boy my age with dark hair and bright turquoise eyes towing a tiny girl with rich chocolate brown curls and deep hazel eyes. She couldn't have been older than seven.

Rebecca introduced herself, Jezzie, and me. The four stood awkwardly in front of us.

"I'm Nathan. I'm from Texas. I accidentally burned someone," the first boy said. His hands lit on fire and he quickly blew them out.

"Jenna. I'm seventeen, from L.A. I can change rocks and dirt and stuff into gems. I got busted for selling them." I glanced again at the piles of sparkling jewelry, and wondered why she decided to come here. The Council wouldn't have insisted that her power be contained, and she didn't look much like a 'amper.

"I'm Alek, and this is Autumn. I'm 16, she's six. We're 'n-"

"Six and a quarter!" the little girl interrupted. Alek rolled his ṣ.

Ne're from Washington State. She can change the color

of things by touching them, and I can move stuff with my mind. Autumn tugged on the bottom of Alek's T-shirt, and the fabric turned rainbow.

"Wainbow!" she squealed.

"She's adorable!" Jezzie exclaimed.

"You can have her," Alek muttered. I smiled.

"Okay, guys, let's figure out cabins," I said. As Rebecca, Jezzie, and I led the procession through camp, we explained how things were.

"This sounds, like, opposite from the brochure," Jenna snapped.

"It is. Under new management," I said.

Rebecca snorted. "That's one way to put it." I glanced back, catching Alek staring at me. Both of us looked sheepishly away. My face burned as I studied the sheet Mr. R. had given us. "Jenna, you can stay in Cabin 14 here, with Tammy. She's at lunch, but we can introduce you guys later," I said. "Autumn? You're staying with Jezzie. I mean, unless you want to stay with your brother or something." Autumn vehemently shook her head and grabbed Jezzie's hand. I looked over at the next name and froze. Rebecca leaned over to see the paper. Her face paled.

"Alek, you get cabin nine. I, um, think someone's stuff might be in there, but work around it for now," she said quietly. I couldn't breathe. Alek was moving into Cole's cabin.

"Dude, it's fine. It's probably the only boy cabin with spot right now. It's not like it's the end of the world. Cole's

isn't going to get moved," Rebecca said. But I was far away, reliving the day I met Cole.

Like it always was at Camp Magic, the weather was perfect. Warm, sunny, not a cloud in the sky. I was on the beach by myself, skipping stones on the placid blue water of the lake.

"The bus is back!" someone called. I jumped up. The bus didn't come often, back when camp was smaller, and new people always brought news of the real world. Sometimes even technology, which was exciting until it got confiscated. I followed half the camp to the dirt parking lot, silent amongst animated conversations.

At that point in my life, I had no friends to talk to. Camp was a sad and unwelcome place for me.

And then a boy stepped off the bus.

Jamie seemed to know that I needed a friend. She asked me to show the boy around. The other two that arrived, two girls, she showed around herself.

The boy introduced himself as Cole. He told me that he could run, fast. I led him around camp, telling him everything I knew about it. I showed him his cabin, and the dining hall, the auditorium, and the training bunker. Once I had showed him all the places I was supposed to, I took Cole to my favorite section of the beach. Quiet, lonely, and secluded.

"This place is so awesome," Cole said. He picked up a flat rock and skipped it miles across the lake. I watched it disappear into the water, leaving only ripples behind.

Chapter Ten

"It's pretty amazing," I agreed quietly.

"How long have you been here?" he asked, flopping down onto the sand. He leaned back on his elbows, looking at me.

"Two and a half years," I replied.

"Wow. That's a crazy long time to be away from home."

"I sort of gave up on home a while ago. I'm happier here."

"I'd miss my family. I promised my sister I'd be home soon," he said.

"Good luck," I said. The dinner bell was ringing. I started to leave.

"Wait! Um, Rachelle? Can I sit with you at dinner?" Cole asked. I turned, catching his hazel-green eyes and feeling a huge smile spread across my face.

"Yeah. Definitely."

That evening was the first time I hadn't eaten alone in months. And in the months that followed, Cole and I had only gotten closer. It was painful, seeing him again. Even if it was only in memory.

His cabin should have been empty. Consecrated. Sacred.

Not occupied by a new kid who hadn't earned a place here yet. Not tainted by the presence of another person.

Cole had made my life worth living.

Alek was another kid with a superpower.

"Rachelle. Come on, dude, wake up." Rebecca waved her

hand in front of my face. I blinked and swatted her hand away.

"I'm fine."

"Right. Of course you are," Rebecca said, her voice dripping with sarcasm.

"I'm fine," I repeated, this time with my power on full strength.

"You are," she agreed.

It was so easy.

CHAPTER ELEVEN

Cole

I was alive.

Barely.

But alive.

It had been a week since I crash-landed onto Planet Oppo. Two days since I let Maddie's screams lure me into a trap.

Two days since I got stabbed.

The bleeding had slowed almost to a stop. My shirt, which I had painfully turned into a makeshift bandage, was soaked all the way through with blood. But I was alive.

Slowly, careful to keep the wad of fabric pressed against the deep gash in my stomach, I sat up. Pain shot through my body, thin daggers. My head spun, and I leaned heavily on one arm. I had been lying down for two days now, and lost a lot

of blood. At this point, though, infection was the thing I most needed to worry about. Not bleeding to death. That threat had passed, at least for the moment.

I needed to get to the first aid kit in the crashed escape pod. It was my only chance. That would involve getting to the crater, lowering myself down, crawling through the crumpled doorway, and digging through debris to get to the cabinet where the kit was. And I couldn't even sit up without seeing spots.

Pressing on the wound with all my strength, I lurched towards the crater. Black spots danced crazily across my vision, and I could feel the gash opening again. I ignored all of it, dragging myself forward with the fingernails of my free hand. I made it halfway before I had to stop. Air tore raggedly through my throat, and every nerve in my body screamed red. I was bleeding again, even against the pressure of the shirt. The distance to the rocket seemed to lengthen, stretching away from me, an endless path. I struggled to breathe, my whole body trembling and shuddering with pain. It didn't help at all that I was dehydrated and hungry. My body was rebelling, and I probably had no more than a few hours to live.

This new thought rang in my head. I needed to get to that hole. I needed food, water, and first aid. So I dragged myself farther, conscious enough to push on, only allowing myself to focus on the thought of safety. I ignored the pain as best I could, focused solely on the ragged edge of the cliff. I was in agony.

I was going to die.

Chapter Eleven

I couldn't do it.

The sun glared down, shining bright in my eyes and burning my skin. Reminding me of the dryness in my mouth and the pounding intensity of the ache in my head. I had eight feet to go.

Seven.

Six and a half.

I paused to rest, but without the single-minded determination of moving forward, the torture was too much to bear. So I pressed on.

Six.

Five.

Four.

Gasping for breath, each slight movement sending the sensation of the dagger through my stomach again, unable to hear through the lion's roar of a million nerves protesting, using all my strength to hold the blood-soaked shirt into the would to staunch the bleeding, I inched closer.

Three.

Two.

One.

My fingers caught the edge of the hole. I struggled to think around the burning red scream in my ears, struggled to find a way down. After a few seconds of muddled logic, I hauled myself over the edge and fell. The ground hit me like a sack of bricks, but the twinge in my shoulder was nothing

compared to the fire in my stomach.

I found the top of the sharp-edged door and hooked my fingers around it. The landslide that had spilled into the rocket made a rough ramp for me to slide down, giving my sore arm a rest.

The ramp ended next to the bed, and I dragged myself onto the dirty white mattress and opened the cabinet. I had made it, somehow. Against all odds.

I opened a can of water and poured it down my throat. Another. I started a packet of food cooking and opened the first aid kit. The items inside had unfamiliar labels, but their purposes were relatively clear. I pulled the bandage away, and my stomach heaved, sending yet another rip of torment through my tortured body. It looked awful. A greenish color shaded the skin around it. Blood was caked everywhere. My skin was swollen and hot. I had wasted too much time. It was infected. Horribly, terribly infected.

Fear and worry sent shivers down my spine. I dug through the kit, searching for a cure that wouldn't exist.

A tube of healing cream fell out of the bag. I picked it up and looked at it. It was too late for it to really help, but a sick sort of hope made me squirt more than was necessary onto the ugly gash. I laid a gauze pad over it and wrapped an Ace bandage around my torso, holding back a scream. I knew it wouldn't help, but I couldn't stand the thought of leaving it.

I slurped down the hot soup, and then more water and

more soup. The pain in my abdomen was fading, both the hunger and the wound. I was almost- almost- comfortable. I decided to get some sleep while I could, before everything started hurting again. I shut my eyes, and it was only a few seconds before I was asleep.

* * *

I woke up to a bright, glaring sunrise. It was hot. Hotter than Camp Magic and hotter than the town. I blinked, trying to focus on my surroundings. Metal. Dirt. More metal. More dirt. The escape pod.

My hand went to the bandage. Disbelief. Confusion.

It didn't hurt.

Fingers flying, I unwound the bandage and stared in incredulity at the place where the gash had been.

It was gone.

Healed.

Leaving only a tiny pink scar.

I pulled out the tube of ointment I had put on it. The only label on it was a tiny sticker that said "for wounds." Nothing hinting that it had some supernatural quality to it. Obviously, though, it did. Otherwise it wouldn't have kept me alive. I stretched and drank two cans of water. The food was almost gone, enough for the two "meals" that I heated up for breakfast. I would need to find more, fast. I had almost died once already on this planet. I would rather not starve to death so far from

206

home.

I pulled the blanket off the bed and dropped the five remaining cans of water and the first aid kit onto it. My shirt was done for, but I still had the sweatshirt I'd left on the escape pod. I pulled it over my head and lifted the blanket by its corners, like a basket. There was nothing else on the rocket I would need.

I climbed the steep face of the crater and back onto normal land. Normal. Ha. The forest was thick, dark, and unrecognizable. Birds sang, but there was no other sound, not even wind. I tied the corners of the blanket into a knot and slung the makeshift backpack over my shoulder. Hoping there weren't any carnivorous beings in the forest that could catch me, I took a tentative step forward.

# Maddie

I brushed my hair and tied it into a ponytail. My eyes roamed over my face in the mirror, searching for something familiar. A month and a half ago, I was a carefree girl with a painful past and superpowers. Innocent, blissful, ignorant. Now, a mere few weeks later, I looked and felt like an entirely different person. The beginnings of wrinkles were forming on my forehead. At age fifteen. My eyes were shadowed and sad. I wondered if I could ever be that bright, happy person again. With all my friends dead, probably not.

Chapter Eleven

I left the bathroom and went back to the creepily familiar bedroom. My closet was as I'd left it all those weeks ago. I tugged an oversized gray sweatshirt over my head and a slightly small pair of jeans over my legs and trotted downstairs.

"Hey, sweetie. Your dad will be down in a minute. You can talk to him about last night." Rosalie told me to sit on the couch and brought me a plate of pancakes.

"I have to go. Work. I'm sure you can find something to do," she said. The front door closed behind her.

I switched on the TV and flipped absently through channels. I found an old Disney movie and stared blankly at the singing characters on the screen.

"Madison." I turned to see my father, in a navy blue suit with a gray tie. He looked haggard and tired.

"Dad."

"I'm sorry. For the way I acted last night."

"What about it?" I turned the volume down on the TV and sat down to face him.

"I'd heard reports from the Earth Other base. Of frauds. The Earth Madison and Earth Cole Quinn supposedly claimed the escape pods you and our Cole Quinn were supposed to take. You and Cole supposedly died, with a few hundred other Others. But you're here. Human Madison and Human Cole were captured and executed. So you must be my Madison," My dad said.

I listened silently, trying to figure out how to get out of

this one.

"I am. I made it onto an escape pod last second. I doubt anyone knows I'm alive. And I think the OPS would arrest me if they knew," I replied.

My dad nodded. "Undoubtedly. All the… Others… are in serious trouble. I can't believe you left us for them."

I wracked my brain for a response. This deception was extremely difficult, when I had absolutely no idea what I was talking about.

"Human Madison went to Camp Magic. I had to go to the Others, right?" I said. It was somewhat risky, using an idea I didn't understand to enforce my argument. But my dad only rubbed the stubble on his chin.

"I know. It's so hard to accept that my daughter is a convict," he said.

"Better than Human Madison. She's not even alive," I said.   My dad rubbed his eyes with the heels of his hands, looking like he was trying to remember an essential detail to the conversation but couldn't.

"You're supposed to be dead. You can't be seen, Madison. Think. If you leave the house and someone recognizes you, and calls the OPS, you're done for. For real. You're in hiding."

I blinked.

"I'm in hiding."

"Yes. I have to go to work now, hon. Stay inside and don't answer the phone or the door. Rose and I will probably be

home around six." With that, my dad turned and left the house.

It was so quiet. The TV blared, the refrigerator hummed, the heater blasted, but it was so quiet.

Quiet enough that I could hear Cole's gasp of pain as the knife cut into his perfect abs.

My stomach turned, and I bolted off the couch and into the bathroom. My breakfast made an unwelcome reappearance. I flushed and rinsed out my mouth. Bracing my arms against the counter, leaning over the sink, I met my own teary gaze. I had gotten the love of my life killed.

It didn't matter that we were fifteen, or that we'd only known each other very long. It didn't matter that he didn't remember me, or that he didn't seem to like me back anymore. He was the one, my first love and my only. The one I wanted to grow old with, the one that I wanted to be with forever.

I dropped my head into my hands and sobbed, crumpling against the polished stone countertop. For close to an hour I stayed there, but by then I was cried out. So I made my way to my bedroom, located my old iPod, and turned it on. I lost myself in the music, skipping all the fast or cheerful or funny songs, only listening to the slow, sad rhythms that matched my mood.

To keep myself from watching Cole's final moments over and over again, I wondered what happened to Rae. Had she gotten far enough away? Did she get back to Camp Magic? That led to other questions. What was camp like without Jamie?

Was Jamie okay? Did she remember anything? Could she find her way home? Could I find my way home? Could I do it without Cole? Cole…

The silver blade of the knife flashed. A small gasp of pain. Cole fell, the man stepped back. The dagger was stained with liquid red.

I found myself screaming, and forced myself to stop. The headphones were across the room, along with the iPod. Tinny music filled the sudden silence. I recognized the song instantly. It used to be one of my favorites. I'd even sung it in a school competition once. *When You're Gone,* by Avril Lavigne.

I played it four times. Every time, it seemed a little closer to my own life. Suddenly, I was worried. My sanity had been slipping when Cole was getting closer to Rae. What would happen now that he was actually gone forever? Halfway through the fifth time, my iPod died. I tossed it on the bed and went back downstairs.

The TV was still on, so I grabbed a huge bag of potato chips and flopped onto the couch. After the three and a half hours of sobbing, I was calm enough to munch on chips and focus on the animated characters bouncing around the screen. I turned the volume up loud enough to drown out my thoughts, and spent the next few hours in blissful, blithe, peaceful ignorance.

 # Rae

Footsteps shook the deck beneath me.

"Rebecca said you might be here," I heard. I pulled my toes out of the water to see who it was.

Alek sat next to me, pulling off his shoes and dipping his own feet in the water.

"I am," I said, instantly cursing myself. Since when did I get awkward in front of guys?

"You are," he said, laughing.

"Can I help you?" I asked. Somehow it came out sounding angry, and I cursed myself again.

"Only if you want me to leave. I can't remember where my cabin is," he joked. He knew where it was. He'd been there a week.

"Then I guess you'll have to stay," I replied. Alek grinned.   The sun was fading fast, and a few stars were visible. If Mr. R. knew we were out here, we would be punished. Especially since we were both out of uniform. For the first time in what seemed like forever, I was wearing short shorts and a tank top and flip-flops. Alek was wearing something that I instantly recognized as Cole's style. They might have even been Cole's clothes.

"I guess you're right. And since we're both here, maybe we could talk a little," he suggested. His hand inched close to mine.

"We could," I said slowly. Alek's eyebrow twitched.

"Yes we could," he repeated. I swished my feet through the water, unable to speak. All I could think of was Cole. He was dead. Gone.

I stared at the stars against the rippling surface of the dark water, wondering which was the sun for Planet Oppo. The people who killed my best friend and the boy I loved. Why didn't Alek see that I didn't want to talk?

Suddenly, I was angry. Alek didn't understand. He needed to leave.

"Your cabin is the one with the huge redwood right next to it and the dead patch of grass in front," I said, getting up and walking away.

"Rachelle? Did I say something wrong?" Alek called.

I started to run. I hugged the shore, stumbling on shifting sand in my flip-flops. Tears stung my eyes.

"Rachelle!" Alek yelled. Another voice echoed his. It was either Rebecca or Jezzie, I couldn't tell which. Hoping to lose them, I veered into the dense forest and kept running.

"Stop! Rae!" the girl screamed. It was definitely Jezzie. I didn't even falter.

My lungs were screaming by the time I reached the fence. I think I'd ripped off a toenail, my knees and palms were scraped raw, and my shins were covered in scratches. I leaned on the rough bark of a redwood tree, panting as I examined the blood on my legs. Running in the dark, in flip-flops, through a

forest…not my most brilliant idea.

"Rachelle! What is wrong with you?" Jezzie hissed. She was at my shoulder, an angry glare in her eyes. I slid down the trunk and sat on the damp earth. My forehead rested on my knees.

"Rachelle! Alek thinks you hate him. Why did you run away?" she snapped. I grabbed her tiny hand and slapped it against the side of my head.

"Do it. Whatever you do, make it happen. I don't want to remember anymore." Jezzie yanked her hand free.

"No! Are you crazy? You remember what happened to Cole!" she shrieked.

"Yes, I do. And I don't want to," I moaned.

"Rachelle, stop. This isn't a game. It's permanent," Jezzie said. As I looked up at her, I was struck by the youngness of her. She was only ten, after all. An old, old ten, but ten nonetheless. She cowered against a tree, watching me with wary eyes. I thought about using my power to talk her into it, but I couldn't focus well enough. And I wasn't entirely convinced that I wanted this to happen yet.

"Rae, what's going on with you?" Jezzie asked gently.

"Cole. Maddie. They're gone. I let them die, Jezzie. I left them. And Alek was trying to … but I couldn't… I still love Cole, and Alek was… he didn't see that… so I left. And then you were all following me, and…" Tears burned my eyes, and I couldn't go on.

"Rae, he wasn't trying to-"

"How do you know? Hmm? You're ten, Jezzie! You don't know!"

"I do. I may be ten, but I haven't had an easy life. I know. I'm not like any other ten year old," she said quietly.

"But you are. You don't understand. I need you to help me, and you won't."

"You are asking me to destroy your life. It's basically suicide, but you still feel the pain and the misery. Did you see Cole after I did what I did? He was miserable. It doesn't help to not have memories. It still hurts."

"I still want to forget. You don't understand. I have lost everything. This place isn't the same. Even if everyone was still here, it wouldn't be."

"I know. I get it. I know exactly how you feel. But I am not going to help you destroy your mind," Jezzie insisted. I was preparing my withering retort when harsh, fluorescent floodlights spilled over the forest. Mr. R. and a group of his followers stepped into view.

"Ah, Rachelle and Jessica."

"Jezzie," Jezzie grumbled under her breath. Mr. R. didn't hear or didn't care, and slowly began walking towards us.

"I would have expected this from you, Rachelle. But sweet, innocent Jessica… never. Such a shame. Out after curfew, out of uniform, in a restricted area. This is very bad, girls." He readjusted the collar of his tweed jacket, mockingly kicked a

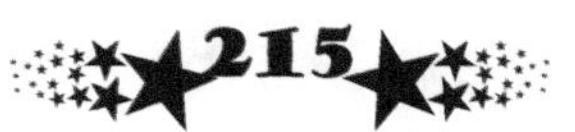

stick at us with his polished brown saddle shoe.

Without turning my head, I glanced at Jezzie. Tears rolled silently down her cheeks. She stared straight ahead, her lower lip trembling.

"For one infraction, I give detention. Three hours in the auditorium, writing a paper on a topic of my choice. Four hours the next day, then five, then six." He paused, studying our faces.

"For two infractions, I believe that the punishment is to be locked in the Box of Shame for two days, no food and little water. A small, cramped wooden box next to the dining hall with only a tiny slot for air and light."

A tiny sob escaped Jezzie, and I caught a fiendish gleam of pleasure in Mr. R.'s eyes.

"I have never encountered an individual with three infractions at once before. I'm not allowed to expel you. I can't give any more detentions or lock you up any longer. So I will spend a few days deciding your fate. Please put on your uniforms and get to your cabins. I will see you tomorrow at training." Mr. R. snapped his fingers and gestured back towards camp. Two of his helpers started to guide us back.

I searched their eyes for any trace of sympathy. These were people that used to play with me on the beach. People I laughed with over the table at lunch. Now they ran around helping Mr. R. run his sick, twisted game.

We passed Jezzie's cabin first, and as the little girl tearfully stumbled inside, I heard Autumn's cheery voice

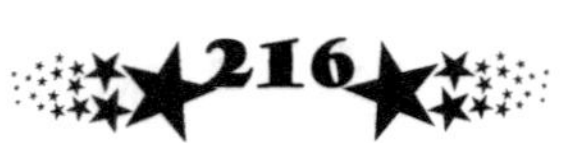

welcome her back. I was deposited in front of my cabin and watched until the door locked.

Immediately I scribbled a note on a stray piece of paper with a half-dead green marker and snuck out again. I ran to Jezzie's cabin, slid the note under the door, and raced back. I was glad Jezzie had refused to help me. She'd been totally right, and the note said so.

The rest of the night passed slowly, fear of Mr. R. and his sick, twisted mind keeping me wide awake. When dawn finally came, I put on my itchy, stiff, gray uniform and the clunky shoes that came with it. I walked to the bunker with a crowd of other kids, every blank stare bleaker than the one before it. Jezzie tried not to look at me, but when she did, she gave me a tight smile and a slight nod. Apology accepted.

Once inside, we all lined up to wait for Mr. R. He came in late, a small piece of paper with faded, smudged green scrawl crumpled in his hand.

"Jessica Mora. You're first today," he yelled. Jezzie's head snapped up. She wasn't allowed to practice at all, because there wasn't anyone willing to risk their life for practice's sake. She only took part in the battle training.

"Jessica. Now." She stumbled on her way to the front of the room. He placed a heavy hand on her shoulder. She cringed.

"Rachelle Levine. Come." My blood turned to ice. The paper. Last night's argument. Our punishment.

"Rachelle." I numbly drifted forward. Mr. R. turned us

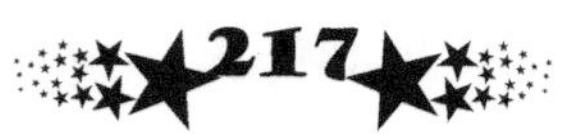

to face each other. He lifted Jezzie's limp hand and placed it against my head. Shock registered on every face as the rest of camp realized what was happening. Whispered conversations drifted through the air. Mr. R. smiled.

"Now, Jessica—"

"My name is Jezzie." She let her hand fall.

"Jezzie. Erase her memory," Mr. R. commanded. He slapped her hand against my head painfully hard.

"But…" Jezzie was pale, teary-eyed, and sweaty.

"Jessica. Now."

Jezzie looked into my eyes, and seemed to be asking a question.

Will you help me fake this?

I gave an almost imperceptible nod. Jezzie's eyes closed, and her forehead creased. I rolled my eyes back in my head and crumpled to the floor. Gasps echoed off of the concrete walls.

"It happened like it did with Cole," Jezzie whispered. I let my eyes open enough to see shapes, but not enough for anyone to see.

"Ah. So it appears. Jessica Mora, do you know what my power is?"

Crap.

"Um…"

"Jacob Stringer. What is my power?" Mr. R. shouted. A boy in the front shakily replied.

"You can read the mind of anyone you are touching."

"That's right. Now, Jessica, please tell me something," Mr. R. said. Realization dawned on Jezzie's face, and she shrank away from him.

"Yes?" she said, almost too quietly to hear.

"Why did you lie to me?" he bellowed. I expected Jezzie to shy away, but instead her face twisted into a sneer. She stood tall and looked directly into Mr. R.'s shallow eyes.

"I am not hurting my friend. And you can't make me," she growled.

It seemed stupid for me to be faking still, so I climbed to my feet and stood behind Jezzie. Mr. R. smiled wickedly.

"Oh can't I?" he said mockingly. He beckoned one of his helpers, a boy whose name I couldn't remember, and whispered instructions into his ear. The boy jogged outside and returned a few long minutes later with something stuffed inside a pillowcase. Mr. R. reached into the pillowcase and pulled out a heavy black object that made every single person in the room cringe.

A gun.

I didn't know much about guns, but it was clearly something dangerous. And deadly.

Faster than I would have expected he could, Mr. R. darted around Jezzie to grab my arm. He pulled my close to him, wrapped his left arm around my chest and arms, and pressed the icy barrel of the gun against my temple.

"Jessica Mora, you will erase this girl's memory or I will

shoot her. And then you." His vocal cords vibrated against the back of my head.

Jezzie was sobbing, and she had an apology written all over her face. But she curled her small hand against my head. As each memory flowed out of my brain, I lived it again. Childhood, parents, friends, school. First days at Camp Magic, first time seeing Cole, Maddie, Amanda, Jamie. Our mission. Amanda dying in my arms. The town, the self-destruct. Alek, Jezzie, Autumn.

Each memory that disappeared left me a little colder, a little dizzier. Jezzie was crying harder than I'd ever seen anyone do, but continued to clear out my mind. With Mr. R. standing there, reading every thought that went through my head. It was too dangerous to keep anything.

After a long, long time, there was nothing left. I couldn't even remember my own name. My eyes rolled back in my head and I passed out.

When I woke up again, two girls leaned over me. One seemed much younger than the other.

"Where am I?" I asked woozily.

"Camp Magic," the younger girl said. The older one shook her head.

"This isn't Camp Magic anymore. This is hell."

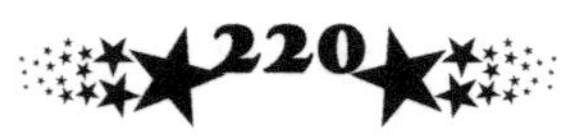

CHAPTER TWELVE

 Cole

Super speed isn't always helpful. But in the wilderness, when you have to make a fire with nothing but two sticks, it's definitely a good thing.

Pine needles blazed, curling red-hot in the pit I'd dug. I dropped some big, flat rocks between the branches to heat them up, and then looked at the birds. Two of them, possibly related to pigeons. I tossed the sharp-edged rock up in my hand and caught it again. Gagging slightly, I began to hack apart the birds.

I'd caught them while trying to fish, moving fast enough that they didn't have time to fly away. I'd jut snapped my wrist, and bam, dinner.

Not that dinner was any fun to cook. I used sticks to dig the rocks out and plopped the gelatinous pink globs of meat onto their smoking surfaces. There was ash all over them, but I was too hungry to care.

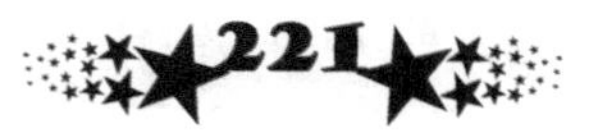

After a few seconds, I flipped the blobs over to cook the other side. I used the sharp rock to check that they were fully cooked, and then choked them down. It was tasteless and had a dry, ashy texture to it, but it was food. Not nearly enough, but food.

I tossed the dirt back into the pit to smother it and continued walking. I hoped to reach some sort of civilization before I starved to death by a wild animal, and therefore spent any spare time I had trudging through the forest. At night, I climbed into a tree and found a place to balance, tucking the filthy once-white blanket around me and looping the drawstring of the medical kit over a higher branch.

Each day, I managed to find some sort of animal or plant to eat, and a pond or stream to drink from. It wasn't ideal, of course, but it was barely enough. It had been close to two weeks since crash-landing here. I'd been able to live off the meals from the destroyed escape pod for a few days, but then I'd been stabbed. And that was when I started walking. And walking. Running expended too much energy; being still was too dangerous. So I walked.

And walked.

And—you guessed it—walked.

I was searching for something. Lost memories, Maddie, a way home. Something I couldn't identify. Whatever it was, it was drawing me to it. I knew I would find it, someday.

Someday.

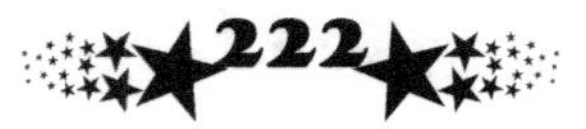

For now, though, I was stuck walking. The forest was dark, trees I couldn't name blocking the sunlight. I hadn't seen many big animals, mostly birds and squirrels and a coyote, though that was only once.

A low sound stopped me dead in my tracks. I spun, eyes locked on the trees. A pale yellow mountain lion crouched on a branch behind me. I skittered back, fumbling for the sharp rock wadded up in the blanket. The giant cat pounced, and I zipped sideways out of the way. The lion snarled, reaching out and swatting me with claws like fishhooks. His huge paw thumped me in the back. I struggled for breath, rolling away as fast as I could as the cat pounced again. It snarled viciously, baring its teeth. I backpedaled, dizzy from hunger and dehydration. I couldn't move anywhere near fast enough, because of the dim lighting and malnourishment. The cat could smell my fear as I wobbled on my feet. Without warning, it leaped, razor-sharp claws outstretched. I ducked and scrambled underneath the lion, running the other way. The lion roared, spinning in air, landing on its feet, and charged me again. I spun around to run, but claws dug into my back. I screamed and pulled free, tearing the hooked claws out of my skin. Black spots danced on the edges of my vision, threatening to drag me into unconsciousness. I grabbed a thick, heavy branch off the ground and held it like an oversized baseball bat. When the cat pounced again, I swung. The branch shattered on impact, and so did the cat's skull. Speed offers force, I guessed. With the cat dead,

Chapter Twelve

I allowed myself to think about the pain of my injuries. And promptly passed out.

I wasn't out long, but when I woke, the dirt around me was a red-stained mud. I crawled through the war zone, passing the corpse of the mountain lion to the place where my makeshift pack had fallen. The medical kit had crashed into a tree, and the thermometer was broken. I picked out the broken glass and tossed it into the woods. The tube of magic healing goop was wrapped in loose Ace bandages. Looking at the little tube, I realized that there wouldn't be enough for my arm and my back. I didn't want to use it up, anyway. That ointment was worth more than gold. So I squeezed out a little, smeared it over the deep, nasty gashes on my back, and simply poured hydrogen peroxide over my arm and wrapped it tightly with an Ace bandage. It hurt. More than I thought anything could. But I couldn't spare the medicine.

Unable to stretch my arm or my back in any way, I spent the night on the cold, rough forest floor. Sticks poked my stomach, rocks jabbed my legs. Worst of all was the fear that anything-mountain lions, coyotes, or worse- could very easily kill me. I was hurt and vulnerable. And terrified.

I didn't sleep more than a few minutes. Every little noise made my heart pound and my blood go cold. My hands and feet were numb from the freezing temperature. By the time the sun finally began to filter down through the leaves of the trees, I was shivering so hard from anxiety and cold that my jaw ached.

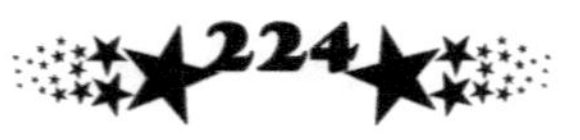

I stood carefully, feeling no pain from my back but an incredible amount from my arm. I delicately peeled the crusted and stained bandage away, wincing and crying out every few centimeters. The four individual gashes were all still bleeding, looking as bad as the day before. Gritting my teeth and biting on my cheek to keep from screaming, I poured a few more drops of hydrogen peroxide on the wounds, watching the white fizz build and dribble away as the sting made my shoulder twitch. I found the nearest stream (there were hundreds of them in this forest, luckily) and rinsed the bandage. It was agony to rewrap it, but I managed. And then I started on the lion. It was huge, enough meat to last days. I built a smoky fire and made sure it kept burning. Messily, with the only tool I had, I tore the skin away and began cooking it. Hours later, I had a tall pile of chunks of meat. I rinsed the lion's blood off my hands in the stream and ate a large portion of the meat.

I wanted to keep walking, so that I could find actual people, but I had no way to carry all the food I now had. And there was no way I was leaving any behind. Eventually I dumped the medical kit's contents into the blanket and packed the food into the bag. To make sure I didn't lose it, I tucked the tube of magic healing stuff into the pocket of my shorts. Gathering the heavy load, I began to walk.

Again.

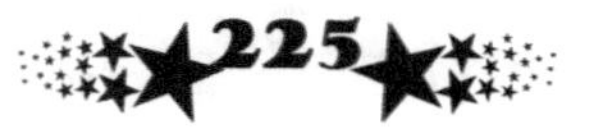

Maddie

The four of us sat at the dinner table; Rosalie, my father, Brittney, and myself. Whenever my half-sister spoke, I heard only the words that had been bouncing around in my head for the past weeks.

It was you.

"No, Dad, it was you. You told me to put in more salt!" Brittney laughed.

Rosalie poked at her over-salted potatoes, beaming at Brittney. At my real home, Rosalie hated Brittney. My sister was a reminder to her that she'd torn a family apart.
Here, though, she adored Brittney. It was confusing and just plain wrong.

"Not that much," my dad said with a smile. I violently stabbed a piece of broccoli and ate it. Everything was backwards. The things I expected never happened. The people I needed didn't exist.

Cole didn't exist.

I spent my days curled in front of the TV, eating ice cream and crackers and trying not to cry. I spent nights with my iPod turned to the highest volume it could go, trying to keep from thinking. Anything to keep from thinking about how things should have been.

"Madison? Are you alright?" Rosalie asked.

I nodded mutely.

"You look a little pale," Brittney said. Rosalie nodded.

"Why don't you go on upstairs, hon. Your father is bringing some schoolbooks home tomorrow. It'll be a big day," she said.

I thankfully pushed my chair away from the table and trotted up the stairs.

"She's so different, Rose. We should never have let her go off with Barker and Thompson. They're absolute madmen," I heard my father say before I closed the door. I paused to listen, so I could know what to do differently.

"Oh, don't be that way, Daniel. You know I trust them," My mother replied. Brittney jumped in.

"And you know how it turned out. She almost died, Rosalie."

"Brittney, please. Daniel, I knew they were doing their best to look out for her. She made it, didn't she?" Rosalie argued.

"More than half the Others are dead, and a few humans as well. Madison's human, in fact. And-" my father's voice broke.   Gasps filtered up the stairwell.

"Her human is dead," Brittney murmured.

"Page one of Opposite Law, " my father said hoarsely, "states that if the human being associated with an Opposite dies, the Opposite will also die."

"A Madison was definitely killed, whether by the OPS or

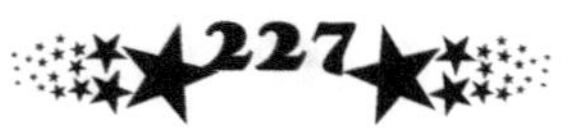

on Earth," Rosalie added.

"And since there is only one Madison alive…"

"It's the human."

I sank to the floor. They knew. Feet pounded up the stairs, but I didn't move.

"Madison," Rosalie said softly, "is it true?" I didn't have to answer. She could clearly see the truth in my expression.

"So my baby… Opposite Madison… she…" I nodded, my knees tucked up to my chest. Rosalie crumpled. Brittney appeared, my father behind her. They carried a weeping Rosalie to her room, and then came back to stand in front of me.

"Why did you lie to us, Madison?" my father asked. I fought back tears as I looked up at his familiar face.

"I didn't know what to do. I had nowhere to go, Dad," I replied quietly.

"I'm not your father. I will allow you to spend tonight here, and then I want you out of this house. What happens to you is not my concern." My father turned and went to console his grieving wife. Brittney glared at me.

"You. It was you that killed my sister." She shook her head, and followed my dad to Rosalie.

I couldn't move. How was I so freaking good at ruining things?

After a few hours, Brittney emerged. She grabbed her bag out of the guest room and left the house without even looking back at me. My parents didn't come out. The night

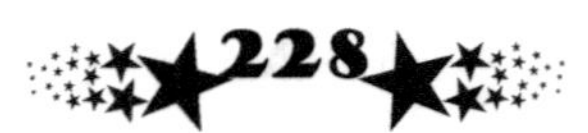

passed slowly. Too slowly. Slowly enough that all the memories I wished I didn't have resurfaced.

When morning finally came, I loaded a backpack with food and clothes and a blanket. I didn't say goodbye to my Opposite parents before I left the house for good.

Careful to hide my face, I walked through town and into the meadow behind it. A deep, dark, gloomy forest loomed ahead. The one I knew like the back of my hand.

I readjusted my backpack over my shoulder and walked through the meadow. Grass was springy under my feet; flowers filled the air wit a sweet, rich smell. But I couldn't feel a thing. It was you. Why did she have to say it? It only brought back everything more clearly. It was me. It always was.

I ruined my father's marriage.

I ruined my sister's life, twice now.

I got my best friend killed. I got my camp director fired and brain-damaged.

I ruined my mother's life.

All in fifteen short years.

I picked a flower and stared at its beautifully blended petals. White to pink to red. I wanted to have it in the woods. I wanted to take a little splash of color where there would be only green and brown. Peering into the dark woods, I saw a figure that didn't belong. Vaguely human, limping, with a huge bundle slung over its shoulder. One arm didn't swing with the walk, staying pinned tightly to its side. As it stepped into

the light, I began to detect finer features. It was a man. Filthy, matted hair stuck out in all directions, and through the layers of dirt and dried blood I saw pale brown. Beneath the dirt on his face, he couldn't have been older than sixteen, probably younger. He wore a shredded, bloodstained sweatshirt and ratty shorts. He was coated in mud and dirt.

Underneath all that, though, I recognized him. I would recognize him anywhere. As his beautiful hazel-green eyes locked onto mine, and an amazed smile lit his face, I felt like I could fly away.

"Cole," I breathed. Alive. So alive.

"Maddie?" he called. Alive.

"Cole!" I shouted, dropping my backpack and starting to run. The bundle, an old blanket, fell from his shoulder and he ran, too. The flower fell from my hand, forgotten. It lay in the grass, surrounded by its peers. Cole slowed from his blinding speed in time for me to crash into him, my arms already around his neck and my lips already locked on his.

If there were ever a moment in my life that I would want to live again, for all eternity, over and over and over until the universe imploded, this would be it. Cole, the only person I could never live without, alive in my arms.

After a few seconds, though, he pulled away. His eyes widened, and he sank into the grass. Horrified, I knelt next to him, asking over and over what was wrong. He squeezed his hands against his head, groaned, and pressed his forehead into the ground.

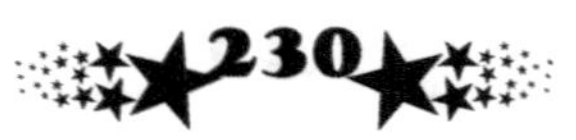

"Cole!" I shrieked. He blindly reached for my hand, squeezing hard enough to almost crack the bones.

After an agonizing minute that stretched for days, he lifted his head. Something in his expression looked whole again.

"I remember you," he said quietly.

Cole

Kissing Maddie felt so right.

That is, until my brain exploded.

It was like tiny bits of shrapnel, tearing hot and sharp through my skull. But instead of killing me, it brought me back to life. Every little piece was another memory rocketing back into place, building me back up. Redefining Cole Quinn. I remembered it all. Every moment was so much clearer than it was even before I lost my memory. My sister, my parents, Jamie, Rae, Amanda, the Others. Maddie. The first night on the dock of Camp Magic with her, staring at the stars and feeling like I'd found my place. Her blue eyes watching me from across the table as Rae and Amanda chattered aimlessly about breakfast.

"You what?" she squealed.

"I remember you. And everything else. I remember," I said. And I did. Everything from my little sister to Rachelle trying to force me to love her. All of it.

"You do?" Maddie breathed. She blinked, fighting back tears.

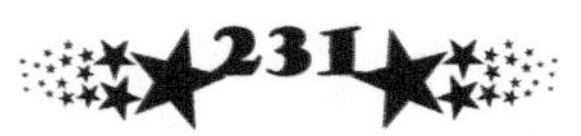

"I do," I replied. She grinned, through her arms around my neck, and kissed me again.

"This is perfect," Maddie said, her forehead touching mine. "You know, except for the fact that you haven't showered in like, two weeks."

"Yeah?"

"Yeah." I didn't have the heart to remind her where we were, or that we couldn't get home. At the moment, I was too overwhelmed to care. The sun shone down on us like a golden spotlight, and the meadow was green and lively under our feet. Everything was perfect. No matter where we were, it was perfect.

"We have to get home," Maddie said. Her voice was soft, gentle. As familiar as the bottomless silver-blue of her eyes and the soft gold of her hair. Home wasn't a building, a country, a planet. Home was right there, clear as day. Home was a girl who could be anything. Home was, and always would be, a girl named Madison Thomas.

"I already am," I said.

She smiled. "Me too. But I mean Camp Magic. Rae. Jamie. Jezzie should know that there's a way to beat her power," she clarified.

"Do you have any suggestions?" I asked.

"I was kind of hoping you would."

"I didn't now my name two minutes ago."

"Yes you did."

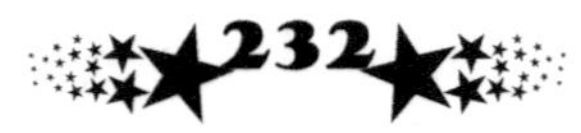

"Only because you told me."

"Whatever. Can you think of any way for us to get back?"

I shrugged. "We could walk."

"You aren't funny."

"On the contrary, I believe myself to be quite the comedian," I said.

Maddie rolled her eyes.

"Okay, okay. We could go into the town here and get some information and a place to sleep. I've kind of been living in the woods for two weeks."

Maddie raised an eyebrow.

"I can tell."

"Hey. Don't be rude. So what do you think?"

She glanced nervously over her shoulder. "I don't think it's such a great idea," she said uneasily. When I didn't say anything, she explained.

"That's my hometown. I've been living there for the last week, and um. They figured out who I am. And kicked me out. I don't think going back there, even if we stay at the motel, is such a great idea."

"Do you know anywhere else we could go?" I asked.

"There's a city maybe ten miles down the freeway. I know a shortcut through the woods my friends and I used to use as a bike path. We could probably make it there in two hours." She pointed to a wide gap in the trees, where a faint path led back into the woods.

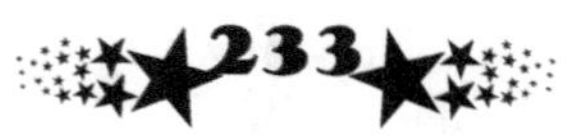

"Let's go," I said.

Maddie glanced sadly at the town in the distance.

"That's not your home, Maddie. They aren't your family. We need to get back to our real home now," I said gently. She didn't look at me, her jaw clenched tight. I reached out my hand, and she took it gratefully.

"Yeah, we do," she said.

CHAPTER THIRTEEN

Rae

"Rachelle."

"What?"

"You have to pay attention," Rebecca insisted. Again.

"I am!" I said. Rebecca and Jezzie were in my cabin again. Trying to help me regain my memory. Again. Summarizing my entire life, hoping to stumble across something I remembered. Again. They wouldn't leave. I couldn't convince them that I really didn't remember anything. Not one single thing.

My head was a black hole. Or a flushed toilet. Yeah, my brain was a toilet.

"You aren't. We're trying to help you, Rae. Jamie isn't here. We're on our own," Jezzie said. I flopped onto my bed and hugged a pillow over my face.

"But you aren't helping," I muttered into the white fabric.

"Come on, Rae. Just a little more," Jezzie pleaded.

I hurled the pillow at the wall, knocking a few unfamiliar pictures to the floor. Jezzie cringed as I turned a fiery glare on her.

"No! I don't remember you, or her, or anyone! You've been trying to 'help' for a week, but it's doing nothing but give me a big fat headache. Every time I turn around, I see something else I should recognize. And it hurts. Like a drill in my skull, twisting a little deeper every day," I hissed.

Was this a punishment for something? Had I done something to deserve this torture? Even the lost, empty expression I saw in the mirror pinged in my mind. Even the black cars in the parking lot. Even the people I saw in the camp.

Trying to acclimate to this place was so much harder than it should have been. Everyone knew me, but I knew no one. And the colorless, dismal landscape felt so wrong.

Yet, somehow, under all the torture and migraines and lack of everything, there was a deep-rooted sense of relief. Like whatever my life had been before was much worse than this.

"Rachelle, we're going to go. Um, see you soon." Rebecca hauled Jezzie from the room. I waved, and once they were gone, I yanked the blanket over my head and closed my eyes. After a few seconds, there was a rapid-fire knocking on my door, followed by the whole plank turning a violent shade of pink.

"Rachelle? Rachelle?" a tiny voice called. More knocking, and the door changed to a rainbow tie-dye pattern. A petite little

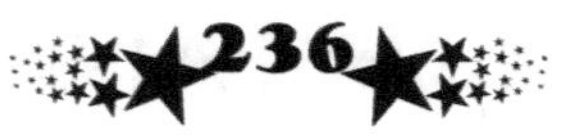

girl, maybe six, stood there in an ill-fitting uniform. She bumped her fists against her thighs, and every time she made contact, the fabric turned a different color.

"My big brother said you're sick, so I brought you a present," she said cheerfully. Triumphantly, she held up a flower. It's petals changed color every time her grip shifted. By the time I took it, they were a blinding shade of neon orange. She reached up to tap the daisy one more time, turning it a soft, pale pink.

"Thank you, sweetie. Um, what's your name?"

"Autumn. I'm Alek's sister. I live with a girl called Jezzie. She's nice. I like changing colors. I do it whenever I touch things," she said brightly. To demonstrate, she grabbed a fistful of my shirt and made it pink and sparkly.

" I love it," I said. Autumn skipped away. I watched her toe catch a rock and she fell flat on her face. I ran out and knelt next to her.

"Careful, cutie," I said as I helped her up.

"I'm not cute. I'm a big girl, and big girls don't need to be cute. They can be beautiful," she protested. Her nose was bleeding. When I told her, she gasped.

"Mommy always gives me a paper towel when my nose bleeds. I need paper towels!" she yelled. Before I could stop her, she ran off again, screaming about paper towels. I stood up, a little confused. Children.

"Rachelle?" I heard. Straightening the awful itchy fabric

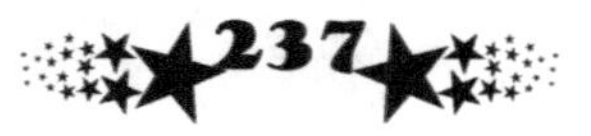

of my uniform, now a far-from-regulation Barbie pink, I turned to the voice. A boy, tall and muscular with turquoise eyes and ebony hair, slowly walked towards me. His hands were out in front of him, like I was a spooky animal he was trying to catch.

"I saw what happened with Jezzie and Mr. R. last week. I know you have no idea who I am, but I wanted to talk to you," he said. I blinked, and shrugged. He stepped closer.

"I'm Alek. Autumn's brother," he said, nodding in the direction little Autumn had run. I glanced at my door.

"She's a feisty one," I said. Alek nodded.

"Yeah, she is."

"So, um, I know this sounds like a weird question, but how well do I know you?" I asked. Alek ran his hand through his hair, and even through the baggy top, I could see the muscle rippling. A shiver went down my spine, and I cursed myself for being such a stereotypical teenager.

"Not super well. I got here a couple weeks ago. We've talked a little. You kind of stopped talking to me, though, so I don't know."

"Oh." What did that mean? How was I supposed to act around this boy?

"Yeah. So, do you want me to tell Autumn to fix your shirt? And your door?" he asked. I glanced down at my shirt, so much brighter in contrast to the rest of the dreary camp.

"Nah. I think I like it." I replied.

Alek smiled. He stretched one arm out towards my cabin.

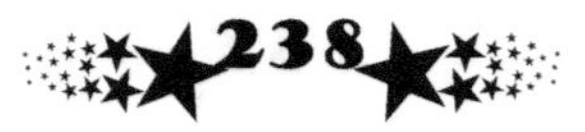

Focus hardened his features, and he slowly swung his arm towards me. Carefully, he pulled at the air, and Autumn's flower drifted into his outstretched hand.

"I think this is yours," he said. A smile lit my face.

"Telekinesis?" I asked.

"Something like that," he replied. I took the flower from his hand. Our fingers touched, and electricity zapped up my arm. Alek's eyes locked on mine, and I looked sheepishly away.

"I, uh, have to go," I said. He nodded, backed up a step.

"Right. Sorry," he said.

"It's fine. All good. See you soon," I answered. We both turned and walked away. I slipped into my cabin and leaned on the vibrant door. I held the flower to my nose and slid down the door onto the floor.

Something in my gut told me that this was wrong. That I was cheating on someone. Someone I really cared about.

But I ignored it. Whoever it was that I was close to, he wasn't here. I couldn't remember him, so he didn't really exist. The flower smelled so sweet.

Alek. Hmm.

# Maddie

"I have a friend here who might help us. On Earth, he loved rules and organization and stuff, and kind of hated me, so here he should be perfect," I said.

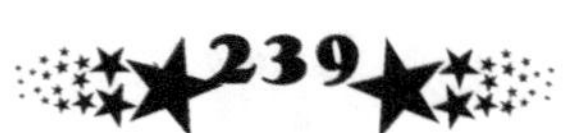

Cole nodded. He looked exhausted. He was malnourished, pale, and coated in dirt and dried blood. Scary cuts covered his body. Four on his arm were particularly bad. It was clear that he hadn't slept well in the weeks we'd been here.

"How much farther?" he asked hoarsely.

"About a mile to his house." The path we were on was well worn, smooth, yet Cole still stumbled. I held his hand tightly, trying to support him. Hopefully, hopefully Oliver would help us. He never, ever would have back home, and that made me pretty confident, but I couldn't be sure.

The next mile was agonizing, watching Cole shuffle along. He was close to unconsciousness by the time we arrived, so I propped him up against a tree and went to the house. It was two stories, with all the bedrooms on the second floor. Oliver's room was on the left side, with two windows overlooking the woods. If it were after 3:00, he would be here. Hopefully it was, because Cole couldn't wait much longer.

I found a small rock and tossed it at the window. It made a loud clinking sound against the glass. A person stepped up to the window. When he saw me, his jaw dropped. I put my finger to my lips and waved him down. He disappeared from the window. A few seconds later, he appeared around the corner.

"Madison?" he called. I nodded.

"What are you doing here?" he asked.

"I need help. My friend and I really need a place to stay. In secret." Oliver's eyes lit up.

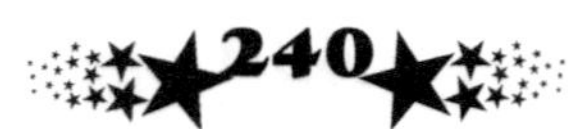

"Secret?" he said.

"Yeah. No one can know we're here," I said.

"Awesome. My parents aren't home right now, so come in," he said. I went back to help Cole to his feet, and we went inside the house. Oliver gave us water and some food, and showed Cole to the shower. The two of us (Oliver and I) sat in his room, waiting for Cole.

"So why are you here? In secret, I mean," Oliver asked. I paused, wondering what to say. A stray Lego was on the carpet. I picked it up and rubbed the knobby surface.

"Have you heard anything about the drama with the Others?" I asked. Oliver shrugged.

"Yeah. A ton of people died. It's been all over the news."

" Madison died there." It took a second to register, but when it did…

"You're human?" he gasped. I nodded.

"Cole too. The Others thought we were Opposite, so they put us on escape pods here," I added. Oliver sat down.

"Humans. Wow," he said.

"We need a place to stay until we can find our way home. Food, water, and beds, that's all," I said.

"Hey, I never said I wasn't helping. I'm all in. There's even a mattress and a bathroom in the basement. My parents never go down there, because I keep all my video games and stuff there. You and what's-his-name can stay down there, and I'll bring you food and drinks and stuff," Oliver said. He

seemed really excited to be helping us.

The shower turned off, and a minute later Cole came back. He was wearing one of Oliver's T-shirts that I recognized from my pre-Camp Magic days and a pair of running shorts. His hair was clean, but stood up in tousled wet spikes all over his head. Now that his face was actually clean, I could see it clearly. That dreaded expression of confusion and self-doubt was gone, replaced by the confident, brave face I had fallen in love with. To say it was a huge weight off my shoulders was a major understatement. Like saying the Black Plague killed a couple people.

"So where are we staying?" he asked.

"Basement. Actually, you guys should really head down there. My parents and my sister are probably coming home soon," Oliver replied. He gave us directions to the basement and went to get blankets and sheets for the mattress. We walked down the steep stairs to the chilly room. It wasn't huge, a couch and the mattress and a TV with video game consoles in a cabinet underneath. A door next to the TV undoubtedly led to the bathroom. Footsteps clopped down the stairs and Oliver came through the door. He dumped wadded up sheets and blankets on the bed and handed us a bag of snack foods and bottles of water. He set to making the bed while he talked.

"This room is basically soundproof, because my parents hate hearing me yell when I play video games. Anyway, you don't have to worry too much about making noise. You can hear

people coming down the stairs really well. If you do, there's a closet back there where I keep extra games. You can hide there if you hear someone coming."

"How do we know it's not you?" I asked.

Oliver thought for a second. "I'll stomp three times at the top of the stairs. If you hear steps but no stomping, hide."

Oliver nodded, his shaggy black hair flopping into his eyes. A door slammed upstairs, and voices filtered down through the open door. Oliver bolted up to the ground floor, slamming the basement door behind him. Cole reached into the bag of food and started chewing on potato chips.

"How are you doing?" I asked.

"Hungry. Tired. Alive." He jumped onto the couch and poured the crumbs from the chip bag into his mouth.

"Any ideas on how we get home?"

"Nope." He dug through the bag and found a box of cereal. He started stuffing it into his mouth, not even glancing my way.

"Aren't you talkative," I said sarcastically.

"Sure," he muttered as he swiped cereal dust off his hands.

"Cole, what's wrong?"

"Do you like Oliver?" The question came out of nowhere.

"Excuse me?"

"He likes you. I don't want to get between you."

"Cole, are you seriously jealous of Oliver?" I asked.

"I don't know. Should I be?"

"No!"

"Don't get like that. I… If you don't like me anymore, I don't want to be obsessing over you in front of other people," Cole said. I almost laughed. Here he was, sheepishly digging through cereal box, wondering if I liked him. After watching me fall apart without him, after all the confessions and feelings and doubts, he was still nervous.

"Cole. I love you. I do and I always will. I don't understand why you doubt that at all, but obviously I'm not being clear enough," I said.

Slow, cautious, crossed the room and sat next to him on the couch. I turned his face towards me and kissed him. It started slow, apprehensive, but intensified, all the emotion from the last few months rushing out in one long, passionate moment. When we finally separated, we were both breathless. I touched my forehead to his.

"I love you," I said.

"Not as much as I love you," Cole replied.

"You have no idea how long I have been waiting to hear you say that," I told him.

"Two months?"

"Fifteen years," I answered. He laughed.

"My friends back home would laugh at me if they heard this," he said.

"Your friends are boring and immature," I retorted.

"Of course."

It was getting late, so we decided to go to bed. Cole wrapped his strong arms around me, and I tucked my hands against his chest and buried my face in his shoulder. He kissed my hair.

For once, I fell asleep feeling safe and comfortable and peaceful.

 # Cole

This day was unparalleled. Aside from the leftover pain from my fight with the mountain lion, I had never felt better. I was reunited with Maddie, I had my memory back, and we had a real chance of getting home.

And I was back with Maddie.

Unlike the memories, which had appeared instantly, old feelings were slower to develop. Fear and hatred of the Others, loneliness without my family. And love.

Cheesy, gooey, mushy, icky, slushy, sappy, corny, sentimental, saccharine love. For one girl. The perfect girl.
Yes, she had gone a little insane. Yes, she had told me she hated me. Yes, she had been rather unpleasant to be around recently.
But I still loved her, and I knew that she loved me too.
We were fifteen. There was no way we could have found the "perfect" person yet, but it was so clear that we had.
Back at home, my friends would have laughed at me. They would have thought it was stupid, girly, and gross.

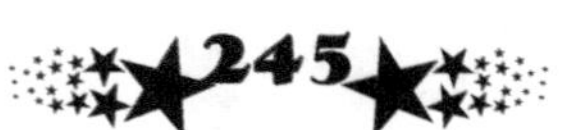

But here, with this girl in my arms, I didn't care.

* * *

The next morning, we woke up to Oliver stomping three times at the top of the stairs. I started to pull away from Maddie, but she twisted her hands into my shirt and buried her face deeper into my chest.

"It's okay," she mumbled.

The door opened, and Oliver came in, precariously balancing two plates. I looked up at him, my face hot, and he glared back at me. We stared each other down until Maddie finally rolled over and got up. Oliver switched his stare to her, watching intently as she tied up her hair.

"Thanks, Oliver," she said. One plate had waffles stacked high on it, and the other was loaded with fruit. Maddie picked up a bunch of grapes and popped one into her mouth.

How did she not notice the way he was staring at her? Was she blind?

"Do you guys mind if I hang out down here for a while? I usually do on Saturday mornings, and I don't want my parents getting suspicious," Oliver said. I glared at him, but Maddie smiled brightly.

"Yeah! Stay as long as you want. It's your house." She disappeared into the bathroom. Oliver smiled faintly.

"Don't even think about it," I growled. He turned towards me, a wicked grin on his face.

"Why not? Are you worried?" he asked.

"Because you don't have a chance. Even if she wasn't with me, she would still have to go back to Earth someday."

"I'll bet I could convince her to stay," he said.

"You think? I don't. Besides, she's going back to Earth- our home- with me. You don't have a choice," I said. Oliver sneered at me.

"Get out of my house."

"Not without her."

"Go!"

"Hell no!"

"Hey, guys. Calm down. What's going on?" Maddie asked. She crossed the room and stood between us.

"Nothing," I said. Oliver glared, but nodded.

"Good. Ooh, lets watch a movie! Oliver, do you have any down here?" she squealed. Oliver pointed to a basket under the TV, and Maddie began digging through it. Totally oblivious.

"Comedy or action?" she called.

"Comedy," Oliver said.

"Action," I answered at the same time.

"Come on, people, pick one," Maddie insisted. Oliver glared at me.

"Omigod! Harry Potter!" She looked back at us for confirmation, and finally sensed the tension in the room.

"What's going on?" she asked.

"Nothing," Oliver said. Maddie stood up and walked

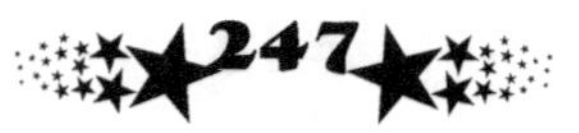

towards him, the Harry Potter DVD in her hand.

"Don't lie to me. Something's happening."

"Let's watch the movie," I cut in. Irritating as it was when she was oblivious to the silent argument going on, she didn't need to be in the middle of it any more than she already was.

Maddie looked at me with narrowed eyes, but then went to put the DVD in to the TV. Oliver flopped onto the couch.

"You could leave, you know," I muttered to him.

"And leave you two alone? Not a chance," he said. I sat on the other end of the couch, leaning into the armrest. Once the movie was starting, Maddie collapsed next to me, leaning into my shoulder. She kicked her feet up onto Oliver's lap. Half an hour in, someone knocked on the door. Oliver waved Maddie and I behind the couch, and went to open the door.

"Ollie, you have to do your chores. You can't spend your whole life down here," a motherly voice said.

"Okay. I'm coming," he answered. I peeked over the top of the couch to see him giving me the finger as he closed the door behind him. Maddie and I climbed back onto the couch.

"Whatever is going on with you guys, it has to stop. We need his help, and I need you," Maddie said. When I didn't reply, she grabbed my face with her hands.

"I'm serious. Now is not the time to be fighting. We need him on our side."

"And I need you on mine," I said.

Maddie looked confused.

"Are you still worried about me falling for him?"

I didn't answer.

"Cole, I thought we went over this last night. I love you. The only reason I'm even being nice to Oliver is so that he continues to let us stay here. I honestly can't stand him half the time. The only reason we're here is because I knew he liked me enough to let us stay. That does not mean I like him. You don't have to be worried," she said. I heard her, and I understood what she said, but I didn't believe it. The look of determination on Oliver's face that I saw and she didn't worried me.

"Yeah, I'm good," I said anyway. Maddie stared unblinkingly into my eyes, her hand still touching my face.

"Don't lie to me, Cole. Why are you worried?"

"You don't see how much Oliver likes you."

"Yes, I do. I ignore it. He needs to think he has a chance in order to keep letting us stay here. But if you want me to stop, I can."

"No, it's fine… yeah." Maddie smiled.

"Of course. You really think you have any competition?" she joked. Someone stomped three times at the top of the stairs. Maddie curled up against me, intent on the movie. Oliver threw the door open and stomped inside.

"I hate chores," he mumbled, flopping onto the couch.

"Who doesn't?" Maddie asked. Oliver smiled at her, and shot me a dirty look.

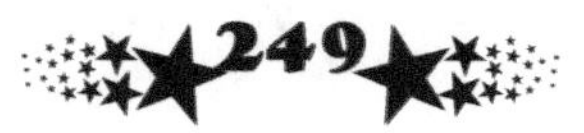

Except for the movie, it was silent in the basement. Maddie shifted so that her foot didn't touch Oliver. He stared at it like it had bit him. And then he glared at me again.

"What movie do we watch now?" Maddie asked as the credits started rolling up the screen. Oliver shrugged. Maddie turned to me.

"Preferences?"

"Whatever you want." She bounced to the TV and ejected the old disc.

"Is another Harry Potter okay?" she asked. Oliver and I both didn't care, so she put the new disc in and sat back down with me. Her head touched my shoulder and her legs curled up next to her. Oliver discreetly scooted closer, until her foot was touching him again. Maddie reached for my hand.

I wondered if this awkwardness was actually worth it.

Rae

Mr. R. glared at me. Alek smiled at me. Everyone else stared in slack-jawed astonishment. The bunker was totally silent. Not even a whisper. My face was red, but not from embarrassment. From anger. Slow, burning anger that led to me hitting Mr. R. with a barrage of verbal abuse so intense that even he was stunned into silence.

You don't hit a six-year-old kid. Not for something as inconsequential as sitting down while waiting for the next 25

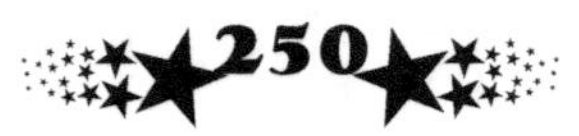

kids to learn to control their powers.

Autumn, the little girl, rubbed the pink handprint on her cheek, crying without making a noise. No one else so much as blinked. Finally Mr. R. took a breath and spoke.

"Rachelle Levine. You are not to speak out of turn or use language like that. Ever. Let alone to me."

"Mr. Riveria, I honestly don't care. Anyone who hits a six-year-old for sitting down when she's been standing for four hours straight and will be for another three deserves about as much respect as a dung beetle," I hissed.

"Rachelle, I am not afraid to report you to the Special Authorities. If I tell them what you have said to me, they will fully support my decision to expel you from this facility," Mr. R. countered.

Something snapped inside me, and power surged through my body like a wildfire, hot and overwhelming. When I talked, it wasn't the senseless stream of profanity it had been before. This time, there was power. Cold and dark and convincing.

"You don't belong here. You are cruel, cold-hearted, vicious, malicious, despicable, vile, loathsome, hateful, rotten, beastly, contemptible man. Every bone in your body is nothing but ice, waiting to melt. Nothing you can say will change that. You have proved yourself unworthy of this camp since the beginning. You belong back with the Council, ruining lives that don't have anything left to strive for." Mr. R.'s face crumpled,

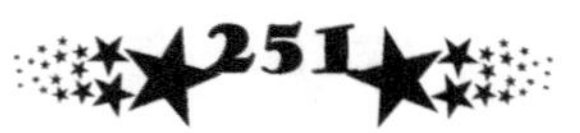

and I watched the confidence melt out of his features as my words sunk in deep.

Alek pulled Autumn towards Rebecca and came to tug me away from Mr. R. I resisted, watching the evil man's face turn an interesting variety of colors under my stare.

"Rachelle. We should go," he whispered into my ear. I wrapped my fingers around his, but didn't move.

"I'm going to say this once. Rachelle, you have crossed the line. From here on out, you are never to leave your cabin. If I or any of my helpers sees you outside, I will kill you myself. Understand?" Mr. R. spat.

He turned his back and waved me away. Suddenly unable to move, even if I wanted to, I only blinked. Alek beckoned his sister, and led us both out of the bunker. Mr. R. told them both to return, but they ignored him and walked me out.

"What were you thinking, Rae?" Alek asked once we were outside. His turquoise eyes met mine, and he gripped my hand tightly.

"I had to stand up for Autumn," I said. Autumn swatted my leg, glaring at me. My pants turned a vibrant green.

'I don't need anyone to stand up for me. I'm a big girl, and I can stand up all by myself!" she insisted. The vibrant green of my pants glowed in the sunlight. Alek tapped her shoulder.

"Fix it, Autumn," he said. The girl patted my leg, and the

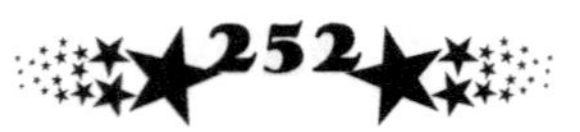

fabric went gray again. Alek led me to my cabin and walked me inside. Autumn followed us, until Alek told her to go to her own cabin. She skipped away.

"Is she okay by herself?" I asked. I watched through the window until Alek turned me towards him. He didn't answer my question, pulled me close and crushed his lips against mine. I pushed him away.

"Alek!"

"Sorry. I thought… you seemed… I'm sorry," he said, and sheepishly strode for the door.

"Alek," I said. He glanced back, and I saw Cole where he stood. I crossed the room and kissed him. It felt amazing. Like I was finding a memory. Like I was finally able to breathe. Like Cole was alive again.

A few seconds later, he started to pull back.

"Cole," I said, stepping back with him. Alek jerked back.

"Cole? Isn't that the other guy you went on that mission with?"

"Yeah. I'm sorry, he was the last one I…"

"Do you remember him?" Alek asked.

And I realized that I did.

"Yes!"

"And Madison and Jamie and Rebecca?"

"Yes!" I remembered it all. Everything from my childhood to this.

"So… you're back then. And you remember Cole and

everything. So I'll see you later," he said. Only the last couple of words were a little muffled, because I was kissing him again.

"You brought me back. I don't know how, but you did. Maybe it's a Disney true love's kiss kind of thing. Whatever it is, if you're sure you like me, I'm yours," I said.

Alek grinned. "Really?" he asked. When I nodded, he laughed.

"Good. Because I was thinking I was going to have to buy you a unicorn or something."

"I want one with a rainbow tail."

"And sparkly gold feet?"

"I wouldn't accept anything else."

"I'll get right on that," he said. He smiled again, and I melted a little inside. I wasn't sure if I was still in love with Cole, but it didn't matter. Cole was gone. Probably in a million pieces in a crater across the country. Alek was here now, and though he was so, so different from the Cole, he was just as amazing.

"Rae?"

"Yeah?"

"You probably shouldn't tell anyone. Mr. R. tried so hard to force you and Jezzie into this. If he finds out it didn't work, he might decide to do it again, and who knows if we'll be able to bring you back again." The genuine concern in his eyes was beautiful.

I would have to fake amnesia. At least I knew what it felt

like. I could do it, easy. But having to pretend I was miserable when I was actually almost happy wouldn't be easy.

"I know it won't be easy, but I can help," Alek said softly. He sat down in my bed. Somehow this felt more intimate than anything else I'd felt. I sat next to him, but discreetly stacked pillows between us. He eyed the barricade, but said nothing.

"Thanks," I said softly.

"Do you think we should go back to the bunker?"

"You could, but I think I need to give him some time to cool off. I don't actually have a death wish. Maybe I could go check on Autumn," I said.

Alek nodded and left the cabin without another word. I waited a few minutes before going to check on Autumn. She was sprawled on the floor, mouthing the repetitive words of a picture book open in front of her. I knocked on the door and she scrambled to open it.

"Hi! I'm reading. My big brother taught me." She turned back to the book, flopping to the floor and dragging the oversized pages into her lap.

"What book is it?" I asked her, sitting down by her side.

"The Lorax," she answered, turning the page. I instantly recognized the abstract illustrations. Every time she touched the book, she had to go back and fix the colors.

Autumn read on, slow and halting, tracing the words with a bookmark so the pages didn't change color. I watched over her shoulder, smiling at the book I'd read so many times when I was her age.

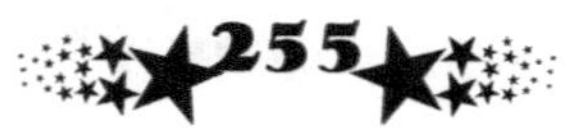

Chapter Thirteen

"What is this word?" Autumn asked me, pointing to the word "bicycle." I repeated and defined it for her.

"My momma used to read this book with me. She told me what all the words meant. But I'm a big girl now, and I can read all my myself." She turned the page and continued. I read with her, smiling at the memories that came with each new page.

The third time through the book, when even I was getting a little sick of it, Jezzie came in, and I left Autumn with her. It was getting dark out, and dozens of campers in gray uniforms raced to get back to their cabins before curfew. I didn't care. Even Mr. R.'s death threat wasn't enough to chase me back indoors. I walked down to the lake, my heart aching. I still loved Cole, more than anything else in the world. But he was gone, and if I was ever going to move on, it needed to happen now. As I stepped onto the pier, I grabbed a handful of rocks. I walked slowly, listening to the water lap against the pilings and the wood creak beneath my feet. Stars glittered like diamonds in the sky, watching my every move. I kicked off the tight black shoes and stood at the very edge, curling my toes over the plank. Sadness gripped my heart, but I ignored it. It was time to say goodbye.

I held one of the rocks in my hand. The biggest and heaviest.

"Cole," I whispered to it. Cole was dead. I loved him. But he was dead. If I was ever going to be something more than a grieving girl stuck at camp, I needed to stop thinking about him.

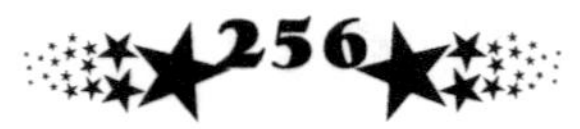

I needed to stop seeing his face everywhere. So, with a squeak of regret, I threw the rock as hard as I could into the lake. The splash was big, and ripples flowed out fast. Within seconds, the tiny wave hit the dock. And then he was gone.

I named the next rock Maddie. And the one after that Amanda.

Jamie.

My family.

My friends back home.

The last one, a dark, almost sparkly one, I called Alek. And I tucked it into my pocket. The sky was a deep, deep black, punctuated only by stars. The chilly light was from the wedge of moon just above the horizon. I shuffled back down the pier with its pale light for guidance. I felt a little lighter, like all the painful goodbyes had pulled those people off my shoulders. I stumbled on the half-dead lawn to the path and then to my cabin. If anyone had noticed my time outside, they hadn't done anything about it. Maybe the poor amnesiac girl got a break.

As I lay in bed, I pictured that first rock sailing out of my fingers. Cole.

But I had given up on him.

It was over.

"We have to get out of here," Cole mumbled into my hair. I snuggled closer to him, not even opening my eyes.

"I'm serious. We have to get home. We've been here five days, Maddie. We're both all healed. If we don't leave now, we never will.

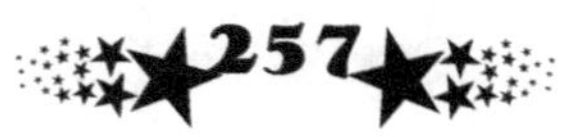

CHAPTER FOURTEEN

Maddie

I knew it was true, but somehow I was okay with that. The last few days, alone with Cole and sometimes Oliver, I'd really gotten close to both of them. That closeness made me hate Oliver and love Cole so much more. Oliver was so pathetic. Everything he did was selfish and self-centered. It got really annoying, really fast.

But there were still twenty hours of each day for me to spend alone with Cole. And instead of getting sick of him, I only became more fascinated by him. All of his stupid jokes, his arms around me, his lips on mine, made my only thoughts of this place good. I didn't want to leave.

Besides, we didn't have any way to get home even if we did leave. I would rather stay here that set out for some intergalactic airport thing and get lost and starve.

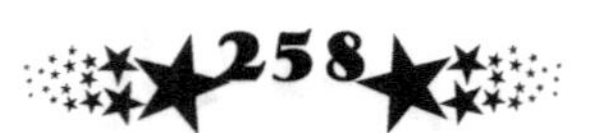

"Maddie," Cole said, pulling away from me. He got up and stretched. Three stomps at the top of the stairs preceded the footsteps pounding down. I pulled the blanket over my head and sighed. The door creaked open.

"Where's Maddie?" Oliver said. Cole must have pointed, because the next question was "is she asleep?" Another silent response. I didn't move.

", I know this sucks, but you guys have to leave. A bunch of my friends are coming over and we're going to need the basement. I'd love to keep helping you guys, but this can't go on forever. You need to go," Oliver said.

Floorboards creaked, and the mattress moved beneath me. Someone sat by my feet.

"Are your parents home?" Cole asked.

"No. You guys can probably take some food and stuff. You have a few hours."

"I'll tell Maddie. You can go. We'll be up soon."

"Thanks."

The mattress moved again, and the floor creaked, and the door opened and slammed shut. The blanket was yanked away, and I winced and blinked at the light.

"Did you hear all that?" Cole asked. I nodded and rolled off the bed. I didn't have anything to pack, but I balled up the blanket and hugged it to my chest. Cole smiled and kissed my forehead.

"I told you we'd have to leave," he said. I told him to

shut up, kicked my feet partway into my shoes, and opened the basement door. Oliver stood at the top, looking down at me. I smiled slightly, and glanced back at Cole. He was tying a new-ish pair of sneakers onto his feet that must have been Oliver's. He waved me out. I shuffled up the stairs, my shoes almost slipping off my feet. I brushed past Oliver and ducked into the kitchen. He had already loaded a backpack with food, water bottles, a flashlight, and a Swiss Army knife. A second backpack held extra clothes, shoes, and two sleeping bags packed into tiny rolls. I put the blanket down, but Oliver rolled it up and stuffed it in the pack.

"I grabbed everything I could think of. It's all old, extra stuff, so don't worry. I don't know how long you'll be on the run, so I got enough for like, a week." His earnest, lovesick puppy expression was almost laughable.

"Thanks. We'll need it. You've been so great, letting us stay here. I can't thank you enough," I replied. Oliver's face lit up.

"Yeah. Anytime." Cole came out of the stairwell.

"Thanks, dude. We owe you," he said, shouldering the heavier of the two bags. I grabbed the other, and we headed for the door. I glanced back only once, to see Oliver staring wistfully at me. I blushed and darted down the driveway. Cole and I walked out into the forest to plan our next move.

"So where do we go?" Cole asked.

"I don't know. There's an airport about fifty miles south,

but I don't know if they have a space rocket thing going there. That Other base was a freakishly long ways away, and I can't remember which direction. So we could-"

"I wonder how common spaceships are. Like, would they be at a regular airport, or-"

"Excuse you, I was talking."
"So was I." Cole smirked at me. I tried to scowl, but failed miserably.

"Anyway, I have no idea where we should start," I said.

"Neither do I. But maybe we should start at that airport, and get an idea of what we have to look for." Cole readjusted his backpack and pulled me to my feet.

"Maybe I can turn into a car or something. Get us there faster," I volunteered. But Cole must have seen the worry on my face, the fear of inanimate objects.

"I can run. I've been cooped up for a week, and it'll be good to stretch my legs. If you have some bird or something you could turn into, that would be even better." I smiled and closed my eyes. It was a little tricky, because I hadn't done a transformation in a while, but within five minutes I had shrunk into the body of a hawk. My backpack melted right into my feathers. I soared up, grateful to finally be able to move again. I screeched, and dove back down again. I buzzed the top of Cole's head and took off south.

"Oh no you don't!" I heard, followed by a whoosh of air beneath my wings. Cole spun to a stop fifty yards ahead of me,

stuck his tongue out, and took off again. We raced through the forest, staying away from roads and populated areas. It was amazing.

Every flap of my wings was another blast of adrenaline, and my laughter was the high-pitched screech of a hawk as I struggled to keep up with Cole. Every so often he would pause for me to catch up, and then zip away again. It didn't take long for us to get to the airport. I changed back, and laughed as I fought to catch my breath.

"You're out of shape. Fifty miles is nothing! This one time, I ran all the way across a country to catch up with this girl, right after saving her from a car crash," Cole mocked. I stuck my tongue out and strutted towards the airport. He caught up easily, spun me around, tripped me into his arm, and kissed me. Just like that. In the middle of the parking lot, with people watching, like he didn't care. Like nothing else mattered. I pulled away, laughing and embarrassed.

"We have to lay low. Both of us are wanted criminals," I said. Cole smiled.

"But we're both dead, so it's okay." I shook my head and continued towards the airport. It was easy to get inside, but we couldn't get through security. So we wandered around inconspicuously, looking at the information boards for interplanetary flights. We were on our way out when we saw a small side building. We snuck towards it, keeping to shadows and making sure we weren't spotted. We were hiding behind a

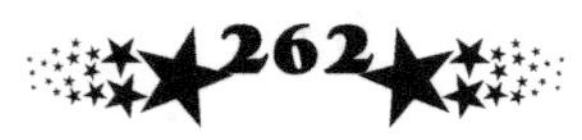

van when a rocket launched out of the top of the building and into the sky. It was the same design as the ones that had brought us here.

"How do we get to one? Or on one? And how do we program it?" I whispered. Cole shrugged. I squeezed my eyes shut. My skin rippled, and warmth spread through my body. I shrank into a hummingbird. At this point, it was a natural choice. They were small, fast, and perfect for spying.

I buzzed in front of Cole before I left, so he wouldn't freak out when he realized I was gone. He cursed and tried to stop me, but I was already halfway to the building. I zipped through and open window and inside.

There was a crowd of people in suits, and maybe twelve rockets. One of the people was talking about the rockets, so I landed on top of a cabinet to listen.

"I know that this is a new installment, but it will be very useful-"

"For what? The humans haven't developed this technology yet. Who is supposed to use them?" an over-made up woman asked. The gray-haired ban shushed her and continued talking.

"We have many agents who have disappeared on Earth but are still alive here. We are using them to explore other galaxies and planets so we can maybe escape this one. Meet Sharpe and McCain, our top trainees." He gestured to two men standing respectfully behind the group.

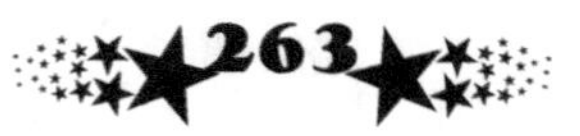

"How do they work?" the same woman asked.

"One simply has to input a password to the computer and then a destination. The rockets are self-driven."

"Can anyone hack it? This building is not well protected," the woman insisted.

"You need a special passcode, key, and registered fingerprint to get to any of these rockets. If anything false is inputted, several alarms will sound. And there will always be guards," the gray-haired man assured her.

"Are you certain?" the woman asked. Everyone in the room looked like they wanted to punch her.

"Yes."

Having heard enough, I jumped off the cabinet and glided out the window. Cole was waiting impatiently behind the van, looking pale and distressed. I changed back and dropped my backpack next to him.

"So? How do we do it?" he asked. I told him what the gray-haired man had said, and watched his face fall.

"All of that? We're screwed."

"Hey. Stop that. We can do it," I said. He glared at me.

"There are these two guys in there. Sharpe and McCain. They have all three, I know it. If we can get one of them to cooperate, we can do this," I explained.

"So we're going to kidnap and torture someone."

"When did I say that?"

"When you said 'get them to cooperate.'"

We argued for a few minutes, and finally started planning what we could do. Sharpe had appeared weaker and less intimidating, so we would go after him. Somehow we would separate him from the group, steal the key, talk the password out of him, and somehow convince him to open the door with his fingerprint.

It was an hour before they all came out, and all piled into separate cars. As the line of vehicles passed, I saw Sharpe alone in a fancy sedan. I pointed him out and morphed back into a hawk. Cole and I chased the car for ten miles before it pulled into a driveway. He got out and walked to the door. McCain pulled into the house next door.

Cole and I ducked behind Sharpe's car.

"They must live next to each other because they both aren't supposed to exist," I whispered.

Cole nodded and tapped his finger against his lips. Once McCain was inside, Cole and I crept up to an open window on the ground floor of Sharpe's house. I peeked inside and saw no one, so Cole boosted me up and I pulled him in after me.

"How are we doing this?" I whispered. Cole shrugged and took the lead. We heard Sharpe clattering around in the kitchen, so we went in that direction. Cole looked at me, and I saw a terrified shadow of guilt under his eyes.

"Can you turn into a wolf or something? You know, something intimidating," he whispered.

I nodded and squeezed my eyes shut. When I opened

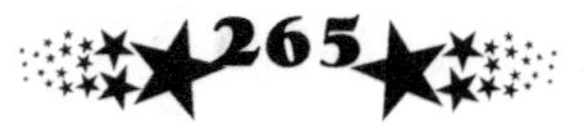

them, I was much closer to the floor. I bumped Cole's leg with my nose and we turned for the kitchen. I stayed back, waiting for a cue.

"Holy… Who are you? What are you doing in my house?" Sharpe shouted.

"We need your help. My friend and I need to get off this planet, and you're going to help," Cole said.

"No. No way. Get the hell out of my house," Sharpe said. Cole called my name. I rounded the corner into the kitchen, growling. Sharpe made a tiny whimpering sound.

"We really need to get on one of those rockets," Cole said. He was still wearing that guilty expression that I didn't understand, and in the dim light of the kitchen, he looked like a psychopath. When Sharpe didn't reply, staring with wide eyes at me, Cole repeated himself. And again. And again.

"I can't help you. Really. I could be executed," he finally said.

I took a silent step forward.

"Seriously! Back off!" he screamed. Cole picked up a knife from the counter. Sharpe backed into a corner.

"We aren't kidding around," Cole growled. He looked at me. I looked at Sharpe. The man was clearly terrified, and I felt awful for scaring him. But I really wanted to get home. So I snarled and concentrated, growing into a full-sized lion. Sharpe let out a terrified squeal and scrambled up onto the countertop. Cole smiled faintly. "We need your help," Cole said. "And we

can force you to give it to us."

I slowly crept forward, a low roar rumbling from my chest. My golden paws were huge against the tiles.

"Okay, okay. The code is 182720789297. The key is in my wallet there," Sharpe said.

Cole picked up the wallet and pulled out a narrow silver key.

"This?"

"Yes."

"Okay. All we need now is a fingerprint. Come with us," Cole said. Sharpe shook his head.

"No. The key and the code could have come from any of the trainees. Fingerprint and I'm done for. They'll know it was me, and I'll be executed," he said.

I glanced at Cole, his face cruel and harsh, and transformed back into myself.

"Listen, dude—"

"Wait, you're those kids! The ones who are supposed to be dead! No, no, no. Oh, God." I glared.

"Listen. We need to get out of here, tonight." Cole zipped forward and seized the man's left index finger, holding the knife underneath it.

"I'll cut it off. I will," he said menacingly.

"Cole, what are you doing?" I hissed.

Sharpe's face went completely white. He trembled, staring wide-eyed and unblinking at the shiny silver blade

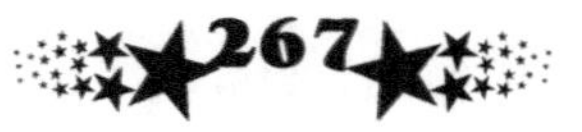

drawing a thin line of red at the base of his finger. Cole's face was made of stone.

"Cole."

His knuckles were white against the red plastic grip of the knife.

"Cole!"

His eyes were dark with fury.

"Cole!"

I didn't recognize this boy.

"Cole, stop!" I screamed. He finally met my gaze. Sharpe looked extremely grateful as the blade pulled back a centimeter. But I knew it wasn't over. There was still a darkness in Cole's eyes that I didn't like.

"I want to go home," he said. And brought the knife down hard. I screamed, Sharpe screamed. Blood spurted. I had to lean against the refrigerator to stay standing. Sharpe's eyes rolled back in his head and he fell forward. Tears falling, I grabbed a dishrag out of the sink and sank to the tile floor next to Sharpe. I pressed the towel against the ugly bleeding stump, pushing hard to stop the bleeding.

"Cole, we have to take him to a hospital. We have to help him. What the hell were you thinking?" I screamed. A hand wrapped tight around my arm.

"We have to go," Cole said. But it wasn't his voice. It was gruff, angry, and too deep.

I was petrified.

"No, are you crazy? We have to help him!"

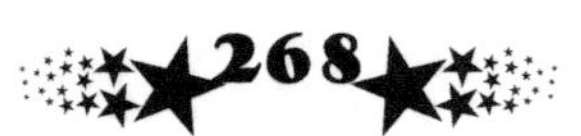

Cole yanked me away. I saw the bundle of red-spattered paper towels in his other hand. My stomach heaved, and I ran to the sink and threw up. Cole came back, gripped my arm tightly enough to leave bruises, and dragged me out of the house. On his way out the door, he snatched Sharpe's car keys off a hook on the wall. He threw me into the front seat and carelessly tossed the bundle into the cup holder. I threw up again out the open window.

Cole started the car and slammed it into reverse. The tires squealed on the pavement as he hit the accelerator. He drove fast, screaming around corners and leaving skid marks in his wake.

He pulled into the airport and slammed on the brakes. He picked up the bundle of paper towels and dragged me out of the car. Despite the gray-haired man's earlier promise, there were no guards. Cole used the key to open the doors and picked a rocket at random. He tapped the keypad on the outside, typed in the password, stuck the key in and turned it, and paused. On the screen, a small square scanner had appeared. I turned away. A small beep, and I was pulled backwards into the rocket. He punched Earth's name into the destination box. Trembling, terrified, sick, I huddled as far from him as I could. I was trapped on an 8x8 rocket with a psychopath. I had never been afraid of him before.

As the machine flew up, I saw helicopters and cars and a thousand flashing lights converging on the airport. Sharpe must have reported us. We would never be safe. The Oppos could

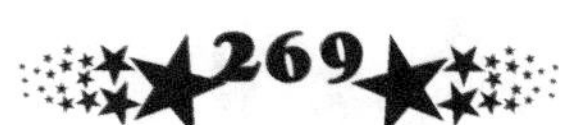

find us. All because Cole decided to maim someone.

I was so afraid.

 Cole

I sat on the bed, watching Maddie. She was crying, shuddering, refusing to look at me. I didn't blame her. Without context, what I'd done seemed crazy, psychopathic, and totally out of character. But I had a reason.

I'd done it for Maddie. While she was in the building, a man had approached the van. I hadn't had time to hide, so I tried to walk away. He caught my arm.

"You're Cole Quinn. I need to speak to you," the man said. I tried to run, but he stopped me.

"I'm trying to help you! See, a boy in the city- an Oliver Ringman-reported you two this morning. Said you were probably headed for an airport. This airport."

"Who are you?" I asked.

"It doesn't matter. Tonight there's a huge team of police and soldiers coming to stop you. You need to leave immediately. They know you'll stay here and be unable to get on a rocket. They're closing in soon. You have to run," he said.

"But..."

"No. When Madison comes out of that building, you run. I'm warning you- if you're here, you'll be killed. So don't be here." With that, the man climbed into an old minivan and

drove away.

So we had to hurry. By the time we reached Sharpe's house, night was falling and we had no time left. It would have taken forever to get the man to the airport, and I had to get Maddie- and myself, I guess- onto the spaceship. So I went a little crazy. If I'd moved any slower, we would have been caught. I'd done the right thing.

But the fear on Maddie's face- fear of me- was painful to see. Especially when it lasted for four hours without her even looking at me.

"Maddie, I finally said. She lifted her head but didn't look at me.

"I… I know what I did was deranged. But you have to understand…"

"Understand what? That you maimed a person for defending himself? That you flat-out refused to even let me help him? That you dragged me away like I was a kidnap victim?" She finally met my eyes, and the fear and rage and betrayal there made me cringe.

"That I was doing it to protect you. The Oppos-"

"You were protecting me? More like traumatizing me!"

"The Oppos were coming to capture and kill us. Your friend Oliver reported us, and we barely made it out."

"You didn't have to maim Sharpe like that! It was unnecessary and cruel! "

"Madison. We were out of time. It would have taken

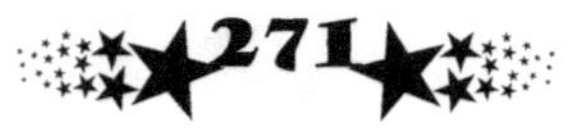

Sharpe forever to get out of there, and we would have been caught!"

"But now we'll be wanted criminals. Now we're even more dangerous. We could have hidden," Maddie said. She was still huddled in the corner, but arguing was somehow making her relax a little bit.

"And if they'd found us? We had a chance to get home, Maddie. Aren't you glad we took it?" I asked, measuring her expression carefully. It wasn't good.

"No. No because it meant ruining someone's career, security, and basically their whole life. I would honestly rather still be there," she said quietly. She turned around to face the wall and lay down. Feeling bad, I pulled the blanket out of the backpack she'd dropped on the floor and draped it over her. She started to throw it off, but her shoulders slouched and she pulled it around her shoulders. I went over to the bed and sat down. As I watched her lying uncomfortably in the corner, I remembered all those nights spent so close together, so recent yet so distant now. How could everything change so quickly?

"I'm sorry," I said, so quiet it was barely a whisper. "I wanted you to be safe. I never meant to hurt you or scare you. I wanted you to be safe." I turned to face the wall and pulled the blanket over myself. I heard the sound of Maddie shifting, probably trying to get comfortable. But then the bed moved beneath me and her lips brushed my cheek.

"I know. Never, ever scare me like that again," she

whispered. She curled up behind me and fell asleep. Just like that, and I was forgiven.

"Never," I whispered. "I promise."

Rae

Mr. R. was yelling again. The bunker was his favorite place to do so, because the sound bounced off the concrete walls so magnificently.

This time, it wasn't directed at me, though, which was new. It was directed at Rebecca, which was really new. But it was my fault, which wasn't new at all. She'd been trying to heal a bruise on my face. One I'd received from Mr. R. the day after I screamed at him.

We weren't allowed to use our powers without special permission. Autumn got in trouble for it every day. Most people never left their cabins anymore, except for training. Camp wasn't camp anymore; it was a dark, lonely, painful dictatorship.

At least I had Alek. In the days since I got my memory back, we'd become really close. As close as Cole and I used to be. But Cole was dead, so there was just Alek. Cole was dead.

As Mr. R. screamed at Rebecca, that burning anger swelled in my chest again. This dictator of a man had no right to do this to us. We were kids, not soldiers. Not a single one of us signed on for this madness.

Chapter Fourteen

I didn't understand how this was legal. The Council couldn't have recommended this. He was hurting innocent people and enforcing rules no one agreed with. It didn't make sense that he was still in charge.

Something touched my leg. I glanced down to see Autumn clinging to me, fear making her face an ashy gray. My pants flicked through colors so fast that it all blended into brown.

"Stop. You don't want to get caught," I whispered frantically. Autumn pulled her hands away, tapping one more time to turn the sparkling Barbie pink back to gray.

"Sorry," she whispered.

"It's okay. Be careful," I replied. Mr. R. spun towards us.

"Who's talking?" he bellowed. Autumn shied away from me and back to her spot. I took a deep breath and prayed that he didn't…

"Rachelle? Autumn? Come here. Now."

Crap.

"I request silence while we are in this room. Is that clear?"

"Yes."

"Then stop talking!" he screamed. Autumn squeaked and ran to her brother. Alek sent me a pleading glance.

"Autumn…" I called.

"Shut up!" Mr. R. growled. He stalked to where Autumn stood and picked her up by the collar of her uniform.

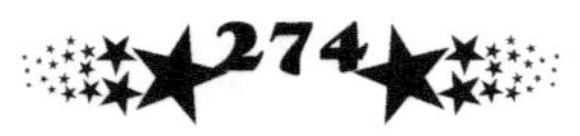

"This is why powers shouldn't develop in children. These toddlers with too much power will be the end of our race," he said, eyebrows set low over his eyes. Autumn whimpered.

"Let her go!" I said. Mr. R. turned to me with fire in his eyes.

"Excuse me?"

"Let her go!" I screamed, all the power I could muster packed into the three words. Autumn fell hard to the floor, but nothing broke. Crying, she ran to her brother.

"You don't use your power on me. Ever," Mr. R. snarled. I bared my teeth.

"Get out of my camp. This is not what Camp Magic is," I hissed.

"I'm here because Camp Magic wasn't working. What you need is discipline and decent training to save this race. I am going to get you there. You, though, have been a pain in my neck since day one. Get out of my camp. The place is mine now."

Mr. R. pointed at the door. I planted my feet.

"Ask anyone here. Camp Magic is about learning, freedom, and friendship. We are here to learn to control our powers, not to become your personal army. I don't know about anyone else, but I am not going to stand here and let you demolish the morals of this camp. I-" I was cut off by a slow applause and cackling laughter from the man in front of me.

"Very nice, Rachelle. What a lovely little show you've

performed for us. But I'm here to tell you that these little revolutionary thoughts of yours aren't getting you anywhere. I have the Council and all of the adult powers standing behind me when I say this: Camp Magic is mine now. I own all of you. I have the right to do whatever I want with this place, and I will. So you get out of my sight." He waved me away. My confidence finally crumbled, and I ran.

I stumbled through the door to my cabin, blinded by hot tears that refused to stop. I was a spineless creature, too afraid to stand up and do what I had to in order to help the ones I cared about.

Camp sucked without Jamie and Maddie and Cole and Amanda. This place wasn't a home anymore, or even a summer camp, or a school.

It was a prison.

Earth was in sight. A small blue dot deep out in space. We were passing what must have been Mars- red, dry, and rocky. So close to home that my stomach hurt.

CHAPTER FIFTEEN

 Maddie

"How much food do we have left?" Cole asked. I opened the cabinet and dug around inside.

"Enough for a few days. Why?

"We don't know where we are going to land. It could be in Australia or something, for all we know. We need to be prepared for a lot of travel," Cole said. I nodded and started stuffing the food in the backpacks.

"We can't use the packets outside the rocket. We should eat those now," I said. Cole was sprawled on the floor, staring blankly at a movie playing on the screen.

"How close are we?" he asked.

"Probably fifteen minutes until we hit the atmosphere," I said, starting to heat the food.

"Mkay. Is everything packed? Depending on where

we land, we might have to make a fast getaway," Cole said. I nodded.

"We need to eat." I put the bowl of noodles in his hand and sat on the bed. I was scared to go home. What if the Oppos followed us? Or what if the Council was angry? Would we be welcomed home, or kicked back out?

"It's going to be okay. Don't worry about them," Cole said. I tore my gaze away from the window and saw him watching me. He smiled reassuringly.

"We can do it. We'll come home heroes." I looked back at the fast growing circle that was our home.

"I hope so."

We anxiously watched the movie while we waited. I joined Cole on the narrow stretch of floor and held his hand. A shudder shook the rocket as we hit the first bit of air in a week. The metal groaned and the wind wailed. But we slowed down, settling gently into an easy, drifting speed as we descended.

I ran to the window, looking down at the shapes of the continents below.

"That looks like Central America. Oh, my go… Oh," I said, staring at the ground below. Only there was no ground. We were headed straight for the Pacific Ocean, off the coast of what looked like Mexico. Miles and miles and miles from land.

"What is it?" Cole asked. He joined me at the tiny window. "Oh."

"What do we do?"

Cole ran to the computer and tried to change the

destination.

"It's not working. We're already too close to the ground. We needed to do this earlier," he said as he frantically tapped the keys. We had minutes.

"We have to think of something!" I gasped.

"Change me."

"What?"

"Madison, do it. We change into fish and we can swim to shore. Change me now, you get the door open, and you change. We jump. It'll be okay," Cole said.

"Are you crazy? The last time I did that, you almost died. You said you would never do it again!"

"I also said that I'd do it if it would save you. I am not leaving you, Madison. Change me. We don't have time to argue." He swung his backpack over his shoulder and held my hands. I looked out the window again. We had seconds.

"Now!" Cole said. He hit the button that opened the door, punched in the password we had stolen from Sharpe, and pulled me over. I squeezed my eyes shut and focused. The wind screamed in my ears, threatened to pull me out. Blankets and empty food packets flew out the door. Cole's skin changed beneath my fingers, and he was out the door. I jumped after him, not remembering what I turned him into, not caring, needing to become something with gills in the few seconds before I hit the cold, white-capped water.

The water hit me with a slap that knocked the wind out of me and sent me rolling through the salty waves. But I had

managed the change. I was a dolphin.

A shockwave from the impact of the rocket on the water caught me, rolling me sideways and making it hard to tell which way was up. As soon as I could get my flippers coordinated again, I started searching for Cole. I tried calling his name, and it came out a high-pitched squeal I wasn't sure he'd recognize. So I tried the telepathic thing we'd discovered at the Other's lair.

Cole? Are you there?

Maddie. Where are you? What are you? I heard.

Um, a dolphin. I think. What are you? I replied. *A tiny orange clownfish swam up to my nose.*

This isn't fair, Cole said. I almost laughed.

Sorry. We were watching Finding Nemo yesterday…

I might want something a little faster. Can you manage that? I touched the little fish with a fin, and pictured it as a dolphin. It grew, becoming sleek and gray and powerful.

Do we swim straight for land or try to swim all the way up towards San Francisco Bay? It'll be faster in the long run if we swim, I think, Cole said.

How long can you stay like this? I replied.

I don't know. I'm hoping it'll last a while.

Let's try San Francisco then. I turned my nose north and took off. We raced for a while, until Cole learned to coordinate this new body and left me far behind as his speed kicked in. He probably could have made it all the way to San Francisco

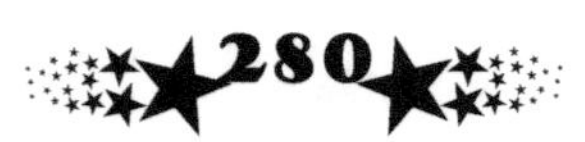

in a couple hours, but he stayed slow and waited for me. We made sure to stay very close to the surface, just in case Cole changed back suddenly. We ran into several schools of fish, a few small sharks, and some whales. Nothing tried to stop us as we raced up the coast, but it was slow going. Despite the sleek, hydrodynamic bodies, swimming wasn't nearly as fast as a car.

Maddie. Maddie, is that a Great White shark? Cole asked uneasily. I looked around me in the salty blue water. Sure enough, there was a huge, scarred, white-bellied shark flying towards us through the water, its jaw wide open and the hundreds of serrated teeth glittering in the dim light. I ducked out of the way, but not fast enough. Razor sharp teeth scraped against my skin as I wriggled free of the powerful mouth. I frantically looked for Cole through the wafting clouds of blood.

I feel it. I'm changing back. Maddie, it's happening, Cole said.

Get to shore. I'm right behind you. Fast as you can, I replied, already turning for the distant beaches of northern Mexico or southern California. The shark charged after me, a little faster. Cole was long gone, getting to safety before he turned human. I dove sideways, avoiding the harsh snap of a million teeth. The whoosh of water sent me spinning out of control, terrified. The red of my own blood was dizzying. I caught my balance, surfaced for a gulp of air, and raced on.

I made it. Any second n- Cole's voice was strained, and then gone. I felt an absence in his place, and knew that he was transformed.

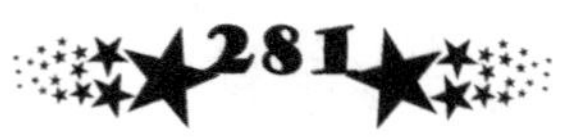

Chapter Fifteen

The shark was giving up. He slowed and turned back for the open sea. But I wasn't out of the woods yet. Blood still streamed from five deep gashes on my right side and three on my left. The clear water was blurring, darkening. The shore only seemed farther and farther away. I swam for my life, knowing it was all I could do. I wasn't going to make it, but I did. Sand scraped my belly. I flopped up the beach, focusing on the change. The ripple was agony, skin tearing further as it shifted. Salt stung the wounds and I cried out.

"Oh, my… Maddie, you're hurt. Really bad," Cole gasped. I panted for breath, pulling my wet shirt up to reveal the eight awful cuts.

"Tell me something I don't know. But I'll be okay. We have to get home." I tried to get up. My head spun wildly, and I vaguely remember hitting the sand.

"You have to get to a hospital," Cole said when I woke up again.

"We're both wanted runaways. We can't," I said through gasps of pain. Cole pulled the slightly damp backpack from his back and unzipped it. He had to dig through it the first aid kit, but he found it pretty quickly.

"There's barely anything in here. Not even that magic healing stuff," Cole said. He helped me wind bandages around the gashes to slow the bleeding. They were soaked through in seconds.

"You need stitches. We need a hospital. I wonder where

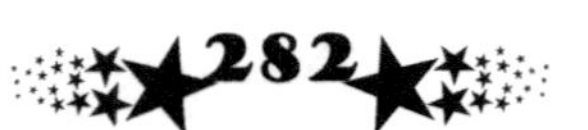

we are? Mexico or America? Cole asked, looking around.

"Rebecca can help me when we get home," I said.

"No, Madison. Hospital. Come on, let's find a phone." He helped me to my feet, supporting me when almost I blacked out again. We slowly shuffled forward, the sand doubling the wobble in my knees. I couldn't continue, but Cole dragged me on. A while later, we met a woman with a cell phone. She confirmed that we were in California, and called 911 for us. Cole told her that we were siblings, and our parents had just been killed in a car crash. We needed a hospital, but then we could find our way to dear Aunt Jamie a few miles away. The ambulance arrived, and I was loaded inside. The pain was unbearable. Despite my urging us to get home, I wouldn't have been able to take another step on my own. I drifted in and out of fiery consciousness, a single red scream punctuating the entire ride. I think I was gripping Cole's hand- I couldn't be sure.

At the hospital, they stabbed an IV into my arm to replace the pints of blood I lost. They pulled off the bandages, anesthetized the area, and madly began stitching the gashes shut. They stitched and bandaged and cleaned for close to an hour. When the doctors asked Cole how it happened, he'd repeated his car crash story. They asked for our names and we gave them fake ones. They asked for an emergency contact and Cole told them about our dear Aunt Jamie. I was okay with all of this, until they told me I had to stay for a few days to keep the injuries clean and free from infection. Not okay.

"I have to get home! Camp Magic needs me… they all need me!" I screamed.

"She's delirious. We're staying. Then we can go to our aunt's," Cole said. I screamed, insisting that I needed to get home. I did. I needed camp. I needed to see Rachelle and Jamie and Rebecca and Jezzie. I needed them to see me.

But in the end, my "delirious" wails only convinced them further- I was staying. And the thick metal cuffs they snapped over my wrists made that very clear.

Cole sat on the cushy gray chair by my head.

"I want to go home," I muttered.

"You have to get better first," he replied, casually to the point. "Why are you so obsessed with getting back there, anyway? Jamie isn't even there. That Mr. Riveria guy is. And I don't know that Rae will have made it back, either. Why do you want to be there so badly?"

"I need to be back there. I want this whole adventure thing done with. I want to be Madison Thomas again."

"Maddie, we have superpowers. For us, the 'adventure thing' is never going to be over."

 Cole

We were in the hospital for four days. Then the nurses really started pushing for information, and we had to avoid answering any questions. So I started planning our escape. It wouldn't be easy, with so many staff members there. But we really needed to get out before they recognized us.

While I sat with Maddie, I "absently" started knotting the sheets together. I stashed what I'd made under a chair. Maddie wasn't healed enough to climb down a rope ladder, so I had to knot a loop she could sit in so I could lower her down. I stole extra towels from supply closets and knotted those in too. We were on the fourth floor, so the rope needed to be long. I spent two days on it, and that night, we made our move. Maddie wasn't plugged into the IV anymore, but she was still cuffed to the bed. As I struggled to pull them free, she pointed out the key on the counter across the room. I sheepishly unlocked them and helped her to her feet. She winced and gasped in pain, the color draining from her face.

"I'm okay. Go," she whispered when I paused. I pulled out the messily tied rope and helped her step through the loop at the end. The window didn't have an alarm, so I yanked out the screen and pushed it open. The hospital was quiet this high up. Careful not to hurt her, I helped Maddie out the window and began lowering her down. The rope slid along the windowsill, catching on the knots as I slowly, holding Maddie's weight with nothing but my own unsteady hands, let it go. It took forever. Every noise, every shift in the rope was the weakened fabric giving up. Every voice was someone seeing us, every footstep someone coming to stop us. Finally, Maddie jerked the rope three times, the signal that she was on

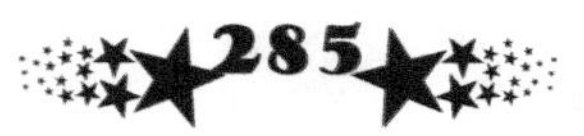

the ground. I tied the rope to the bed and to the heavy chair that sat next to it. Quickly, but careful not to slip, I scrambled down. Maddie met me at the ground, uncomfortable in the blue hospital gown they had given her.

"Let's go," she said.

We started down the road. Slowly, so that Maddie wouldn't be in pain. We walked along the road, following street signs to the coast. Once we had the ocean in sight, it was easy to follow it north towards camp Magic. Towards home. It was slow, slow going. Maddie could only move so fast. Already the wounds were reopening, dark red seeping through the blue hospital gown. She really needed normal clothes if we were going to stay inconspicuous. For now, though, in the bleached blue dark of night, we were able to sneak along the coastline towards our home.

"We are going the right way, right?" Maddie asked. Her breathing was shallow, her mouth pinched. She was hurting.

"Yes. It should only take, like a week to walk there," I said, trying for a joke. She faked a smile.

"Sorry about this. I should have swum faster," she gasped.

"Hey, you aren't me. There wasn't much you could have done," I replied. The soft sound of waves crashing on the beach was the only sound for a while as we stumbled along the winding sidewalk.

"You should go. Get home. Leave one of the backpacks

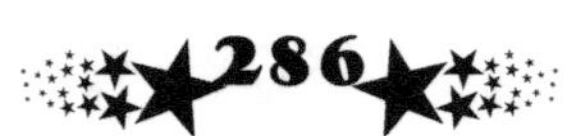

and go. You deserve to be there," she finally said. I stopped walking. She turned to face me, the harsh glow of streetlights turning her face into a pit of shadows.

"Excuse me?"

"You should go. I don't want you to have to stay with me and risk everything when you should be home," she said.

"Maddie, I can't leave you. With that injury, you could die out here," I said. Her eyes met mine, and I saw a haunted, terrified blackness rooted there.

"I will anyways. Can't you see it? I might as well already be dead. This is my end, Cole. I'm not going to get back to Camp Magic," she insisted. I watched in horror as she pulled the bandages away from her body. Blood flowed freely, darkening the ground in neat puddles. I ran to her, held the bandages against her body, tried to stop the steady spill of life from her body. She pushed me away with strength she couldn't have and fell to the cement sidewalk. Her eyes locked onto mine as I continued to try, try to save her. Had to save her.

But her eyes were still locked on mine when the life left them. I screamed, crying, unbelieving. She couldn't be gone. She couldn't be.

"Cole? Is that you?" I heard. I spun, and saw a shadowy figure approaching. Hair the color of a sunset over the Grand Canyon.

"Amanda?" I gasped.

"What happened to Maddie?" Amanda asked. Her

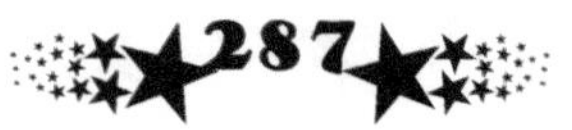

eyebrows lowered.

"How are you alive?" I whispered.

"What?"

"How are you alive?" I repeated.

"That healing stuff. The Others found me after Rae left and saved me. I ran away and tried to come home, but I got lost, so I stayed here." She knelt down next to me and looked down at Maddie's body.

"What did you do to her?" she gasped. My eyes stung.

"Me? Nothing. It was a shark," I stammered.

"You killed her," Amanda said. I shook my head violently.

"No! I would never… It was that shark!" I screamed. I looked up at Amanda. Her eyes glowed green as they bored into mine. My face solidified, my body hardening as I turned to stone.

"Good luck getting home now, lover boy," Amanda hissed as she ran off towards the sea.

* * *

I opened my eyes.

Maddie was there, leaning over me, her face framed by sunlight. She smiled.

"Finally. I didn't think people actually slept that long," she said. I jolted upright, and automatically I glanced at her stomach where the shark bite had been.

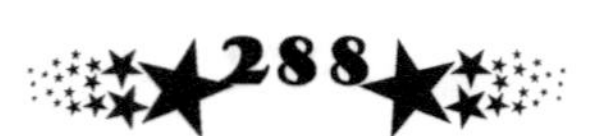

"Dude. What's wrong?" she asked. I fell back onto my elbows. There was no blood.

"How—" My thoughts were dry leaves, scattered so far by the wind that I couldn't catch them.

"Cole? Are you okay?"

"The shark," I managed to say.

"What shark?" Maddie asked, confused.

"The one that attacked you. You died," I said.

"Clearly I did not. I am very much alive, thank you."

"And then… Amanda showed up, and froze me," I said. Doubt was inching into my brain.

"Amanda died weeks ago," Maddie said carefully. "Are you okay?"

"What actually happened?" I asked. "We made the flying leap of faith out of the escape pod, turned into dolphins, and started swimming up the coast. After a while, you started twitching, and then you passed out and started doing that rapid-fire change thing. I dragged you here and pulled you up the beach, and you stopped shifting after maybe an hour and then…"

"No shark?" I interrupted.

"No. You didn't wake up for like, a day after you stopped shifting. No shark. What happened in your dream?"

"We saw this shark, and it bit you. The change was happening, so I took off. We made it back to shore, and you went to the hospital." I paused to dust sand off my clothes,

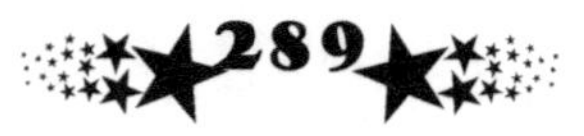

continuing between ragged breaths. Maddie looked horrified.

"That's one hell of a nightmare," she said quietly.

"Yeah. I guess it is," I said. I thought of Amanda, the way her eyes had glowed.

There had to be a hidden meaning to all of this, but I couldn't imagine what it could be.

Maddie

I lied.

So what?

There had been a shark.

We escaped the hospital.

We went and slept on the beach.

His crazy me-dying-and-Amanda-appearing thing wasn't real, so it worked. I'd found some crazy magic healing stuff in the first aid kit and used it, and found some spare clothes in the bottom of a backpack, and I was good as new. I was fine. Cole was fine. He didn't need to remember that I almost died. We could move on.

We were fine, especially now that we could keep moving without me holding us up. I was grateful for Cole's "dream," because he didn't want to get back in the ocean, and I really didn't want to. But I couldn't tell him that. So we moved up the coast. I changed into a bird and raced Cole again, miles and miles beside the sea. No matter what I turned into, though, he

was always faster. Nothing on land or sea could beat him. Not even a cheetah (I tried).

With the two of us going as fast as we could, we had to stop somewhat often for breaks. I carried both backpacks because they didn't weigh me down. We'd had to throw away some of the food that got wet, but most of it was fine. We ate and rested in shadowy places, away from people, and then left again. I flew as high as I could to scope out the land for Cole, making sure we were taking the shortest routes possible. The ocean was our guide. I had no idea where we were, but only that we hadn't reached San Francisco yet. From the bay, it was a two and a half hour drive to Camp Magic- I had no idea how long it would take for Cole and me. We probably had a long ways to go.

Since Cole couldn't run in the dark, we decided to try to get some sleep. I scoped out a secluded beach, guarded by cliffs. We laid out blankets and curled up next to each other, the smell of salt and seaweed ever-present and overwhelming.

"One of us should stay awake and guard," I said.

"I will. I got all that sleep after we got out of the ocean," Cole said. I bit my lip. I'd gotten more sleep in the hospital than he had on the beach. But from his expression, I knew it would do no good to argue. So I rolled over and closed my eyes.

"Wake me up when you get tired," I murmured. He mumbled a quiet "sure," but I knew he wouldn't. I knew he would stay awake all night, staring out over the wind-tossed sea, the dark hiding the expression that darkened his face. It

was exactly what I would do if I were the one awake. Especially after lying to him.

* * *

I woke up to the brilliant yellow-orange glow of the sun over my face. Sand was everywhere- caked between my toes, grinding between my fingers, itching on my legs. I sat up and brushed it off, immediately looking for Cole. He was on the cliffs, throwing stones into the waves. I rolled up the sandy blanket and tossed it on top of the two backpacks nearby, and climbed up to the cliff. Cole didn't see me, bent down for another rock. When he threw, his arm moved so fast that I lost sight of it. The rock went for miles out to sea. I watched him throw, silent and still. Finally he saw me. His face changed, but I couldn't tell how. He walked over; dead, salted cliff grass crunching under his shoes. The sun was climbing in the sky, leaving a long, glowing trail across the water. Cole's hand in mine, I walked to the crumbling edge and stared. The dark back of a whale crested, a spray of water cascaded into the air. I turned to Cole, to see if he saw it, and found his lips instead. This was perfect.

I forgot where we were; I forgot what we were doing. I forgot everything, except for Cole and his taste and his touch and his smell. Cole.

Cole and me, finally, together, inseparable

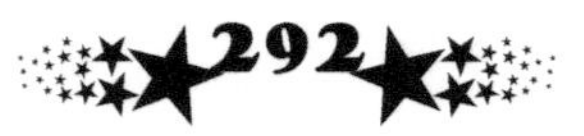